PRACTICAL USES FOR PRINCES WITH POINTED EARS

Otherworld Realms: Book One

Isabelle Saint-Michael

Otherworld Romance, LLC

Published by Otherworld Romance, llc
www.otherworldromance.com
www.elvenlife.com

ISBN 978-0-9908665-0-3

Dreams start in the heart but manifest with hard work and dedication. Mine certainly wouldn't be coming true without the help and talents of Lisa my editor, Chas my fixer and James my cover designer. I wrote a story and you helped me share it with the world. With all my heart I truly thank you.

To all of my family and friends that have cheered me on through all these years, thank you for the love and support. You let me be myself even when that meant you had to be my kite string.

Finally, to my readers:

You are never too old for fairytales or happy endings. My stories are for every Changeling that is walking around in the world and still not sure how they got where they are. Magic is real within you don't be afraid to dream. Hold it in your heart and never let go. Dream big and then give it all you've got.

Love Always,

Isabelle

Chapter One

"Are you ready, Lilly?" I gave an unsure nod. I felt Cedrick's hand slide along my back, forcing me to straighten up and align my elbow. "Good, now STRIKE!"

With all the force of my body, I snapped my arm forward, transferred my weight onto my lead foot and connected my sword with the combatant in front of me. There was a loud crack as his body shook and he was knocked off balance by a foot or so. I pulled my hand back, let my weight settle back into my knees and prepared to press him again with another blow. It was then I heard a shaky voice from the man before me as he cried out "Good!" and cringed away from me.

Cedrick's heavy hand clapped down on my shoulder reassuringly. "Excellent, Lil! You keep this up and those boys on the field are going to go home with all sorts of new bruises." I turned to look at the older man beside me. Pride filled me, causing my chest to swell. From my first day in the Living History group, I had respected Cedrick. He made me feel less like a stranger and more like a little sister than I could have ever imagined. With one last clap to my shoulder he smiled fondly and moved on to another warrior.

I pulled off my gauntlets and unstrapped my helmet, then began to peel out of my armor. It had been a great practice. I glanced over at Tommy, the unfortunate soul who had found himself at the other end of my practice sword. His armor was off and he had managed to find an ice pack he now pressed to his ribs. "Are you going to live?" I asked, trying not to let the amusement from the mishap slip onto my voice.

He chuckled. "I hope so. I'm just glad that we fight on the same side." As if to prove a point, he tried to move and flinched from his new injury. "That one will be purple tomorrow." I laughed, glad he was taking it all in stride. I was thankful that my brothers in the war band had always taken kindly to a woman fighting alongside them. It hadn't been my experience in every group I participated with. Like many historical reenactment groups, we had a heavy focus on period related combat. Many of the ancient cultures didn't paint pictures of strong female warriors. For that reason, many historical groups were greatly against women on the battlefield. That was not the case here, though.

With the help of a nearby onlooker I managed to escape the heat and weight of my armor. I was sliding it back into its bag when I heard another loud crack behind me. I turned just in time to see a fighter in green fall to the ground in mock death. A smile curled my lips as I resisted the urge to laugh. I looked at the victor who was already taking further instruction from Cedrick. We were all lucky to have a knight who took more joy in teaching than fighting. His years of knowledge and discipline were always laid before us like an open book. His wisdom enlightened us and his words inspired us to push ourselves week in and week out.

I tucked the last of my armor in my bag and was reaching for my sword when someone called my name. "Lillian Chambers!" My head snapped up as I surveyed the busy gym. Most people were in various states of packing or removing armor, but at the center of the floor stood a single man in heavy plate armor. I didn't need to see his face under the heavy steel helm to know who it was.

"Yes, Erik! Do you feel bad I didn't give you your weekly beat-down?" I picked up my heavy sword from where it rested on the ground and rose to my feet. Erik stood there shaking with laughter.

He dropped his own sword, threw his arms wide and purposely left himself wide open. "Let's see if that new shot lands on me!" From several places in the gym I heard shouts of warning, telling me to stop as I was unarmored. My feet swiftly carried me the short distance and rather than slash, I lunged deeply and thrust with all of my momentum and weight.

My sword tip connected firmly with his armor, knocking him back, but it was too late for me to catch myself. I had tossed too much of my own weight in that direction to try and compensate. I followed my sword and connected with him, this time knocking him completely to the ground with me on top. He connected with the floor and my head connected with his armored shoulder. I quickly scrambled to get off of him.

"Are you alright?" I asked frantically.

He was laughing as he fought to sit up. "Of course I'm all right, I'm the one wearing armor." I breathed a sigh of relief only to hear him swear, "Freaking hell, Lil, does that hurt?" It was only then I realized that the vision in my left eye was blurred slightly by a red stinging liquid.

"Dammit!" I clapped a hand to my head wincing as a sharp pain ran through my wrist. Cautiously I felt my brow, ignoring the throbbing from both my head and hand. My fingers ran over the cut as I tried not to wince at the pressure. "Oh, it feels small." As I struggled to my feet, Cedrick was there with a hand under my elbow to help me up. "Thanks," I mumbled.

"I ought to beat you senseless. What were you two thinking? Neither of you are twelve - why are you acting like you are? What is our number one rule?" Cedrick bellowed.

I fought the urge to roll my eyes. "Safety," both Erik and I spit out.

"I should pull both your cards and ground you from practice for the next two weeks, since you both insist on acting like children." His words were harsh and justified. He seemed to forget them, though, as he turned me in his grip and started to inspect my head wound. "Go sit down. I'll get the first aid kit and ice pack." Before I could protest, he had walked off.

I picked up my sword in my non-injured hand and slid it into my bag before zipping the bag closed. I then plopped down on top of it and prepared myself for the rest of my lecture and the less than gentle first aid that would accompany it.

An hour later, I pushed my way through the front door of my home. I kicked off my shoes, dropped my gear bag and wandered into the kitchen, hell-bent on finding something to eat. After poking through the poor selection in my fridge, I decided on a bowl of cereal and milk. I made quick work of my impromptu dinner, rinsed the dishes before loading them into the dishwasher, and then headed for the bathroom.

My bathroom was small, but right now it held the keys I needed to unlock a good night of sleep. I turned on the shower, setting it to the hottest setting. I peeled out of my sweaty clothes and looked at myself in the mirror. Bruises were already showing up and covering my body. I could make out where armor had been or see the marks left from a sword impact. They wrapped around my arms, outlined my ribs and dotted my upper thighs. I leaned close to the mirror to look at the gash that ran just above my eyebrow. A thick coat of Vaseline had prevented it from bleeding while I drove home. I sighed at the thought of more marks, cuts and bruises to explain at work.

I cautiously stepped in under the stream of steaming water, testing the temperature. The water ran over my body, stinging my new injuries and massaging away the tension. Carefully, I ran soft smelling soap over myself with my uninjured hand. An earthy scent of sandalwood and jasmine mixed with the steam. I ducked my head back under the water, doing my best to wash my hair with one hand. I sucked in air when the hot soapy water ran over my cut and washed away all the residue from the Vaseline.

With a flip of my uninjured wrist, the water stopped and I fumbled with the towel, doing my best to pat away the worst of the water droplets. Moments later I stepped free of the bathroom fog, clean, dry and sporting a pink bandage on my newest injury. Without consideration for my looks I pulled on a well-loved t-shirt and turned down the silky soft sheets of my bed.

Sinking deeply into the pillows and beneath my covers, I surfaced long enough to click off the light on my bedside table and fill my room with darkness. It surrounded me and cradled me as if it was a long awaited lover. It tempted me into closing my eyes and drifting quickly into a deep, satisfying sleep. Now came my favorite part of my day. The moments when my dreams would return and I would see "him".

Tallyn swung his sword again, repeating the same motions over and over. His shoulder ached and his back throbbed in complaint. Every day for the last hundred years he had pushed his body harder. Reaching for a new best. Struggling to be faster, stronger and more agile than the day before. He knew one day all the training would save his life. With one last thrust he allowed his muscles to relax and slid his sword back into his belt.

Casually Tallyn made for the river, stopping at the edge only long enough to remove his boots, belt and pants. His shirt and doublet were tucked carefully into the bag attached to his saddle. Without another moment of hesitation, he slid into the cool water, allowing it to caress his sore muscles and wash away the sweat of the day. With a tug, he freed his long, dark hair from its leather tie. The dark locks fell freely around his shoulders and down his back like a curtain shading him from the sun.

Taking a deep breath, he dove below the surface of the water. Its chill numbed the aches of the day and urged him to relax. Its coolness on this early fall day pricked at his face and ears, causing him to sputter and suck in air when he reemerged from below its surface. Dipping his hand, he lifted it to his lips and drank deeply. With a heavy sigh, he relaxed as the flowing water washed over him, and closed his eyes.

The feeling had returned. Every day for what had to be over a year, around this same time, he would get the feeling he was being watched. At first he was unnerved and sought the source of his unease, hoping to unmask this unnamed person who would dare to spy on him. He never saw a shadow. With time, he grew to realize whoever was watching meant no harm, and he felt as if he was being admired. *Perhaps a spirit of the forest watches over me?* he asked himself.

Tallyn climbed out of the river and pulled a blanket from his saddlebag where his mare waited patiently for him. The horse nuzzled at him, looking for treats, as he wiped away most of the water. After an affectionate pat to the nose, the horse resumed its stance of disinterest while he changed into his dry clothes. Quickly he pulled his wet hair back, pulling it free of his pointed ears before securing it at the nape of his neck.

With one last look at the forest, he pulled himself up into the saddle and urged his horse Mavba forward. At a slow and leisurely pace, he rode through the trees and along the riverbank towards home. The feeling of the watcher's eyes never left him.

I awoke the next morning as my alarm clock yanked me cruelly from my dream world. I watched over my handsome dream stranger every night when I closed my eyes. We had never met, not even in my perfect dreams. I was helpless to only watch him each day from afar.

At first he looked for me, and I called to him each time, hoping we would find each other, but never did we meet. We were always so close and yet so far. I would wake up each morning and his name was on my lips but I could never quite remember it. I felt like I'd known him a dozen lifetimes, and though I could feel him deep within my heart, I knew he was only a dream. A figment of my imagination, put in place to give me something to aspire to.

He practiced tirelessly each day so that he would be able to defend himself and the ones he loved. He moved like a battle-hardened warrior but acted with the gentleness of a youth who has maintained his innocence. His eyes were as crisp and green as spring, his hair dark as espresso and skin so pale it looks like fresh cream.

There was something so otherworldly about him that I knew he could never be more than a dream.

Slowly I dressed for work, staring longingly at my bed. I wished nothing more than to return to it and immerse myself in dreams again. However, duty called and there were teenagers to teach. Without me, who would teach them that "The Three Musketeers" and "Harry Potter" weren't just movies?

The drive was a quiet one. I refused to turn on the radio or play an audio book. My thoughts were consumed with my dreams or with my fighting. I had always loved teaching. In fact, until recently I had never been more passionate about anything. It had all changed two years ago when my husband at the time decided he needed space. Which really meant he needed space in the bed of a co-worker.

I ignored it for a while. I thought maybe it was a phase and that because we were in love it would get better. When he told me he was moving out I was devastated. I always figured we would grow old together. I wanted to be mad at him and hate him, but no matter how hard I tried I couldn't. I was a failure as a wife.

When he left, all my dreams of the future left with him, and I'd been trying to fill a void ever since. The passion for my job or for much of anything never really came back.

I parked in the lot behind the school and quietly made my way in. My classroom was empty and would be for at least another hour still. I dropped my bags and coat and went in search of the life giving nectar called COFFEE.

I could smell it wafting down the hall from the teacher's lounge.

I politely said hello to a few of the early morning murmurs that greeted me. Many of us didn't become human until after the first cup. I picked up my mail from the box and took a seat at one of the tables. There were flyers begging for homecoming chaperones, information about mandatory in-service days, my pay stub from last week and a large brown envelope.

The envelope was the size of a catalog and my name and school address were scribbled across the front with a handwriting that looked vaguely outdated. In the upper left-hand corner there was a coat of arms for *The Essex Historical Society* and a return mailing address from England. I pondered the name for a moment before ripping away the flap and pulling out its contents.

I felt like I was a high school student open a college brochure. There was a folder filled with colorful pictures and articles about gray and historic England. Then there was the letter:

Practical Uses for Princes with Pointed Ears

September 17th, 2014

Dear Ms. Lillian Chambers,

It is with great pleasure that we write to you today. After months of discussion and years without adding new members to our ranks, we have decided to invite fresh minds into our fold. Many times your name has been mentioned by our members due to your work on the Tower of London project you were part of at Oxford in 2005.

It is our sincerest hope and deepest wish that you will consider joining our mission to expand the world's knowledge of historical sites and texts through our ongoing research efforts.

We look forward to seeing you at our Annual Masquerade Ball at the end of October.

Sincerely yours,

Randall Edwin Dukes
President of the Essex Historical Society

Beneath the letter was a small gold envelope holding two tickets to the ball.

I leaned back in my chair and took a sip of my cooling coffee, and flipped through the folder before me. I had submitted a request while working on my Masters at Oxford years ago. At the time I had figured I was too young and inexperienced, but perhaps they just weren't taking members then. Either way, there was no way I was going to get my principal to approve time off to go to Europe.

I slid the information back into the envelope, gathered my mail and coffee, and then headed back to my classroom. Kids would start rolling in for homeroom in about half an hour and I wanted to get a little bit of grading done before I had to enforce dress codes, unlock lockers and lecture about PDA on school grounds. When had I become such a stick-in-the-mud prude?

During my third period freshman lit class, I had a girl stand up to read a journal response about last night's reading only to have a panic attack and faint. I quickly sent one boy to fetch the school nurse and another to go get a vice principal. I dialed 911 and gave the school address and classroom info.

Moments later my classroom was filled with paramedics, administration and rowdy teens. Once I was assured the girl was going to be all right but was being taken to the hospital for liability reasons, I ushered the extra people out and took another quick roll call to see if I was missing anyone. I was missing three.

I made note of the names and then picked back up with class after I let everyone know the girl would be alright. The rest of the day was rather uneventful after that.

I went home, changed into workout clothes and went for a run. Thanks to my iPod, I tuned the world out and focused on my next five miles. They passed quickly and soon I was home again, sweaty and tired. I practiced my footwork before dinner, then took a shower and finished up some grading. By the time I slid between the covers of my bed, not only was I looking forward to my dreams, but also my long awaited sleep.

With my head pressed against my pillow and the darkness wrapped around me like a beloved childhood blanket, I considered my letter from the historic society. *Maybe I need a break?* I thought to myself. *Perhaps it's burnout?* I pictured myself traveling around the UK, looking at historical documents, working with some of the top minds in the field and I finally realized, I was right. I did need a break. This fall was out of the question, but maybe next summer I could do that rather than teach summer school. My mind made up, I allowed sleep to overtake me and dreams to fill my vision.

Chapter Two

When I arrived at the school the next morning, things just seemed "off". The air smelled more like oppression and panic than usual, and it was nowhere near midterms yet. I quietly glided down the empty hallways feeling more and more like I was stuck in a slasher movie. As I rounded the last corner leading to my classroom, I was surprised to find the door open and the light on.

"Hello?" I called as I stepped through the door. Sitting at my desk was a pretty young woman with red hair dressed in gray slacks and a green cardigan. "Can I help you?" I asked.

She looked up, startled. "Hi there. Are you Ms. Chambers?"

Her voice was sickeningly sweet. I was willing to bet she had been a cheerleader in high school and had one of those popular girl names. I nodded. She smiled warmly.

"I'm your substitute, Tiffany Williams." Score one for me and the name, I thought.

I processed the words. "I didn't call for a substitute?" The question in my voice and on my face was enough to make her break eye contact with me.

"You haven't met with Principal Macabre yet, have you...?" Her words trailed off. "I think you should go see her first."

"I will." I kept my words short. I took off my coat and hung it in *my* closet along with *my* bags, then marched out the door and down the hall to battle. The principal's name didn't just strike fear into disruptive teens, it worked well on staff too.

Principal Eleanor Macabre was not an unkind woman. She was just very strict, with many no-nonsense policies. She surrounded herself with a team of Vice Principals that tended to be softer and more forgiving. When I arrived at her door, I knocked quietly hoping she wasn't in yet. "Yes, please come in," called a voice from within, dashing those hopes.

I took a deep breath and opened the door, stepping into her office. Her office was decorated in shades of grey and white, making me feel like I was in a sterile environment more befitting of a hospital. Principal Macabre sat behind her desk sifting through some papers. When she looked up at me, she looked a little startled and motioned for me to have a seat.

"Ms. Chambers, you should be taking advantage of the day off. I hadn't expected to see you today. I trusted we would talk this afternoon when I called you." There was an uneasy hesitance in her voice.

"Principal Macabre, why is there a substitute here today? I didn't call for one." My words came out with an edge of frustration that I hadn't meant for them to have.

The older woman's eyes softened. "Please, call me Eleanor. We've worked together nine years." She took a sip of tea from the mug on her desk. "Lillian, I called the substitute. I also left you a voicemail last night giving you the day off today with a message about talking this afternoon. My apologies, it doesn't seem like you received it."

"No, I'm sorry. I didn't see any voice mails or missed calls." I quickly developed one of those sinking feelings you get in the pit of your stomach right before something terrible happens.

"The girl who collapsed in your class yesterday, Stacy, is being treated for PTSD." She paused.

"Is she recovering? The paramedics said she was going to be fine. Did something else happen to cause her PTSD?" My mind flew at a million miles a minute.

"Her parents called the school board and said that you had created a hostile class environment by making students read out loud in front of classmates. They believe you gave their daughter too heavy a workload and caused her unhealthy stress levels. They claim it's why she collapsed." Her tone sounded as exasperated as I felt.

"I caused her breakdown by asking her to read twelve pages of a novel required by the state and asked her to write a one to two page journal response where she wrote about her feelings towards the book?" I wanted to scream. "That is so LUDICRIOUS! Are you saying I can no longer assign homework anymore, because students may have to take thirty minutes out of their day to THINK?" My blood boiled within my veins.

"I agree with you. You are here to teach them, and what you asked of them was by no means excessive or overly challenging. The problem is her parents are boosters. The school board received so many phone calls last night from parents whose teens are now complaining they are overly stressed that they are calling for action to be taken." She cleared her throat. "I told them that you were an excellent teacher who has been recognized for her classroom excellence and a determining factor for so many of our students doing so well on the SATs."

"But?" I knew there was a *but*, because there was always a but at times like these.

"But they don't want you teaching their children until things are fully settled. I have convinced the board that getting rid of you so close to your ten year mark would look like they were trying to avoid giving you the benefits you are entitled to. I am prepared to offer you a paid sabbatical through the end of this term. Hopefully by next semester this will have all blown over and you can return to your duties. In the meantime, please consider doing something worthy of a paid sabbatical, so I don't need to explain why taxpayers are watching you tan." Her eyes pleaded for understanding.

I looked down at my hands and then to hers. There were no visible ropes but I could tell they were tied. "I understand. I will gather my personal things from the classroom before the students arrive. I wouldn't want to damage their psyches before the day even begins." I rose from the chair and opened the door.

"Lillian?" I looked over my shoulder. "Every member of the staff looks forward to your return. We all believe this is a gross misstep on the board's part and I will continue to support you on this matter. If you need anything, please let us know?"

I nodded and left.

Tiffany watched with interest as I gathered my personal belongings in three bags and two file boxes, huffing each time I took something she had eyed for herself. My goal of escaping before any students arrived was a passing dream. Two of my homeroom boys helped me carry my belongings to the car.

"Are you coming back, Ms. Chambers?" Mike asked. It was his senior year and I had taught him all four years as a student in one of my classes. I had written a letter of recommendation for him to Reed.

"I hope so." I couldn't quite bring myself to make eye contact.

"This is so lame. Someone doesn't do their homework, freaks out, and then blames you for their issues. I'm a student and even I know that's messed up. What are you going to do until you come back to teaching?" He was such a nice young man. I promised myself that even if I didn't come back to teach, I would come back for graduation to see all my students.

"I've been offered a chance to go to Europe. I think I may try and do some work on some recently found historical documents. Don't worry too much about me." With those last words, both boys gave me a big hug before running back inside before the bell.

The drive home seemed to take more time than it normally did. It could be the influx of traffic that was the morning commute which I normally beat. It could have also just seemed longer because I felt numb. My whole body felt foreign to me as I drove home that day. By the time I got home I was cursing myself for thinking about being burnt-out the night before. Had I wished something like this upon myself? Was this my fault?

Once home, I stripped out of my clothes, wandered into the bathroom and climbed into the shower. It didn't take long before the tears started. All the pain that I had bottled up for the past two years came gushing out. I sank to the floor of the tub with the warm water washing over me in a storm of self-pity and loathing. I was a scapegoat because parents didn't know how to discipline or raise their children anymore and it was heart breaking.

Tallyn awoke with a start. His heart beat heavy in his chest and an overwhelming sense of pain washed through him. He heard a cry in the night and then realized it was his own. Tears streamed down his face and he was filled with immense despair and he wasn't sure why.

There were pounding sounds before the door of his chamber burst open. Two tall elves pushed through the door, swords in hand, alarm in their eyes. "Sir, we heard you cry out. What's going on? Have you been injured?" They quickly looked over the room, searching for the invader who had tried to do damage to their captain.

A blush started at the tips of his ears and washed over him. Tears still streamed down his face. "I'm fine, I'm fine. I'm sorry to have woken you up." He gulped back a sob and did his best to ignore the glances his soldiers exchanged. "I'm not under attack, but if you could call the physician?" he sobbed. His men made haste for the door, stumbling over themselves.

Moments later an older Elf appeared at the door. His hair was grayed and tied back in a braid that ran down along his spine. His eyes were a dark brown filled with warmth and concern. "Sire, you called for me?"

Tallyn motioned him over. "Please don't call me Sire. That title belongs to my father and brother." He struggled to get his breathing under control. "I feel like my heart is being ripped from my chest. Sorrow has consumed me for no reason I can see. I just woke up like this, suddenly." Tallyn didn't resist as the old Elf pushed him back down on the bed.

Leaning close the physician listened to his heart. He stroked the younger man's wrist while checking his pulse. "Are you sure you didn't just have a dream, Sire? Nightmares can affect us in peculiar ways."

Tallyn snatched his wrist back and sat up with a snap. "Grelyem, you have been the royal physician for what... five hundred years?" The old man gave a nod. "You've known me my entire life, right?" He paused for confirmation. "I've had plenty of bad dreams in my time. Have I ever called for you because of them?"

Grelyem looked startled. "No, you haven't." He looked over Tallyn again. "Have you met a young maid recently?"

Confusion creased Tallyn's brow. "I meet new people all the time. I'm Captain of the Guard and the youngest son of the King."

"Not to alarm you, but could you have developed a psychic link?" The older Elf lowered his head, breaking eye contact.

"Why would I have a psychic link to a maiden?" He asked. "Did she bewitch me?" Anger coursed through him.

"Well, a psychic link to a Soul Mate could cause such a reaction. If she were in so much pain that it was overwhelming her, she may be reaching out to you for comfort. You may be feeling part of her pain." He straightened a fold in his robe, refusing to make eye contact with the prince.

"That's impossible. There hasn't been a Soul Mate in the family for at least three generations. Remember the King and my mother?" The tears had finally stopped and Tallyn was flooded with anger.

"The King loved your mother, but she wasn't a noble and she wasn't his Soul Mate so she couldn't become his wife and queen," Grelyem said to Tallyn.

"No, she was a commoner, and so I enjoy the looks filled with pity from the court as they gaze upon the King's bastard son. I know my father loves me. I know my brother loves me, but it doesn't change the fact that I am not a prince and therefore am not entitled to a Soul Mate." It was true that only "real" members of the royal family had Soul Mates. Tallyn carried royal blood, which he couldn't deny, but he was not courtly. He had no real claim to the throne and so no need for a Soul Mate. Soul Mates were meant to unite kingdoms and bring fresh blood to the throne. They completed you in a way that no other would ever be able to. They were meant to create a leader that was stronger and more complete.

The physician clapped a hand on the young man's shoulder. "Perhaps then, it was just a bad dream?"

Tallyn was so unnerved he was shaking. Looking around the room, his eyes settled on the open window. "Perhaps it was."

Grelyem left without another word and Tallyn was no longer able to sleep. He pulled on a shirt and breeches before he headed out into the hall to find some of his men. Ale! Ale, the company of friends and maybe a pretty lady were the answer for the foul mood he now found himself in.

Hours later, when the first rays of sunlight began to caress the night sky, Tallyn stumbled back into his bedchamber. He had washed away his tears with ale and worked off the remnants of his anger by burying himself in the arms of a sweet-smelling kitchen girl. His limbs felt heavy as he dragged himself into bed. Sleep came quickly.

Alone in his dreams, he raced through the forest on Mavba's back. The air was crisp and filled with excitement. He had no idea where he was headed, but his heart swelled with anticipation. He drew to a stop when he felt another presence. Tossing both legs over one side of the horse, he slid off gracefully and looked around with caution.

Finally he cast his gaze down, looking into the river. There he saw her. Golden brown waves tumbled over her shoulders halfway down her back. Two large violet eyes read from a book intently. A soft smile gently curved her lips. Her body was abundant with curves, like a woman's should be. The type of body that welcomes a man home from battle or hugs a child close to wipe away tears. She was clothed like a man in tight-fitting blue breeches and a hip-length black knitted tunic. She radiated beauty. He touched the water and her image disappeared.

Tallyn bolted upright in his bed. He had seen the face of the watcher. He knew it was her by her very presence, but she had only been an image in a dream. He looked at the window. The sun was already high in the vivid blue sky and smells of the midday meal were filling the air. *Who is this mystery woman and how did I find her?*

After a good cry and a dose of anger over the whole situation, I had managed to collect myself. I took a long nap, setting my alarm for nine AM in the UK, and snuggled in. When I woke up I was going to let them know I would attend the ball and see if there were any projects I could work on this fall.

With the buzz of my phone's alarm I woke up and checked the time on the phone. It was one AM. There were plenty of times while I was attending university in the UK that I was still awake at one AM. Now, in my early thirties, it definitely felt more like a time better suited for sleep.

I got up out of bed, made a pot of coffee, and then pulled on some clothes. I just always felt more awake and alive out of my pajamas. I snagged a few books and sat down on the couch to read for a few minutes to get my brain engaged before I made the phone call. I stared down at the pages, letting my mind wander feverishly to a time of old, where honor and chivalry still meant something to most and not just a select few.

When next I looked up I realized more than two hours had passed. I took a deep breath for confidence and picked up the phone. If I didn't call now I would have to wait until after lunch. I punched in the country code and the number from the bottom of the letter I had received.

After two rings a chipper British voice answered. "Good morning, this is the Essex Historical Society. Iris speaking."

I swallowed and opened my mouth. "Good morning Iris. Is Mr. Dukes available?"

"One moment and I'll check for you. Please hold." With a click she was gone, replaced by music one might find in an elevator. After a few moments she returned. "Thank you for holding. He will take your call."

Before I could thank her there was a click, then a ring and suddenly a deep male voice was on the phone. "Hello, this Randall Dukes."

My brain went on autopilot. I had met Mr. Dukes while I helped with the tomes that were found at the Tower of London. "Good morning Mr. Dukes, this is Lillian Chambers. I worked under your tutelage for the translation of the twelfth century tomes that were found at the Tower of London a number of years ago. I was also just offered membership into the Historical Society."

Mr. Dukes was quiet for a minute, most likely trying to remember me. "Lillian Chambers - you were the American at Oxford working on her Master's Degree in European Literature, am I correct?"

"Yes, sir," I answered quickly.

"Excellent, I thought I recognized your name when we sent out our letters this fall extending membership to a handful of new people. You're probably one of our youngest prospects, my dear. Are you going to be able to make it to our yearly ball?" His voice was warm and inviting, like a welcoming grandfather you haven't spoken to for a while.

"Yes, I will be attending, but that's not the purpose of my call." I gave it a moment to sink in.

"It's not? What can I do for you my dear?" His question hung in the air. *What could* he do for me?

"I'm taking a sabbatical from teaching at the moment and I'm looking for something to keep me entertained. I was curious if you knew of any existing projects that could use a researcher?" Sure, the jobs never paid well, but it would keep me busy and look good on the resume if I wasn't to return to teaching at the beginning of next semester.

"Hmmmm..." he quietly pondered on the phone. "I might have something that your talents could prove useful on. The title would be researcher, so I apologize that it wouldn't pay very much. Only £1800 a month. Room and board would not be included, but I could ask Iris to help locate some flats in the town you would be working in."

I quickly did the math. Provided I didn't do anything too crazy I could afford to live on that. "I can do that. How soon would you need me?"

There was no hesitation on his part. "Can you be here Monday? I can help you take care of your visa when you arrive. Since you attended university here it shouldn't be too difficult."

I was shocked. Monday was three days away. "I can do that, but I need to price tickets."

"Scan me your passport and I will have Iris book the ticket for you. I don't need to remind you what autumn and winter are like here. You will also be spending a fair amount of time in Scotland with this project, so pack warmly." He finished off by giving me some details about what-all to scan and send so he could begin work on my visa before I arrived.

By the time I had hung up the phone with Mr. Dukes' assistant Iris, I had a confirmation number for my ticket, an email box full of papers to print, sign and bring with me to Europe and a thousand things to do before I left Monday morning. I sat for a moment catching my breath from the whirlwind that had just taken place.

I have always hated believing in forces such as fate. It's a hard pill to swallow that we may not always be in control of our destiny. With recent events lining up as they had, it left me to wonder if I was truly the one in the driver's seat.

Chapter Three

Tallyn swung his sword at the boy in front of him. He pulled back some of his force as the swords collided. The young man was barely an adolescent, but had insisted on learning to fight with a real sword. As captain of the guard he had humored him after the young lad had shown up every day for a week, rain or shine, just to watch the guards practice. The boy stumbled to the ground under the weight of the blow and dropped to his knee.

Without hesitation the lad accepted the hand that Tallyn offered. "Will I be ready to join the guard soon, Sire?" Tallyn sucked in a deep breath and reminded himself the boy was trying to be polite.

"If you keep working at it I'm sure you will be one of the King's men in no time." Tallyn started to turn away, then stopped. "Also, you should just call me Tallyn, sir or Captain. I don't sit on the throne, nor will I, and Sire should be reserved for those more deserving of the title."

The lad looked as if he were going to argue but thought better of it. "Yes sir, thank you." Then he was off, headed for his mother's dinner.

Tallyn had just sat down and was taking a sip of water when a large, heavy hand clapped down on his shoulder, causing him to spill the contents across his lap. He swore as he turned, drawing his blade, ready to give a thrashing. The sound of deep laughter filled his ears.

"Calm down little brother. It was merely an accident." With a resounding thud Maerryn dropped on the seat beside him. His older brother's dark features were made golden by the setting sun. "I wasn't trying to startle you." He raised his hands innocently while laughter played through his eyes.

With an annoyed sigh Tallyn sheathed his sword. "What can I do for you, brother?" The words drained the last of his annoyance.

"I heard that you have a Soul Mate!" When Maerryn smiled so broadly it was said that every woman in the Kingdom swooned.

Tallyn rolled his eyes. "Have I guarded the Kingdom so well that all you courtly fellows have left to do is gossip like the laundry maids?"

Maerryn roared with laughter. "Are you going to mount a search, go look for your other half? Perhaps the other half of your soul is the well-tempered and polite half?" he teased.

"I don't have a Soul Mate. It was just a dream. Besides, aren't you worried that if I have a Soul Mate it would give me some claim to the throne? Only those with claim would have a Soul Mate." Tallyn tried to forget about the vision of the woman he had seen in his dream this morning.

"Do you want to be King?" Maerryn asked in a rather sobering tone.

Tallyn's mouth dropped open in disgust. "A politician I am not. I will leave the fancy clothes, polite words and ego-stroking to you and father."

"And that is why I'm not worried. Besides, Father isn't even over two thousand yet. We have a long time before we have to worry about it. Especially with you leading the guard to keep us all safe." Maerryn took a sip of water from the nearby jug.

"Even if you don't like it, you do have claim. The King named you a son. You are a prince of the land, a son of the King and my only slightly-less-handsome little brother." Maerryn gave one last hard thump to Tallyn's back before getting up to go prepare for dinner.

Tallyn considered his recent dreams. Turning, he hurled a few more words in his brother's direction. "Perhaps a few days away to clear my head is in order. What do you say, Prince? Are you too courtly to get dirty with the guards and have some fun in the woods? Maybe a little wenching with the locals?"

Maerryn turned to toss a mischievous grin over his shoulder. "I'm in. We'll leave in two days' time!"

The next few days passed in a blur for me. I ran around town gathering up things I needed. I moved many of my belongings into storage and planned to sublet my home while I was gone. If I ended up not coming back to the States for the new term, the extra income from renting a place I wouldn't be using anyway would come in handy. In the meantime, it would mean not needing to touch my savings, and as the school was still paying me, I would actually have a little bit more money to spend.

Much to my dismay, when I checked in I found out I was sandwiched in a middle seat for the next eleven hours. It was the only direct flight from Seattle to London - everything else had a connection. I rummaged through my purse, looking for my wallet. When I found it at the bottom of my purse, I dug out the frequent flyer card for the airline I was flying.

I patiently waited for the gate agent to look like she was less busy. "Excuse me, would it be possible to have you add my frequent flyer number to the reservation? I just remembered I had a card with you."

She looked up at me from under her heavy black frames, offering a smile. "Sure thing. May I have your ticket and card please?" I handed them over obediently. "Ms. Chambers, are you aware you have a free upgrade available?"

"Oh, really? I haven't flown with you in a very long time," I responded excitedly.

"Yes, would you like to use it today? I have a seat available in first," she said with a wink.

I blinked at her. "That would be wonderful. Thank you." She punched a few keys and printed another ticket, handing it to me with my card.

I thanked her again as I boarded the plane. I quickly imbibed a glass of wine and closed my eyes, determined to sleep as much of the flight as possible.

My dreams were more vivid than usual. It was like I was standing there with my dream man. He and several others were packing up horses. There was a great deal of laughter and teasing among the men. They poked at each other until finally he had to step in and tell them to calm down. Even as he reprimanded them his smile shone brightly. I had never seen him smile with such a youthful presence.

Moments later another man appeared, just as handsome as my dream guy. "Tallyn!" he called, and my heart skipped a beat as I watched the man of my dreams turn to wave.

"Tallyn," I could feel myself whispering. He turned and looked in my direction, as if he had heard me. His face fell a little when he couldn't see me standing there.

"What's wrong?" the taller man asked him.

I watched as Tallyn shrugged. "I was just thinking about how I was going to have to see your face every morning for the next few days and it quashed all the fun out of our camping trip."

The taller man laughed, only to turn when someone called, "Maerryn!" which I guessed was his name.

I could feel the cool breeze on my skin, causing the hair on my arms to stand up. I watched with interest as the men finished packing up and began to ride away. I followed them through the forest I had seen a hundred times in my dreams. After a few hours they crossed the river in a shallow area then headed up a steep cliff, guiding their horses one at a time along the narrow ledge.

By midday the group reached the top of the cliff and stopped for lunch. The food smelled amazing cooked over the open fire. I felt my stomach rumble. When it did, Tallyn placed a hand on his stomach and looked around with confusion.

He was beautiful to look at, even with uncertainty creasing his brow. His green eyes deepened in color and his breath stilled. It was like he was looking right at me but couldn't see me. With a shake of his head, he rejoined the conversation around him.

They packed up and left, heading across a path at the top of the cliff that led into another forest. The group seemed more hesitant when they entered the new area. They rode close together for hours, and when darkness finally threatened, they found flat ground and made camp. The horses were tied up, dinner was caught and prepared, and then the wine came out.

Boys will be boys, I thought to myself as they laughed, sang and passed around the bottles.

Behind me I heard the crack of twigs underfoot. Suddenly, I sensed someone else was there. I turned, looking in the direction of the sound, and I saw shadows moving through the woods towards the encampment. Panic filled me and I tried to scream, but I was just a watcher without a voice.

Without warning a hand latched onto my shoulder, shaking me. "Miss! Miss, please wake up. You need to put your seat back up - we're getting ready to land."

I nodded as I came back to the world of the waking. I was on a plane surrounded by other passengers, many of whom were staring at me like I had three heads.

I thanked the flight attendant and noticed she had brought me meals that sat untouched. No wonder I had smelled food. She removed the trays as they did their final sweeps.

My heart started pounding and adrenaline was running through me. I had that feeling every time I put on my armor and picked a sword. I did my best to keep my reactions in check - it had just been a dream.

I exited the plane as quickly as possible, dragging my carryon behind me. In the terminal I made a beeline for the ladies room. I needed a pit stop and a moment to calm myself down. I was filled with rage, fear, and determination. I felt as if I had raced into battle, and found I was gasping for air.

I splashed cold water on my face, applied fresh makeup and pulled my hair up into a neat bun. I took a moment to find all my paperwork: passport, old alien registration card and customs forms. I walked quickly through the terminal towards customs.

The customs agent flipped through my paperwork and looked up at me. "You were here on a student visa last time. What is the purpose of your visit this time?" His eyes were gray and his mouth was hidden under a thick white mustache.

I looked at my stack of paperwork. "I am here on holiday as well as for research."

He looked me over closely. "You can't begin work until you take this paperwork to immigration tomorrow. If you are caught working without the proper visa you will be deported."

"Scouts honor, I will not so much as touch anything work related until my visa is issued." I raised my right hand, holding up three fingers, and offered what I hoped was a reassuring smile. It must have done the trick because the agent scanned my fingers, took my picture, and then put two new stamps in my passport.

Twenty minutes later, after I had wrangled my other two bags from the claim, I headed for the nearest taxi stand. It was pushing midnight and despite all the sleep I had gotten on the plane, I was exhausted... and hungry. My stomach growled in protest, demanding food just as a black taxi pulled up to the curb to collect me.

The driver hopped out to help me with my bags and open the door. "Where to, Missus?" he asked. His accent made me smile.

I looked down at the papers in my hand and tried to sound confident. "The Savoy please." Quicker than I could snap we were out and on our way. The Savoy was, and still is, an amazing hotel in London, but nights there do not come cheap. I didn't want to think about what Mr. Dukes was paying to put me up there until my visa was ready and we had found me a place to stay.

At some point during the ride I fell asleep, and when I woke up again it was because the doorman was opening the taxi door for me. I blinked, handing my credit card to the driver along with a few pounds for a tip before stepping out. With a polite word of thanks the taxi sped off.

A young man in a bellhop uniform collected my bags onto a trolley then followed me inside while I checked in.

The girl behind the counter checked me in and handed me my key cards. "You're on the sixth floor, here are your keys, and we will have your bags delivered to your room right away Miss Chambers. If there is anything we can do to make your stay more pleasant please don't hesitate to ask." Her voice was far friendlier than mine would have been at that time of night.

The trip from the lobby to my room was uneventful but grueling because I was hungry. I had just slid my shoes off when there was a knock at the door. I opened it, and like clockwork the young bellhop who had taken my bags brought them in, setting them on the luggage rack for me. With a smile and a nod he asked me, "Is there anything else I can help you with tonight Miss Chambers?"

I started to say no, then stopped. "Is room service still available?" I asked as hope crept into my voice.

"No, I'm afraid not miss. Are you hungry?" His smile was still firmly in place.

"Starved. I haven't eaten in over thirteen hours." I grabbed my purse from where I had dropped it on the desk and pulled out money for a tip.

"How about this, do you like fish and chips?" He had hardly finished the words and I was already vigorously nodding my approval.

"I know a place just down the street. My shift ended five minutes ago. If you don't mind the wait I will run out and grab some for you. My girl gets off in thirty minutes and I would just be banging around till then, when she finished up." Without question I pushed money for food and a large tip into the young man's hand. He laughed and assured me he would be back soon.

Once he was gone I began to unpack. I hung my clothes in the small closet then slid my suitcases into the bottom. I watched the clock, and true to his word, there was soon a knock on the door. I flung it open, delighted by the smell of fried fish and vinegar.

"You're my hero!" I exclaimed as I threw my arms around him. I remembered my place quickly, dropping my arms and stepping back.

"Give me your supervisor's name and I will make sure he hears of your good deeds." The young man blushed, pressing the take-out container into my hands along with a bottle of ale.

"The stuff in the mini-fridge isn't as good and it's overpriced." He gave me a wink. I offered him another tip and he just smiled and walked away without it.

I quickly gobbled down the food and enjoyed the beer. It had been so long since I last enjoyed a good fish n' chips. Sighing happily, I pulled my pajamas out from the closet and went on a quest to find my bathroom, desperately in need of a bath or shower.

The bathroom was gorgeous. Marble countertops and floors, with a claw-foot tub that sparkled under the lights. I ran a hot bath, taking full advantage of the bubble bath that was provided by the hotel. Moments later I was neck deep in warm lavender and vanilla scented bubbles. The water swirled around me, caressing away the soreness caused by long hours of travel. I leaned back against the wall and closed my eyes.

Tallyn sat around the fire with his fellow guards and brother; they had gotten lucky. A sudden feeling of panic had flooded him, causing him to reach for his sword just seconds before a band of thieving sprites jumped out of the shadows. His reaction had sent his men scattering for their own weapons, and the attackers had come face-to-face with a prepared guard.

The battle hadn't lasted long. The sprites had outnumbered the six Elves, but the Elves by nature were much faster and stronger. The trained soldiers had easily overpowered their attackers, but it was enough of a scare that they had decided to sleep in shifts. All the soldiers had clapped him on the back, commenting on his great prowess, but he knew it had been his watcher that had alerted him and saved them from ambush.

"I think I'm going to turn in," he said to the group before he headed to his tent.

"Good night, Captain!" they all called after him

From within the tent he could still hear them talking, the crack of the fire, and the sounds of the forest at night. He closed his eyes and quickly fell asleep, where he found his way back into his dream world.

Steam surrounded him and obscured his vision, but he could sense he wasn't alone. He pushed through the sweet-smelling fog, deeper into the unknown. He was aware that he was dreaming, but he felt as if he were awake and somewhere far away.

His breath caught in his throat as he realized that in front of him was a large bathtub filled with bubbles - and at the back of it sat the woman he had seen in his dreams just a few days before. Her cheeks glowed a rosy pink thanks to the heat of the bathwater. Her skin looked soft and smooth. Her dark lashes cast shadows on her cheeks where they were closed.

He then realized that there were sounds other than that of his heart beating quickly. Forcing himself to be calm, he was able to hear her humming softly. Occasionally she would splash a little water with her toes in rhythm to her wordless hums.

"Beautiful," he whispered.

Her head shot up from its resting place, her eyes wide awake and alert, looking over the room. At first he started to turn away, only to realize she couldn't see him.

"Hello?" her voice called softly.

He wanted desperately to answer back but was unable to. He turned, blushing, as she stood to rinse off and wrap a towel around herself. Even if she couldn't see him, he was still a gentlemen, and a lady deserved some bit of modesty.

He waited for the sounds of her leaving the bathroom, then followed her footsteps into a softly lit room. The furnishings were elegant, mixing cream with rich hues.

Surely the woman was a Lady or Queen to have such finery. He watched with interest as she climbed into a large bed and folded the covers around her. With a flick of her wrist the lights in the room dimmed. He was amazed at how she made such a feat of magic look so simple.

As she slept he looked at her closely. She didn't appear to be Elven or Fae. She looked... Human?

He watched with genuine fascination as she slept. He had a desire to stand vigil over her and protect against nightmares. His heart stopped and the world went dark when she whispered his name, then fell effortlessly to sleep.

Darkness overtook him, and the dream was gone.

Chapter Four

The next morning I woke up to the sound of the phone on my bedside table ringing. "Hello?" I said groggily into the receiver.

A chipper voice greeted me. "Good morning Miss Chambers! There is a Miss Iris Capanelli here in the lobby waiting to meet with you. May I let her know you will be down shortly?"

I processed the information. "No, please give her my room information and send her up." I hung up the phone and quickly bounced out of bed to brush my teeth and pull on clothes.

I had just finished getting dressed when I heard a knock on the door. I looked at the unmade bed with a grimace, then opened the door. The girl that stood there towered over me. She was slender, with dark olive skin and wild brown hair tucked back in a messy yet sexy ponytail. She looked like she had stepped off a poster for an Italian vineyard. "Hello, Iris?" I asked.

The girl smiled, revealing a row of perfectly white and straight teeth. "Yes, you must be Lillian then?" I nodded, stepping out of the doorway and motioning her into the room.

I looked at the clock and noticed it was a little after nine. "I apologize for not being downstairs to meet you earlier. With the late flight last night and time change I totally forgot to set an alarm."

Iris laughed - her voice sounded almost like wind chimes. "It's quite alright. Honestly, I thought Randall would give you a few days to settle in, but he seems rather excited to get you to work. If you have all the paperwork needed I can take you to immigration so we can take care of your work visa. After that, we can go look at a few flats I've already called on. Does that sound good?"

I breathed a sigh of relief and nodded. "That sounds perfect. Let me just grab my purse, pull on my boots and then we'll be off."

Iris paused for a moment. "May I ask you a personal question, Ms. Chambers?"

I nodded. "Of course, and please call me Lillian."

"You are obviously American, but you speak with the slightest hint of an accent and use some phrases that are far more UK than Colonial. Why is that?" she asked curiously.

"Well, for one, I attended University here and two, my ex-husband was British. When you hear the accent day and night for several years, you tend to adopt certain phrases and sounds without realizing it." The mention of my ex-husband made my skin crawl. While I didn't hate him, I didn't like thinking about him either.

She seemed satisfied with my answer and sat quietly in one of the chairs as I finished getting ready. I gave myself one last look-over in the mirror before I pulled on my coat. "I think this is as good as I'm going to get for the day, so let's get out of here." Iris smiled at my very American accent and phrase approvingly.

I waved to the bellhop from the prior night as we headed out. The poor guy must be tired having two shifts so close together. The doorman gave us a nod as we passed through the revolving door. We rushed to the car that pulled up to greet us. As gracefully as I could, I slid in after Iris, noting that even in three inch heels I only reached her shoulder.

The town car had a gray leather interior, an automatic screen between the front and back seat, and a fold down monitor in the ceiling. "Is this Mr. Dukes' car?" I wondered out loud.

"Yes, he gave us its use for the next few days, provided we make sure it is available to take him to and from work." Iris pulled a compact out from her purse and quietly checked her makeup.

The sky was already gray when we left that morning, and with each passing minute it grew darker, threatening to rain on us. This was the England I knew. Full of gray clouds, raindrops, and people in a hurry. It felt like I had come home.

The car pulled up in front of a gray stone building. The front was rather unimpressive, with only a sign indicating it was the immigration office. Inside Iris made quick work of securing a queue ticket for me. I glanced at the number on the slip and noticed there were at least thirty people in front of us. Prepared to wait, I sank down onto one of the hard plastic chairs in the waiting area.

"It looks like we have a little bit of a wait ahead of us. Have a seat." I smiled at her but she just looked at the chair beside me.

"Fifteen minutes, tops," she said.

I laughed. "No way. Last time I was here I sat around most of the day."

"Yes, but you are meant to be here now." Iris's words were filled with a sort of untold secret. "Besides, I hate waiting."

"What do you mean, I'm meant to be here?" I studied her carefully.

She gave me a shrug and sat in the chair beside me, her eyes never leaving the monitors overhead. "Just that. You are meant to be here. When you follow the path the world designs for you, the travel is much easier."

I thought for a moment, of the way it had seemed the stars had aligned for me over the last few days. "I like to think I am the master of my own destiny."

"We are all our own masters when it comes to the journey, but when it comes to the destination there are fewer options. Happy or Unhappy. Success or Failure. You get the idea." The numbers above rolled over. "Ah, we're up!"

With a ding overhead, I looked at the television above us, and there was my number displayed for all to see. Iris and I approached the counter. An older woman stood behind it. Her hair was graying mixed with a mousy brown. Her eyes were a pale blue and her lips showed no emotion. "Passport and paperwork please."

Iris took the paperwork I had signed along with a few others she had brought and my passport, then slid them under the barrier to the woman on the other side. "I am a representative from the Essex Historical Society. I have come on behalf of Randall Dukes to confirm this sponsorship."

The worker flipped through the papers, noticing the check on the sponsorship letter. "Everything looks in order. You can pick up the visa at the end of the day or first thing in the morning."

Iris cleared her throat. "We have included her hotel information. Can you have it couriered over to the Savoy when it is finished?"

The Immigration representative blinked as if surprised for a moment, then agreed. Iris turned, flashing me a wicked smile. "Guess we're all set here. Like I said, no more than fifteen minutes. Come along. Let's go take a look at the flats."

I felt my mouth go slack-jawed despite my best efforts to do otherwise. I'm not sure how it had happened, but it had. Nothing was ever easy with Immigration departments in ANY country. I couldn't help but acknowledge I had recently run upon an uncharacteristic lucky streak.

I watched as Iris slid into the back seat of the town car, motioning for me to join her. "How long is the drive? Is it possible to stop and grab a coffee and bagel?" My stomach grumbled on cue.

Iris looked at my vocal abdomen. "It's a few hours' drive out to the town you are going to be working in. We can stop and pick up some take-away." Iris tapped on the glass and gave the driver directions to stop so we could pick up some breakfast for the trip.

Twenty minutes later I had a cup of coffee in one hand and a scone in the other. Iris seemed self-absorbed in her mirror and smart phone so I quietly watched out the window as we crept closer to the city limits before passing through the smaller towns that made up the suburbs.

The rain started to fall in fat droplets, hitting the car windows with a satisfying slap. I watched as the heavy rain skewed the view of the countryside we passed. Green fields stretched on for great distances, marked only by the houses, animals and fences that inhabited the region. Wherever I was going was out in the middle of nowhere.

I started counting sheep in fields, either out of boredom or morbid curiosity, remembering the tales of lonely sheep herders. I shivered at the thought of the poor sheep. It was a fun joke to make in university if a guy turned out to be Scottish. The handsome ones always laughed and said their mother was a ewe. I smiled at the memories.

Suddenly on the horizon of a far hill I saw what looked like old ruins. They were too far to make out, but I was confident it was the remains of an old castle. "Where exactly are we?" I asked.

"Almost to your new home," Iris declared abruptly.

She motioned with her hand to the window I had been staring through. "Those ruins you see over there have some unknown inscriptions on them. They haven't meant much to us until recently. A few old tomes were found in northern Scotland at another site, which match the inscriptions. Your job will be to help connect and decipher them. The professor leading this project has been struggling with understanding the context behind the inscriptions."

Already my mind was teeming with questions and excitement. New tomes, secret inscriptions... my heart skipped a beat when I considered the possibilities. Who knew what secrets we would learn about the past? I thought of all the stories we had with no factual evidence. What if it was proof of Robin Hood or Arthur? A smile was plastered on my face and growing wider with each passing kilometer.

I was so deep in thought I hadn't noticed the car had stopped in a small town. The driver parked and came around, opening the door to let us out. "We're here, ladies," he explained as I stepped from the car and did my best to take in my surroundings.

The town looked like it had been pulled out of the pages of a fairytale and seemed untouched by the centuries. I would have considered time travel as an option if I hadn't seen a WiFi sign in a nearby café window. I looked at Iris, who seemed to be considering the town with an expression of disgust I didn't understand.

"This way. The realtor is expecting us." I followed obediently as she led me up a set of stairs to a small office.

As we stepped in the office I closed my umbrella, leaving it by the door. The woman that stood before us reminded me of my mother: soft eyes, rosy cheeks and a welcoming smile. "Would you girls like a spot of tea to warm you up before we go?" she asked.

Iris and I both agreed, sinking into the large, overly stuffed pale pink chairs that faced the agent's desk. We sat around sipping the tea quietly. The agent introduced herself as Molly before dropping lightly into her own chair.

"I have a half a dozen places to show you but perhaps if you tell me what you're looking for I can narrow that number down." She took a sip of her tea, looking at me over the rim of the cup.

I looked to Iris, who seemed uninterested, then back to Molly. "Well, it needs to be affordable. No more than five hundred pounds a month. Warm and dry," I said looking out the window. "Fully furnished and have internet access. I don't care about television but it needs internet access." I thought for a moment. "Oh, and quiet would be nice."

Molly smiled. "I was going to show you several flats - most of which were above restaurants and shops - but now I think I have a better idea. How do you feel about being off the beaten path a bit?"

"I'm fine with it so long as it doesn't mean wading through a foot of mud or solid ice," I said hesitantly.

"There's a cottage just on the edge of town. It's set back off the road a bit in the woods. Most people feel secluded back in there, but if you're wanting quiet I think it may be a good fit. The owner had high-speed wireless internet installed two years ago when her son was living there. The rent is four hundred and eighty pounds a month. The one catch is it has a fireplace and pellet stove for its only heating. Interested?" She gave me a wink.

"Let's go!" I said, already standing and reaching for my coat.

Half an hour later, I stood at the mouth of a paved pathway leading into the woods. I followed Molly down the path noticing I didn't need the umbrella as much under the cover of the trees. Tucked out of sight was a small cottage just as Molly had said.

The front had golden wood, an arched door and a large picture window. I closed my umbrella and wiped my feet before I stepped inside. I felt like I was stepping into Snow White's cottage. The first floor was separated into two large rooms. One half was a kitchen with an old stove and range, a porcelain sink, a few cupboards filled with dishes and a blue refrigerator that seemed strangely out of place, but retro at the same time. The other room was a large living room with a fluffy floral couch and matching chair centered in front of a fireplace on the far wall. Every available wall was covered in bookshelves, filled with colorful books on every subject. The back of the cottage was dominated by a large window looking out into the woods. Tucked back in the corner of the room was a small table big enough for a few people to sit around for a meal.

Molly motioned to the corner of the kitchen. "There is a small water closet in the kitchen and a full bathroom up stairs." I followed Molly up the small staircase leading to the second floor. The room ran most of the length of the cottage except for a small room at the end which I guessed was the bathroom.

A large iron bed sat in the center of the room. Another window running along the back of the cottage looked into the woods. In one corner was the pellet stove Molly had mentioned, and in another stood a large armoire. In front of the window sat a small writing desk and two short bookshelves filled with more books.

I walked across the bedroom and opened the door to the bathroom. It was a small, with skylights, and had walls made of white-washed wood. One side housed the sink, toilet, and a small cabinet with towels and toiletries. On the other side was a large claw-foot bathtub that overlooked a small garden below. Above the tub was a shower head that jetted out of the wall to rain upon you.

I looked at Molly with a smile. "It's perfect! I'll take it."

She smiled brightly and led us back downstairs. "Let's head back to the office and take care of the paperwork. You can move in as soon as Friday - is that going to work for you?"

I glanced at Iris who gave me a nod. "You begin work Monday so it will give you the weekend to get settled in. I will make arrangements for the driver to pick you up at the hotel and bring you and your luggage here."

I'm sure the smile on my face was beaming. The rest of the day went just as smoothly. We returned to the office, I signed some paperwork, wrote banknotes for the deposit and first month's rent, and then signed the lease. As I waved goodbye to Molly, climbing back into the car I once again found myself considering my recent good fortune.

The drive back was just as boring as the drive there, only instead of watching civilization disappear I watched as it became more and more prevalent. Soon we were back within the city limits and headed for the Savoy.

"Iris, would you like to join me for dinner? I would like to thank you for all your help."

She smiled sweetly at me. "I would but I have a lot of work to catch up on. Perhaps you would consider taking Mr. Dukes in my place? He doesn't get out much and I'm sure he would appreciate the company."

"I like that idea. I'll give him a call this evening and make arrangements for a night that is convenient for him." She nodded approval for a question I didn't ask.

"What will you do with your free time in London, Lillian?" Curiosity had finally gotten the better of her.

"Well, I have friends who live here in the city, so I'm going to get together with them for a few meals and some shopping. There are a couple old haunts I want to go check out while I'm here, and I also need to find something for the ball." I hadn't had time to find anything before leaving the States - not that full out ball gowns were easy to find there.

"You should get on that. If you like I can recommend some stores?" she offered. "It can sometimes take a few weeks to get things altered."

"Thank you, I would appreciate that." I turned and looked out the window. The raindrops were rolling off the car as we passed over the stone streets.

Finally the Savoy appeared in view. We pulled up under its large awning and the doorman rushed to open the car door for me.

"Would you like to come in?" I asked, but Iris shook her head.

"I'll email you the list of shops but I need to get the car back for Mr. Dukes. It's already after three." She waved to me as the door shut.

I turned on my heel and marched through the revolving door into the lobby. A rush of warm air washed over me and I smiled at the girl behind the desk as I approached. "I'm expecting a delivery this evening of some important documents. Could you call me when they arrive?"

"I would be happy to make sure that is taken care of. Your name and room number?" she asked politely.

"Lillian Chambers. Room six hundred eleven." I watched as she paused for a moment, turning and shuffling through papers. When she turned around she handed me a large blue envelope.

I quickly peeked in the envelope to find my approval papers and passport. "This is it, never mind then. Thank you so much." She gave me a confirming nod then looked at the customer behind me.

I hustled into the elevator area, checking my phone for any messages. I had left word with my school that I would be going to Europe for a research opportunity and had expected to hear something back from them. There was nothing. I let out the breath I realized I had been holding. I loved teaching, but this had me excited. I entered an elevator with a number of other guests letting the attendant know my floor number.

A few moments later I was in my room pulling off my boots. "What a day!"

I started considering another bath when the memories of the night before came rushing back. It felt like someone had been there with me. It wasn't a threatening feeling or even that of a perverted peeping tom. It had still been unnerving. I could have sworn I had heard someone speak softly. Maybe I had imagined it. Or maybe I had overheard another guest from the room next door.

❧

Maerryn and Tallyn sat at the front of the group of men on horses. They were riding much slower today, letting caution be their guide. While most Fae were welcoming, some resented the Elves for the power they held.

This land was divided into four kingdoms. The Elven lands lay in the south ruled by their King Naelym, Maerryn and Tallyn's father. In the high, snow-covered mountains of the north lived the Dwarven King, Kenthur, and his Queen Ethba. Along the great distances of the eastern coastline the Fairies held power, ruled by their Queen, Mab. Then there was the west, controlled by the Were.

There were many other kingdoms that lay beyond the oceans, but these four had banded together to form close ties and better control the land they shared. Each was responsible for its own border defenses. It was how they had maintained peace for so long - by working together. Trade was open between the kingdoms and most lived and flourished happily, but in recent times there had been rumors of a band of less-than-happy Fae that wanted to see all of the people under one ruler, in the hopes that local governing would be given to the villages.

Maerryn was the first to speak. "So, how did you know about the band of cutthroats last night? Did you just hear them before us?"

Tallyn cleared his throat. "My watcher warned me. I sensed her panic, alerting me that something was wrong."

"Is this the unseen presence that watches you each day? Did you say she?" The grin on Maerryn's face was spreading.

"Yes, I believe it is a woman. The presence is somehow nurturing and protective, like that of a mother or a lover." Tallyn started looking all around for anything to change the subject.

"You can now sense her feelings, and you doubt that you have a Soul Mate?" There was no stopping it now. Maerryn's face was beaming with laughter. Amusement was written there like a sign on a pub.

Tallyn rolled his eyes. "No, she is not my Soul Mate. I don't have one of those. You might, though."

Maerryn considered his brother's words. "I hope so. I hope she's a Fairy or a Pixie princess. Wings are so...

alluring." His eyes glazed over with daydreams and Tallyn knew he had lost him- thankfully. Maybe now he would drop the Soul Mate business.

"You know they like it when you trace the designs of their wings with your fingertips, or after you make love to them you stroke the muscles between their wings. It drives them wild and gets them ready to go again."

Tallyn resisted the urge to shove Maerryn out of his saddle. Several years ago a party of dignitaries from Fae lands had come to the castle. The rumor was that his brother had sampled all in attendance. "You know, if you would put half the effort you spend on women into your sword work, you would be the finest swordsman in all of the kingdoms."

"I put all my efforts into my sword work brother. Just because I choose a different sword than you doesn't make me any less deadly with it." Maerryn waggled his eyebrows at his brother. A few of the men behind them laughed.

In disgust Tallyn pushed his horse further ahead until he broke through a wall of trees. They had finally arrived at their destination.

There was a cliff face with a beautiful waterfall that marked the edge of the sacred space. A ring of trees protected the area. None with ill intent in their heart could enter through the magical barrier that surrounded this place. It was one of the ten magical Fairy Circles in the land and its magic was as old and powerful as the Fairy race for which it was named. For thousands of years the Fae had come to these places to relax peacefully.

The circles were safe havens even in times of war. They offered transport to distant lands, kept out those with ill intent, and rejuvenated the Fae who visited with fresh magic. They were holy places filled with joy.

Tallyn slid off of his horse and led her to the far side of the pool where she could drink easily. He began to unload his gear, setting up camp in an alcove of trees. Soon his men and brother joined him and before long a camp had been established.

While some of the Elves stripped down to swim in the pools Tallyn retrieved his sword and began to go through his daily practice. It wasn't long before his brother, wet and wearing only his breeches, approached with his own sword.

"We come all this way to relax and have fun and what do you do? You work and practice," Maerryn teased.

Tallyn lunged with a thrust, piercing the heart of his imaginary opponent. "It is your job to lead the kingdom and my job to protect it. You may be able to break from politics but I cannot break from practice. Diligence is what keeps our people and lands safe."

Maerryn brought his sword down with force on his younger brother. Tallyn smiled and countered the blow. It had been too long since the two had fought.

Maerryn pushed Tallyn back toward a group of trees. His smile broadened now that he had his brother on the run. When Tallyn's back foot connected with a tree trunk he smiled before jumping and pulling himself up onto a tree branch, barely missing the sting of his brother's sword. The two grown Elves laughed like children.

"For someone who doubted my ability with a sword it seems to me I hold my own."

Tallyn grinned wickedly down. "Maybe I just let you push me here so I could get you into the trees. Coming up?"

The branch beneath Tallyn shook as Maerryn dragged himself up, into the tree with far less grace.

"Oh no, I can keep up." With those words Maerryn thrust his sword at his brother, catching the edge of Tallyn's shirt.

"Do mind the clothes. Unlike you I don't bed the castle's seamstresses and so I must repair my own clothes." He watched as Maerryn's eyes flared with humor.

Tallyn backed out further along the branch. When he looked down it was a ten or twelve foot drop into the waters of the pool below. He took one more step backwards, forcing his brother to come out further on the branch.

Maerryn took the bait and lunged with his entire body. Tallyn jumped, using an overhead branch to help him swing over his older brother, landing behind him.

Maerryn whirled around to face him but it was too late. Tallyn rushed under his brother's sword, knocking it from his grip. He quickly caught it with his free hand. Maerryn's eyes glowed when he realized he had been bested.

"Now what little brother? You win, I forfeit." He smiled his charming grin.

Something wicked crossed Tallyn's mind as he held his brother's gaze. Without warning Tallyn jumped and landed with as much force as he could on the branch. He was rewarded with the desired outcome.

Maerryn's face filled with shock as the branch moved suddenly under him and he found he was standing on only air. A second later he crashed into the pool of water below. He was sputtering water and gasping for air as he resurfaced.

"Now, I have won!" Tallyn called down to him, laughter dancing across his face.

Once Tallyn had left the tree and Maerryn had dried off, they sat down along with the other Elven men to enjoy some warm soup and each other's company.

It was then that Tallyn noticed there were half a dozen nymphs in camp, cooking, rubbing shoulders, and flirting. He smiled politely then turned his gaze on Maerryn.

"Who are they?" Tallyn asked.

Maerryn smiled at one nearby. "This is what I had intended to tell you when I came over to talk before our little game. These ladies are camping here as well. Of course, when they heard we were two Elven princes and members of the Guard they wanted to meet us, thank us and make sure we were well cared for while on our vacation."

As if on cue one came over with a bowl of soup, sat on Maerryn's lap and began feeding him.

"Do you like it, Sire?" she asked, her voice filled with flirtatious laughter.

Another Nymph, who looked more Sprite than Nymph came over, sinking to the ground beside Tallyn with a bowl of soup.

"Are you hungry, Sire?" she asked politely.

Tallyn grimaced at the word Sire. "You can just call me Tallyn. I am hungry, but I would prefer to feed myself, if that's alright?" He glanced at his brother, who looked as if he was having far too much fun.

Tallyn noticed her shoulder slumped at his lack of enthusiasm.

Nymphs had delicate emotions and needed to feel appreciated or desired. Tallyn was uninterested in the girl, but didn't want her to feel underappreciated when all the other girls seemed to be preoccupied. He cleared his throat uncomfortably. "Umm, maybe I could try letting someone else do it once."

The Nymph's face lit up as she spooned a small amount of soup from the bowl and blew on it gently. She carefully raised it to Tallyn's mouth so he could eat. The soup tasted wonderful, full of fall vegetables and soft handmade noodles. He swallowed.

"What is your name?" he asked the nymph.

"Arinella, my lord." Tallyn could accept this title.

"Do you visit here often?" He kept his voice soft and considerate.

"A few times a year." She fed him another spoonful of soup.

"Are these ladies your sisters?" he asked after swallowing his latest mouthful.

"No, just my friends. We're leaving tomorrow morning to return to the coast. Misha is expected in the Queen's court in two days' time." Arinella smiled at Tallyn.

"I see. Are you part of her retinue?" Tallyn reached out and swept a lock of hair back behind her ear. Arinella nodded.

He sensed an unease in the nymph. "Don't be scared of any of us. We are all gentlemen, I assure you."

Arinella blushed and smiled. "It's not that. I am a new courtesan for the Fairy Court. I'm just nervous. Misha said I should ask you or your brother to take me first. It would be most honorable to have my first be of royal blood." She lifted Tallyn's palm and pressed a kiss to it, then gave him another bite of soup.

"Is this a life you have chosen for yourself or was it chosen for you?" His words had an edge to them though still spoken softly.

"It is the life I have dreamed of. I will be a consort to those who need me. I will be reserved only for the highest members of the court. I've waited years to be chosen. Misha finally saw my beauty and picked me." Her conviction burned in her eyes.

Tallyn noticed as he looked around that everyone else had disappeared. He could hear a mixture of moans and laughter coming from the woods and water. Carefully he rose then and allowed her to lead him back to his tent where he fell into her arms, knowing full well that her claim of a prince would indeed make her more valuable in the Queen's eyes.

Chapter Five

I pressed my nose against the glass of another dress shop. I had been looking for three days. If I didn't find a dress before leaving London tomorrow afternoon, I was screwed. The problem was none of the shops carried stock in my size. They all needed to be special ordered. Which took six to eight weeks minimum.

With a deep breath I sucked in my tummy and marched into the last dress shop. It smelled like lilacs within. A black and white cat sat on a chair beside a sewing machine. Moments later a small old woman of shocking beauty appeared at the front of the store. "Can I help you, miss?"

I marveled at her otherworldly features, almost unable to breathe. "Yes, I need a ball gown for an event in two weeks. Everyplace I go doesn't carry my size and would need to order it for me which will take too long."

"Why didn't you order one sooner, dear?" The woman's voice didn't seem to match her apparent age.

"I didn't expect to be able to go to the masquerade ball. If you can't tell by the accent, I'm American, and it just wasn't possible for me to travel to Europe for a party. Circumstances have changed and I'm now staying for a couple of months." A certain level of hopelessness flooded me as I looked around the shop not seeing any dress that appeared to be bigger than a size small.

The woman considered me for a moment and disappeared into the back room. I began to wonder if I would be attending the ball in a toga made from bed sheets. Suddenly the woman pushed through the curtained door dragging two bagged petticoats and a corset under her arm. "I think I've got something perfect for you, dear."

Moments later I was clinging to a door frame for dear life as the old woman cinched my waist tighter and tighter into a corset. My bosom was spilling out over the top. The doubled layer of petticoats kept me from being able to get close enough to the frame for a more secure hold. "One last deep breath, dear," she commanded over my shoulder.

I took a deep breath and with a hard tug was tied into my corset. My spine was forced rigidly straight as I stood there. I placed my hands on my hips, which were now exaggerated by the corset and petticoats. I ran my hands up over my waist to the curve of my chest. No wonder women wore these things. I couldn't breathe but I felt empowered, sexy, and in control. I smiled, picturing myself standing like Wonder Woman.

"Foot, please!" The woman stooped before me and held out an ice blue shoe covered in crystals. To my surprise the shoes fit perfectly and despite their high, narrow heel were insanely comfortable.

"Now put your arms straight up over your head, dear." I did as instructed and watched as the shop woman lowered a sky blue gown over my head. It was trimmed in ice blue and silver embroidery covered in clear crystals. The full ball gown skirt had a train behind it and a swoop in the front. She quickly laced up the back of the dress and finished smoothing out the wrinkles.

I turned to face the mirror. The dress fit me perfectly, as if it had been made for me. With the shoes, the hem was perfect. The neckline was low without being too revealing. The final touches were a lace and crystal mask that had been made to match and a tiara that sparkled like ice. I could hardly believe it was me standing there. It was as if this shop owner had reached into the secret place in my mind and pulled out a dress from my dreams.

Reality quickly set back in. "I hate to ask, but how much will it cost to take Cinderella to the ball?" My excitement was fading as I realized a dress of this quality and beauty wouldn't come cheap.

The old woman walked around me, looking at me carefully. "This dress has already been paid for once. It was made for a young bride that ended up fleeing the country with her groom to avoid her family. The dress was never worn even though it was paid for. Now, I have stored it all these years and have never found another that it was meant for until today." She paused, rubbing her chin for a moment as she considered the dress. "I will sell it to you at the price that was originally paid all those years ago. £100."

My jaw dropped. "How old is this dress?" I asked, amazed at the price. I had expected at least another zero and wouldn't have been surprised had it been two.

She pulled a bill of sale off the hanger handing it to me. It was dated March 14th, 1938. At the time the price of this dress would have been extravagant. I reached for my purse and without hesitation dug the cash out to cover the purchase. To my surprise the corset, petticoats, shoes, mask and tiara were all included. The shopkeeper explained that in the era it was how things were done. People ordered complete sets to be made.

After thanking the shopkeeper three more times, I left. My arms were filled with two large boxes housing the dress and three large shopping bags containing the accessories. It didn't take long for me to hail a cab. With the driver's help I carefully wrangled the oversized purchases into the cab.

I sat quietly in the taxi as we drove back to the Savoy hotel. I had dinner plans with Mr. Dukes tonight and wanted to be ready on time. I was overjoyed with my dress and couldn't wait to try it on again. Tomorrow I would move into the small English cottage which was to be my home. Could things get much better than this?

As the taxi pulled up to the Savoy, the doorman rushed forward, opening the door for me. I paid the taxi driver and retrieved my packages from shopping. I felt like I was almost floating to the elevator, I was so happy. When I saw my favorite bellhop, I said hello with a big smile. He winked and gave me a nod as he tugged at a trolley loaded with luggage.

Once in my room I carefully stacked my purchases in a corner. I looked over the small pile I had already accumulated of daily use items. In my shopping adventures I had purchased a wheeled shopping cart for groceries, towels and bathroom toiletries, a pair of warm, heavy slippers and a coffee maker.

I looked at the clock on the bedside table. I had two hours before Mr. Dukes would be here. I went and began running a hot bath before returning to the bedroom. I had wanted to make the dinner reservations but Mr. Dukes had insisted. He was crazy though if he thought I was letting him pay after all the help he had given me.

I considered all the clothes in the closet that I had brought with me. Finally I decided on a brown sweater dress, dark tights and boots. I laid them out neatly on the bed, then stripped down and headed for my bath. I practically skipped into the bathroom. I turned the water off, set an alarm on the clock by the sink and happily sank into the warm tub of sudsy water. *I could really get used to this,* I thought to myself.

"All I need now is a book and a glass of wine." With one last self-fulfilling laugh I dunked my head below the surface of the water.

Two hours later I stepped into the lobby of the hotel dressed and ready to meet my English host. As I headed for the door I noticed Mr. Dukes standing by the fireplace in the lobby. He held in his arms a bouquet of Tiger Lilies.

He smiled and laughed as I approached saying, "Mr. Dukes, it's so nice to see you again." He gave me an affectionate hug. My experiences had taught me most Englishmen did not hug. At least, not people they barely knew.

"I hope you don't think this is too forward of me, but in my day we always brought a lady flowers before we took her out. My granddaughters still love the tradition, as antiquated as it is. I thought you may as well." He handed me the bouquet and I smiled.

"It's funny, my grandfather used to always call me his favorite Tiger Lily. This was thoughtful, thank you." I walked over to the desk and asked if they could have them put in a vase in my room. The girl agreed, smiling at me as she took them.

I looked back at Mr. Dukes. "Shall we go, sir?" He gave me grin and offered me an arm.

He opened the car door for me, making sure I was situated before closing it. Giving the driver directions he then turned to me. "Do you eat Italian?"

I smiled at him. "I eat just about anything, but it doesn't have to be fancy. I'm just as happy with fish n' chips and an ale at the pub as I am anything else."

He laughed. "You are so much like your grandmother it's scary sometimes."

I was unable to keep the confusion off my face. "You knew my grandmother?"

"Of course, she was my older sister." He took my hand and patted it. "Your grandparents, much to the family's dismay, decided to move to the United States after World War II ended. Surely you knew that?"

I had known that. "We as a family just never really talked about it. I knew Mother's parents had been older when they had her, and I knew they were from the UK, but I had never met them."

They hadn't spoken to my mother since she married my father, whom they didn't approve of. Then they passed away. I studied my hands trying to find the words. "Was that part of why you took a special interest in me during University, and now?"

"Yes. Also, you showed a lot of promise and we're family. Your family here would love to get to know you, your siblings and your parents." His voice was even but not devoid of emotion.

I thought about his words for a moment. What had happened, happened a long time ago. Perhaps it was time to put the disagreements behind us. Then I remembered something. "Are you the Uncle Randy that sends Christmas and birthday cards each year?"

"One and the same," he answered.

For years, cards had come for all of us in the family from an uncle none of us knew. It suddenly made sense. "So you've met and spoken with my mother?"

"Of course. How do you think you got into Oxford?" He said it matter-of-factly.

"My own merit?" I asked hoping.

"Well, that did help, but so did having alumni on the board." He gave me a wink.

Things suddenly made more sense to me then they had in years. I can't say I loved the idea that I had help getting into Oxford, but I do believe I made a solid reputation for myself. Something else hit me. "Why did you act like you didn't know me? Why all the secrecy?"

"That was done more for your own good. I knew you would work harder if you thought you were on your own.

Not to say you would have goofed off, but your mother said you always felt added pressure from family. I wanted to see you shine." There was compassion in his tone as he gave my hand a squeeze.

"What about this new project?" I asked.

"This just happened to work out with perfect timing. I had just found out the night before that the professor needed someone. Then you called and it seemed like a good fit." He laughed a little. "Funny how things sometimes just work out."

The ride was short and soon we arrived at the restaurant. We were in a district known for its food. As I climbed out of the car, smells from the Indian place next door mingled with the French bakery across the street and then danced with the garlic from the Italian restaurant in front of me. It felt as if I was taking a bath in a cultural stew.

Mr. Dukes tucked my hand around his arm and walked me in. The maitre d' wasted no time in seating us. Wine and water were poured and a list of the evening specials were read off flawlessly. I closed my eyes and breathed deep the scents of the Italian kitchen. The herbs and spices mingled with the acidic smell of cooking vegetables. My stomach roared, demanding satisfaction. Since coming to England I had eaten less and less, too busy to be bothered with food. However, now for the first time in several days I realized how foolish that was.

My uncle placed the order for both of us, and moments later fresh bread and a large salad was brought to the table along with two bowls of soup. I leaned forward and smelled the soup. It was filled with fall vegetables in a tomato base. "Wow, this smells amazing." Looking up with a smile I reached for my spoon, trying not to eat like a famished vagabond.

The broth was light and the vegetables were still firm enough to add texture to the dish. It was perfect. Everything about that meal was perfect. I had reunited with lost family, returned to a country that made me feel at peace, and the food was amazing.

The pasta fulfilled every flavor need I was craving. The chef even came out and spoke with us. I assured him that the food had been top notch.

After dinner my uncle took me to London Bridge, where we purchased a few cups of coffee and discussed everything that had happened to me over the last thirty-two years of life. What holidays had been like. Where we went as a family on vacations. I even told him about my ex-husband and my return to the single life.

"You were married before?" he asked, sensing my hesitation to talk about it.

"Yes, I met him while I was here studying for my master's degree." I stared at the water.

"So he was an Englishman?" He pursed his lips together.

"Yes, and I thought we were growing old together and he thought we were growing apart." Even now, I couldn't make the words sound less bitter.

"So he found someone else and left. Did you see it coming?" he asked as he took a sip from his cup.

I shrugged. "Yes and no. Looking back I saw the signs and chose to ignore them. I thought it was a phase. When it happened I was shocked. Now I know, I think my head was just trying to protect my heart, as long as it could."

He nodded as if he understood. "Sometimes we let the wool be pulled over our eyes, because we hope it will hurt less if we don't see it coming. The problem is, if someone swings a sword at you and you don't see it, you can't defend against it."

I laughed, having had real world experience with exactly that. "Are you jaded and sick of love then?" His words were feather light as he tried to assess the damage done.

"No, I think I'm just tired. I think ever since it happened I've just been empty inside. It wouldn't be so bad if I could just get mad, but I can't even do that." I wrapped both hands around the cup hoping its warmth would fill me where I now felt hollow within.

"Well, I believe you are here for a reason. I'm sure if you let it, Britain will wash away your sadness with its rain, and the winds from Scotland will fill you with new life." He gave me a wink.

I laughed loudly. "You should sell that logo to the travel administration."

"Too much?" he asked.

I held up my fingers to indicate just a little. He had a laugh with me and patted me on the back. "It's getting cold, you should get back to the hotel and pack up. I'll send the car early tomorrow. That way if you need anything once you get there, the driver can take you to the market and what not. There's a Tesco not far from where you'll be."

❧

The next morning Tallyn awoke slowly. His head was pounding, no doubt from too much wine. He reached out, looking for the young nymph who had shared his bed the prior night. When all his hand found was blankets he opened his eyes. Sure enough, his bed was empty. Quickly he grabbed his breeches and pulled them on, then began to search through his belongings in the tent. Sure enough his purse was gone. Luckily all his other belongings seemed to be accounted for.

Angrily, he stormed out of his tent. Maerryn was sitting by the cooking fire with a rather smug grin on his face. "What has you so angry so early in the morning?"

"That little Nymph stole my purse. I knew better and still I went along with it. Karma has a way of reminding you when you step out of line." Tallyn kicked at the dirt before sitting down on the ground beside his brother and reaching for a cup to make tea in.

"You did hear the part where she said you were her first, right?" Maerryn took another sip.

"Yes, of course." Tallyn crumbled up tea leaves and poured boiling water over them.

"Not only did you take her innocence, but she gets the bragging rights that her first was a prince. Your purse bore the royal seal. She took it for payment and proof that it was you who bedded her." His chest rumbled with soft laughter.

"Great, lucky me." Tallyn winced as he burned his tongue on the still boiling tea. He wasn't so much angry with her as he was with himself. Then again he had known what he was getting into. "So did we all lose our coins or just me?"

"Oh we all lost our purses, but not to worry, I have coin hidden away. Should the occasion arise I have enough to meet our needs. They were also kind enough to leave our horses. That was my biggest fear this morning when I discovered they had taken our purses." Maerryn smiled to himself, very amused by the whole situation.

Tallyn, still grumpy, got up and headed back to his tent. "Where are you going, brother?" Maerryn called after him.

"To wash her off of me and my sheets." He ignored Maerryn's laughter behind him.

Tallyn finished hanging his clean wet sheets on a nearby tree before stripping down and diving for the warm water at the base of the waterfall. Hot springs under the mountain kept the pool steaming warm even in the coldest of winters. The waterfall, while it was cold water, never seemed to freeze. Strange magic indeed.

Tallyn allowed himself to float mindlessly in the pool. Soon his thoughts drifted to his strange dream girl. *Where was she? Who was she? Did she even exist?* He had never considered the possibility of love. No woman wants to love a soldier, but too many wanted to love a prince. He didn't think he had it in him to love or let someone love him like that.

The cool fall air, mixing with the warmth of the spring lulled him into the lightest of sleeps. He could see her. She was in a dirty gray place. She stepped into what appeared to be a shop. The saleswoman there was shrouded in magic. There was something about her that seemed familiar and slightly dangerous. His imaginary beauty shifted nervously, waiting for the woman to return.

Tallyn bit back laughter as he watched her being laced into a corset. Here was a woman who didn't do such things regularly and it showed. She wore men's clothing and looked baffled by a corset. She had no concept of her own beauty. His breath caught in his throat as he watched her in the gown. Tallyn wanted nothing more to reach out and touch her. To prove to himself she was real.

He felt her heartbeat quicken and a moment of concern touch her as she asked about the price. At that moment he knew that were she his, he would gladly pay a king's ransom to watch her smile like that again. He would bid her to dress in whatever made her feel the most beautiful. Whether dressed in the breeches of a man or the gown of a woman her beauty would dazzle the court.

It was at that moment he realized the shopkeeper's cat was staring at him. He could see it in its eyes. Its gaze followed his every motion, never blinking.

The cat walked towards him and it was then he felt it brush up against him. It was otherworldly, which meant it was most likely the familiar of the shop keeper. Either there was a Fae out there playing a trick on him or his dream girl was real. With another brush of the cat he was jerked back to reality. He was alone, drifting along in the pool of water, inside a sacred circle.

Tallyn swam to the edge of the pool and pulled himself out. He picked up his breeches and marched naked back into camp. Everyone came to a halt from what they were doing when they saw him parade naked to his tent. When he exited he was dressed again.

Considering his words carefully he looked at Maerryn. "I need to talk to you."

Maerryn shrugged and got to his feet to follow his younger brother. "What's this all about? None of us care that you're running around naked, you're just normally more conservative than that."

"I saw a woman," Tallyn said. "And I think she was real."

Maerryn laughed. "Most of them are."

"No, that's not what I mean. I've seen this girl in my dreams before. I just watched her purchase a gown from what I believe was a witch." Tallyn then recounted the dream he had just had, including the experience with the cat.

"Hmmmm, and you believe she is in trouble?" Maerryn asked.

"No. I don't believes she knows she was in danger though." Tallyn realized the situation was beyond his control.

"Has it occurred to you yet, that maybe this woman is your Soul Mate? Perhaps if you can see her, she can see you. Your watcher," Maerryn offered.

Tallyn pondered that idea for a moment. "Maybe she is my watcher, but she certainly isn't my Soul Mate. If one of us has one, it would be you, but there hasn't been a Soul Mate within our family in three generations - four if you include us."

"Alright, whatever you say. So, where is she? We will mount a rescue party and keep her safe from the witch." Maerryn turned back towards camp.

Tallyn's jaw hardened. "I don't know. It is like no place I have ever seen before. For now all I can do is wait."

Maerryn considered his brother carefully. "Are you sure she's not in trouble? We are half a day's ride to the Fairies. Queen Mab can see between worlds. Perhaps she is in a different realm?"

"No, I don't want to involve the Fairies if at all possible. I will wait. Night is coming and hopefully I will reach her again in my dreams."

Despite Tallyn's concern, he felt she wasn't in immediate danger. Maybe a good night's sleep and a fresh head would do him good. He stopped long enough to gather his now dry bedding before returning to camp.

Dinner, games and boasting were as they normally were when the males of any race got together. Loud and filled with laughter. Soon the heavy drinks did what they do best and sent them all off to deep sleep.

Chapter Six

I awoke early the next morning. I wanted one last bath in the giant bathtub before I retreated to my cute country cottage. I had packed all my belongings last night, except for the clothes I planned to wear today, and had them by the door ready for the bellhop to pick up. I had finished writing a letter to the manager detailing the exceptional service of the bellhop who went above and beyond the call of duty for me the first night. After sealing the letter, I ducked into the bathroom to run a bath.

As I settled into the oversized tub I thought about how much my life had changed in such a short period of time. A little over a week ago I had watched a girl pass out in my class. Who knew that one event would set off this entire chain reaction?

I closed my eyes and thought of my handsome dream warrior. I pictured his face, his smile, and his laugh. I could feel him like he was near but all I could see was darkness. I concentrated deeply on the darkness around me, willing it to reveal something that would act like a beacon to guide me. There before me I thought I sensed something. I reached out towards it.

Suddenly something grabbed my wrist, biting deeply into it and piercing the skin. I was reminded of my injury last week where I had sprained it. I had been careless with it in all the excitement, and now it hurt worse than ever before. I was tugged forward by something large. I fought against the pull, trying to regain control over my body. I could feel hot sticky liquid running down my hand. Fear took over and I cried out, making one last pull to free my wrist.

I awoke with a splash, sliding under the surface of the water and gasping for air as I resurfaced. There was a loud pounding on the door accompanied by a voice filled with concern. I flung myself out of the tub, grabbing the robe on the back of the bathroom door. I peeked out the front door. The manager was standing there with deep worry lines creasing his face. "Miss Chambers, is everything ok in there? We received reports of a scream from your room."

I pulled the robe around me tighter. "I'm fine, I just fell asleep in the bathtub. I'm so sorry...." My words trailed off as I realized the manager was staring with horror at the hand that held my robe closed. I looked down at it. It had a bruised handprint on it and several deep gashes that were now bleeding on the white robe. "I'll pay for this," I offered.

"Miss Chambers, if you are in danger or someone else is in there, don't say anything, just blink twice," he whispered. I stared at him wide eyed, then back down at my wrist.

"I'm in here alone, but perhaps if you could bring me a first aid kit I could make use of?" He nodded and immediately made a call on his cell phone. In just a few short minutes a paramedic and police officer had arrived.

A nice young man in a white uniform finished giving me stitches, then bandaged my wrist. "Miss, if you're in trouble we can help you. Just let one of us know." His eyes were pleading with me.

"I really don't know what happened. One moment I was in the tub the next I was like this. I had a bad dream that someone had a hold of me, but that's all I can remember." I tried to look reassuringly at him. The fact that I had remnants of scars and bruises covering my body from my extracurricular activities wasn't helping my case. I even pulled out my laptop and showed them pictures of me fighting in armor.

After an hour of explaining myself, I was able to get changed and make my way to the checkout desk. My uncle's car had arrived and I was glad to be heading out of the city for some peace and quiet. This had been a frightening but weird experience and obviously required more thought.

A few hours later my Uncle's driver helped me carry my belongings into the cottage. The realtor stopped by and was startled to find I was injured. I assured her it wasn't worth worrying about but it didn't stop her from helping me unpack. With her help I also compiled a grocery list for the market. I didn't even object when the driver offered to go to the store so I could get settled in.

I sat alone on the couch and peeled back the bandages on my wrist. It looked like a bruise from a four-fingered hand. Sharp talons or claws had sunk deep into my flesh and peeled away layers. If the one on the inside of my wrist had severed my veins I may not have made it. I would have bled to death and no doubt been counted a "mysterious suicide" found floating in a hotel bathtub.

I had refused to see a doctor until I saw the bloody tub. With the amount that had spilled out over the soft terrycloth robe and the floor, it's no wonder I was lightheaded even now. I had promised to take it easy for the next few days and if I had any swelling, excessive pain, or additional redness I would come into a hospital. Eighteen tiny stitches is what it had taken to close the four gashes that cut deep into my skin. The worst part is I had no way to explain it.

The police that were called thought maybe someone had drugged me and tried to take advantage of me. I knew that was crazy. They inspected my other hand and realized quickly there was no way I could have done this to myself.

Thinking about it now caused me to shake with fear. For the first time since I was a child I was afraid of the boogieman, an unknown evil that tried to get me as I slept. The hair on my arms and the back of my neck stood up and a chill ran down my spine.

Not ready to face bed, as the afternoon had just turned to evening, I opened up my laptop and connected to the WiFi to check my email. There was an email from one of my fellow teachers in the States, an ad for free shipping on my next order of international baking supplies, and an email from Professor James Scott.

Practical Uses for Princes with Pointed Ears

From: Rose Oswald
Subject: Your substitute sucks

Dear Lil,

We were just filled in at the staff meeting this afternoon as to what happened. Aside from all of us being banned from giving homework for the next few weeks while the school district handles this court case (Oh yes, the parents are suing),we heard you were sent on a sabbatical.

Not to tell you that you're doing it wrong but if I was still on the district's dime I would have opted for someplace sunny and warm rather than England, where the weather is almost identical to Seattle. I heard you're doing research on old texts found in a castle or something? Sounds pretty neat. Maybe if things don't work out you can get a well-deserved University gig where they respect you.

Your replacement is a sad attempt at even babysitter status. I swear I can feel the kids in your classroom actually dropping IQ points. She has your AP English course reading The Boxcar Children because it was one of her favorites growing up. I guess they won't be getting college credit. It would serve the district right if the GPA of the entire school plummeted. Then they may realize how stupid all this is. I mostly feel bad for the students though. They're the ones who are missing out.

Anyway, hang in there and wanted to let you know you were missed,

Rose

I quickly hit reply on the message.

From: Lillian Chambers
Subject: Yes, I know she sucks. If she were better at it she would make more than a teacher's salary.

Hi Rose,

I'm doing well. As you know I attended University here, so it has been nice to meet up with friends and visit old haunts. It's funny how life works out sometimes. This opportunity came to me the same day the student passed out. I guess what they say about one door closing and another opening is true.

To be totally honest I'm not sure they will have me come back next term, so I am playing it by ear. You should come visit over winter break. I'm renting a cute little cottage and have to split my time between England and Scotland. Have you SEEN Scottish men? Let me tell you.

Let everyone know they are missed except George, I hate that guy. Haha. Ok, you can even tell him too. Hang in there and remember killing the students a crime. Encouraging them to do stupid things that may get them expelled with no reliable proof is the better option. (jk)
Take care,

Lily

I smiled as I hit the send button. Rose and I had started the same year at the school and were close in age. We had helped each other through our rough divorces. If I didn't go back to teaching I would no doubt miss her terribly. I hoped she would consider my offer and come visit. I just wasn't sure the UK was ready for her.

I deleted the ad then considering the email from Professor Scott. *It would be better if I ate something before I dug into the email,* I remember thinking. I could already see that it had an attachment which probably meant I would be distracted from food very soon.

I stood up and went to the kitchen. I grabbed a can of soup from the cabinet and tossed in a pan. I then made a quick salad and broke off a chunk of bread from the baguette that the driver had been kind enough to pick up for me. Balancing everything with my good hand, I went and had a seat at the small table by the window. The sun wasn't quite ready to set when I finally sat down.

I ate in silence, my eyes never leaving the trees behind the house. I had been so excited at the idea of having solitude that I never considered solitude could be bad. I paused long enough to touch my wrist. Whatever had happened was a fluke, it was unexplained, but that was alright. I was more than strong enough to handle anything life could throw at me. Without realizing it I had finished my dinner and just sat staring out at the forest around me. There was an almost magical element to it, which lured me into almost believing in fairy tales.

When I was finally able to break the hypnotic trance the woods had over me, I put my dishes in the sink and returned to the couch and my email.

From: Prof. James E Scott
Subject: Welcome to Seelie Keep

Dear Ms. Lillian Chambers,

I have received a glowing recommendation of you from Mr. Randall Dukes. He assures me that you are a much needed asset to my team. Near you is a castle that the locals call Seelie Keep. The folklore says that once upon a time, an Elven King made his home on the cliffs to watch over all the people of this land. When he left, the castle was handed over to mankind, which allowed it to fall into ruins.

What makes Seelie Keep so interesting is that recently in Northern Scotland we unearthed some ancient tomes that have the same writing that was found on the walls. We have also found this same writing on a castle in the Netherlands and on a rock at Stonehenge. We believe it all predates or coincides with the Iron Age.

I have sent photos of some of the tomes. The first thing I need you to do is go over the ruins with a fine tooth comb and photograph any markings that match up. You don't need to start this project until Monday if you don't want, as that is when you are officially listed to begin work. However, if you are anything like me, this is exciting and the sooner you can dig in the better.

Please be careful at the ruins, as there are several that are crumbling and no longer safe to bear weight upon. Also be mindful that on the other side of the ruins happens to be a cliff. No plummeting to your doom. I've heard good things, and it sounds like you may be difficult to replace.

I will be back from Scotland at the end of next week. Take lots of pictures and let's make plans to meet next Friday afternoon at 2 in the Brisbane Café.

Sincerely yours,

James

I opened the attachments on the email. The markings felt familiar but I was unable to read them. They didn't appear to be related to Old English or Old French, which was the majority of my ancient text focus. I did have some experience with Ancient Celtic which this sort of reminded me of, but it was still not the same. I twisted my family crest ring, which I was still wearing on my hand with the injured wrist. It had become a nervous habit of mine in college whenever I was studying.

I looked at the window again. From where my cottage was I was only a ten minute walk to the ruins. The sky was just starting to darken but the sun still hadn't set. I grabbed my coat and shoved my phone in my pocket. I also took a flashlight from under the kitchen sink, checking to make sure it worked. Just in case I got caught out later than I intended to.

Locking the door behind me, I set out around the back of the cottage through the trees in the direction of the ruins. The sun was finally setting thirty minutes later when I broke through the trees almost at a run. I wanted to make it to the ruins before sunset. I approached the castle remnants with caution, watching the play of colors painted across the clouds over the cliff. The ruins were beautifully silhouetted against the sky. The windows and cracks allowed color and light to seep through the dark stone.

Stepping forward I ran my hand along what was once a great wall. My fingertips danced across the surface as I walked, dragging my hand. I would hit bumps and dips where the stone had crumbled away. Then, suddenly something pricked at my fingertips, causing me to pull them back in discomfort. I stopped and looked at the stone but didn't see anything there.

I turned my flashlight on, shining it over the spot. Nothing was there. When I ran my fingers over it again sure enough something was pricking at them. I placed my face near the wall, squinting with one eye to see if I could see the cause of the pricks. I turned my flashlight on the spot again, this time laying it flat against the wall. I could see the slight edges and bumps from this angle but when I looked up I suddenly realized what was going on.

When the light shined across the flat surface it projected an old script onto the corner wall about twelve feet away. I stood amazed for a moment until reality slapped me in the back of the head. I fumbled with my bad hand to pull out my phone and snap some pictures, all while not allowing the flashlight to drop. Five photos later I was feeling pretty good about my accidental find.

The sun was now totally gone. I clicked the flashlight off and let the darkness surround me. I could hear the wind running through the grass and the waves crashing against the cliff face below. The sky was lit brightly with thousands of twinkling stars tossed about the black velvet sky. The moon was a thin white sliver in the ocean of black and glitter.

This was not the darkness that had threatened me. It was one that sang to me like a lullaby, telling me everything was alright. I took a deep breath and let all my fear out with it.

I flipped the flashlight back on and shined it towards the wall of trees. Carefully I made my way back to the woods. I hadn't noticed a path before when I came through, but now that I was looking I could see one. "I probably didn't see it because it wasn't in the line of sight for my cottage. Which means, that doesn't lead back to my place." I examined the trees carefully, trying to enter close to where I had exited. I had pushed straight through and that's what I was going to do now.

I entered the woods and began walking in a straight line. When half an hour passed and I was still deep within the woods I decided I should try and put some sort of marker out. Under the forest cover I could see very few stars because the canopy was so thick.

I found a few large branches and laid them out like an arrow pointing the direction I was headed. Hopefully I wouldn't come across them until another walk. I then kept heading straight again. Ten minutes later I still wasn't out and had come face to face with a large boulder. I started to go around it, but something caught my eye.

The moss that grew on it looked like it had a pattern in its growth. I brushed away the moss and stared at it in surprise. Quickly I pulled out my phone and looked at the pictures I had taken. There, carved into the boulder was the same inscription. I quickly snapped a few more pictures.

It was then I realized the trees around me formed a perfect circle. There was a thick green grass within this circle and the stars were visible. At the center stood this large, smooth, white boulder. I felt like I was in some sort of sacred place. I closed my eyes and let the feeling of the area wash over me.

It was then I heard the crack of a branch. I turned to see what had caused it. Two glowing red eyes looked back at me from the darkness of the forest. I turned my flashlight towards them. A large shadowy creature charged forward, but as it hit the edge of the tree line it stopped abruptly, as if it had hit a wall. As I moved about the circle it followed along the perimeter. Each time it tried to pass through the trees the air in that area seemed to shimmer and glow.

My heart was pumping so fast all I could hear was its thunder pounding in my ears. "Whatever you are, go away! Leave me alone!" I yelled loudly at the shadow.

It let out a loud ear-piercing screech and pushed into the barrier that the trees made. The air seemed to be filled with electricity. I could now see long, blood-red claws ripping at the barrier. I backed up, leaning into the bolder. My hand slid across the inscription and the boulder began to hum and glow a soft blue color.

The walls of the barrier shimmered more and more until they began to look solid. I heard a scream of pain in the direction of the monster and noticed a severed claw on the ground of the circle. Without warning, there was a flash of light and my world went black.

Last night was quiet and peaceful. Tallyn had fallen asleep without a problem, and though the night brought him no dreams he could feel the peace of the world around him. However, this morning he had woken up clutching his wrist, his body wracked with fear. Somewhere, his watcher was in trouble.

He closed his eyes and tried to find her in the darkness. He could feel her pain and fear. They were overwhelming. Then, just as quickly as it had started, it was gone. Tallyn sat in his tent gasping for breath. He had never experienced such terror in all his life.

He rolled off his cot and wandered into the camp. He wasn't surprised when he found his men doing all the work and his brother reading a book.

Maerryn looked up at his younger brother, closing the book with a snap. "You're pale as linen. Are you feeling unwell?" Concerned was laced through his words.

"It was the watcher. She was in trouble, scared, and in pain. Something is wrong and there is nothing I can do to help her." Tallyn was so frustrated his hands were shaking.

"Calm down. If there is nothing you can do, then there is nothing you can do. I think we should pack up and head for Queen Mab. Surely, she can see between the realms and find out what is going on." Maerryn climbed to his feet and offered his brother a reassuring hug with a pat on the back. Tallyn was helpless in his brother's grip.

Elves by nature were very touchy-feely, but Tallyn had never become quite as comfortable with it as his brother. He had no problem hugging his brother, his friends or his father. He just didn't like doing it very often, or with an audience. Finally he sighed and hugged back. It was his only means of escape.

Leaning back he looked at Maerryn. "Ride on ahead. Something about this place makes me feel more in tune with her somehow. I'm safe within the circle, so take the guard. See if the Queen can grant us the use of one of her talented seers for help? I want to continue to try and stay connected. "

Maerryn agreed and in less than an hour he was riding out with the guards. "Be safe and well. We probably won't be back until tomorrow."

Tallyn nodded and looked at his men. "Keep the Prince safe at all costs. Godspeed to you all."

With that they rode out. He followed them with his eyes until they passed too deeply into the forest and out of the Fairy Circle.

"Now what?" he asked the silence that greeted him. Tallyn went to retrieve his sword and practice down by the waterfall pool. The hours seemed to pass slowly. After practice he sat by the water to meditate. Maybe he could commune with her if he focused.

By late afternoon he had given up meditation and was hungry. Tallyn walked back to the encampment and rummaged through the bags. He found a loaf of bread, a few pieces of fruit and some cheese. A simple but filling meal. He sat by the fire, eating in silence. When the sun finally began to sink in the sky and the colors of dusk filled the air, he finally realized he was still covered in sweat.

Making a snap decision, he grabbed a clean change of clothes and some soap, then headed to the waterfall. Darkness was sinking faster and faster upon him as he rushed to wash away the dirt of the day. He finished pulling on his clean, dry clothes as the stars began to shine. He headed back to camp but something in the woods called to him.

He looked in the direction of the tents then to the woods. "Why not?" he asked himself as he walked deeper and deeper into the forest. The further he walked, the closer to the edge of the barrier he came. Finally he stopped. There was a hum in the air. It seemed as if the violet moon that hung in the sky illuminated a large rock.

He studied the rock carefully before approaching it closely. There was an old Elven inscription on it. "Where hands of the lovers meet, so shall their..." Moss had grown over the last part. He reached out, pulling the moss away and running his fingers over the last words of the inscriptions. "...hearts."

His heart began pounding harder and harder. Fear swept through him again. Her fear. He reached out his hand to lean on the rock for support. "I'm here," he whispered.

The stone under his hand began to glow a soft blue color. The air around him seemed to sizzle. The wall of the barrier shimmered to life. There was a sudden flash of light emitted from the stone. A form began to materialize beside the rock and become Fae shaped. Then he saw her. In a sparkle of what looked like starlight she was there standing before him.

She began to collapse as soon as she was solid. She hit the ground with a thud, her head making contact with the stone. He winced for her and immediately knelt at her side. "My Lady, are you alright?" She lay lifeless on the ground. Fearing the worst he reached for her neck to see if her heart was still beating. Relief flooded him when he felt her pulse beating strongly and could feel her breath on the back of his hand.

Her head was bleeding from where she had hit the stone. Carefully, he scooped her into his arms and carried her back towards camp. The travel was slower than he would have liked but he didn't want to jostle her too much. With her cradled against his chest her head rested against his shoulder. He could feel each of her slow breaths on his neck.

He laid her down gently on his cot, wrapping her tightly in blankets to keep her warm. He cleaned her cut and applied salve to it, stopping the bleeding. He carefully pulled her boots from her legs then tucked her feet under the warm covers as well.

For a while he sat there watching her. He could hardly believe she was real. He reached out to brush hair from her face and his hand stopped when he saw her ears. Curiously he ran his finger over the curve of her upper ear.

They weren't pointed. She wasn't Fae. They looked like those of the dwarves, but she was far too tall. Then again she was considerably shorter than most Elven women. Maybe fairy height. He looked at her features. "I wonder if she has wings," he finally said. "Halfling, definitely a Halfling. Dwarven and maybe Nymph or Pixie." Satisfied he had solved the mystery he tucked the covers around her one last time and left to sleep in his brother's tent.

Chapter Seven

I woke up the next morning to a dull throb in my head. *I had the craziest dream ever,* I thought to myself. I snuggled deep into the pillows and blankets around me, breathing deeply. There was something earthy and masculine to their scent. *The owner probably forgot to wash them after her son moved out. I should do that later today. For now, I think I may just enjoy this secret shame.* My thoughts trickled out like water from a faucet.

Suddenly the thought of water made me all too aware that I needed the bathroom. The air was cool and I began to wonder how long I could go before needing to leave the warmth of my bed. I heard a rustle of fabric beside me which didn't make sense. Slowly I opened one eye and then the other quickly.

There in front of me in perfect glory was the most magnificent butt I had ever seen. The leather pants that clung to it hugged its every manly curve. Without realizing it, I was staring.

"Oh, rhasha jo mtut ghar ilm," A rich male voice mumbled.

I looked up at where the sounds were coming from, dragging my eyes over a perfect chest and pale beautiful skin stretched tautly over finely-toned muscle. His dark hair was a mix of braids, which tumbled down his back.

He had two perfectly formed lips meant to kiss a woman until she was dizzy, and piercing vivid green eyes that seemed to glow against his pale skin. "It's you!" I squeaked.

"Ahl lahm sheili migwah?" I could tell he was asking me some sort of question but I was unsure what. Frustration was written on his face as he realized I didn't understand.

"I'm sorry," I said softly. I tried to sit up but winced when I put pressure on my hand.

Concern washed over his features and he gently urged me to lay back.

I sighed and rolled my eyes at him, then tried to sit up again. This time he held me in place with light pressure on one shoulder. "Tek," he said shaking his head. Well, at least now I knew the word "no".

"I need to go to the bathroom. Please move or I will move you," I said to him calmly.

Confusion knit across his perfect features again. Looking at him I gave him what I hoped was my best apologetic look. Then as quickly as I could I lifted my feet and pushed against his chest. It successfully knocked him off of me but didn't seem to hurt him. With my momentum, I rolled off the bed and dashed out the door of what appeared to be a tent.

Once outside I realized I was still in the woods and dashed toward some shrubs. I made it a few steps and discovered I was incredibly woozy. I felt myself sinking to the ground. Just as I was about to land face first into a camp fire, two strong arms wrapped around my waist and I was hauled back against his chest.

For a moment I thought about how nice it felt pressed against him but it was short lived. He spun me in his arms. "Lehm na ja?" I blinked and he quickly looked me over for injuries. Once he made sure I was uninjured he checked I was stable on my feet and carefully let me go. His hands hovered, in case he needed to save me again.

I looked into his eyes, then pointed at the trees near camp. I made a pleading motion with my hands then danced around like a young child does when they need to pee.

Suddenly, the light dawned and he blushed, motioning me towards the trees. He even turned his back and walked a little further away. I resisted the urge to giggle and made my way into the woods.

When I returned, my dream guy was sitting in front of the fire. He patted the ground beside him, and pointed at a selection of food. I nodded and sank to the ground close to his side. Cautiously, he handed me a bowl of warm soup. I leaned forward, breathing in its aroma. I couldn't help but smile. It smelled wonderful and looked like it was full of vegetables. I tried using the spoon but my hand and wrist were so stiff that I couldn't seem to get a grip on it.

I looked up at him helplessly. At first he seemed perplexed but then his eyes narrowed, looking at my hand. He picked up my soup bowl and set it down behind him. He reached out and tried to push the coat off my shoulders. With his help I wiggled out of my wool coat and he laid it to the side. Gently, he took my hand and unwrapped the bandages around it.

To my shock and evidentially his, the stitches were all inflamed. The skin looked yellow and was puffy. This was bad. "Kretah! Ithie-gah." I blinked at him. The first part sounded like a curse but I knew the second word from folklore.

"Itheaga," I whispered. It was a shadowy creature that resembled a cross between a bird and snake.

He nodded then motioned for me to stay sitting. A few moments later he returned with a bowl of water and a sack. He submerged my wrist in the cool water and gently rubbed it, then dried it with a clean towel. He pulled a jar from the sack and opened it, lifting it to my nose, the smell burning my nostrils. Motioning to the jar he winced and acted like he was blowing on his wrist. I nodded, understanding that this was going to burn.

I watched as he smeared a large glob onto the first gash, then the second, third and fourth. He quickly and gently as possible rubbed the ointment in, taking extra care to really work it into the gash and stitches. The pain didn't hit immediately but it grew until tears streamed down my face. He looked as if he felt the pain too as he held my hand and blew on it. Finally when the worst of the burning had stopped he rewrapped my wrist in clean cloth bandages. I noticed most of the yellow color had already faded back to red and pink.

He then rinsed his hands and picked up the towel he had used to dry my wrist. With extreme care, not wanting to upset me, he wiped the tears off my face. He then placed the water and towel to the side and picked the soup bowl back up. He checked to make sure it was still warm and then without words began feeding me the soup. He did it in such a way that it didn't seem like an act of pity, but rather one of compassion.

We ate soup, cured meat, dried fruit, and some stinky cheese that reminded me of gorgonzola. When we finished he gathered up all the dishes and put them in a bucket of water to deal with later.

He threw another log on the fire before he sat down to face me. "Tall-Hyen," he said pointing to himself.

I smiled. I had heard his name before. In my dreams I could understand him, but here and now language was a barrier we had to overcome.

"Tall-Hyen," I repeated pointing at him. He nodded agreement.

I then pointed to myself. "Lillian."

He pointed at me and said, "Lil-li-hyen." I smiled. It was close enough so I nodded.

Next he made a cross with his arms and shook his head no and said, "Tek."

I repeated the word back to him, then did the same motion and said, "No".

"No!" he said in a commanding voice, then laughed.

Next he put both hands up and nodded his head in an agreeable motion. "Shav."

I repeated the word back nodding agreement. "Shav." I then did the same motions he had and said, "Yes".

"Yesh?" he said, questioning his pronunciation.

Smiling I offered the "Ssssssss" sound to him feeling like a snake.

"Shhhhhhh..." he said again.

I shook my head and said "Tek. Sssssss," making the sound again.

He shook his head no and whispered the word, "Tek," back to me then placed a finger over both his and my lips and quietly said "shhhhhh" again.

I almost laughed. I guess some things are universal.

He closed his eyes, listening. I watched a string of emotions cross his face and then he seemed to relax. He pointed back over my shoulder. As I turned curiously I heard the sound of horses approaching and then saw a string of six people on horseback.

As the riders drew closer he stood up and offered me a hand to get to my feet. They stopped several paces away and slid off of their horses. A tall man with similar features to Tallyn approached. I smiled remembering him from my dreams. "Maer-ryen!" I pointed and laughed. Tallyn looked at me with shock but the man approaching just grinned wider.

The three of us were joined by four more pointy-eared men and a woman with wings. A Fairy, a real honest to god Fairy. Her wings sparkled in the sunlight. Tallyn leaned close and whispered, "Tek," in my ear. I snapped my jaw shut and looked up at him.

Everyone in the group looked at me, and the air was suddenly filled with a flood of questions in a language I couldn't speak. Tallyn quickly stepped in front of me and put up his hands. He conversed with the others, their eyes skirting back and forth from me to him. Finally, the Fairy spoke again.

"Rej-tah!" Her voice sounded like a bell, soft to my ears, but I didn't need to understand to know she had just given an order.

"Tek," Tallyn argued. Suddenly Maerryn stepped towards me, a large grin on his face, and reached for me. Tallyn shoved him back. "Tek! Li mah rej-tah." Tallyn turned to face me, his eyes meeting mine. "Mia," he whispered and I knew immediately it was an apology.

Before I could try to understand what he was apologizing for he slid an arm around my waist and pulled me against him. He lowered his head brushing his lips against mine, pressing them to encourage me to open to him. Without hesitation I opened my kiss to him, allowing my tongue to daringly jet out and taste him. He slid his other hand up to the nape of my neck drawing me in closer as we drank of each other. When finally he lifted his head, breaking the kiss, he kept me pressed against his body. I couldn't tell if it was for his benefit or mine.

"Is that better?" he whispered.

"Yes," I breathed. My eyes flared. "I understand you!" Shock rolled through me.

There was a slight rumble of laughter in his chest. He then slowly released me and turned back to face the others. They stared at me for a moment and then the list of questions came again, only this time I understood them. "Are you a Halfling? Are you Human? What realm are you from? How do you know my name? What happened? How did you get here?"

I closed my eyes, processing all the information. I was woozy. "If you don't mind I'm going to sit down. I lost a lot of blood yesterday and sustained a head injury last night." Tallyn sank to the ground with me, offering me support so I didn't just collapse there. Everyone exchanged looks. One man went to get more wood to build up the fire and everyone else settled in around it.

I took a deep breath. "I don't know what a Halfling is so I'm going to go with no, I'm not one of those. I am Human. I come from a realm currently called Earth. My Kingdom is the United States, but I fell through the Fairy Circle in England." I reached for the cup of water that Tallyn offered to me, taking a sip.

I looked at Maerryn. "I know your name because when I dream at night I can see Tallyn. I heard him and others call your name before. I knew his as well." I looked around the group. "As for what happened... I was out looking at some ruins when it got dark. On the way home I got lost in the woods and found a large alcove of trees with a big white boulder in the center with an inscription on it. Something big and scary followed me to the circle but some sort of barrier prevented it from entering. The rock began to glow, there was a flash of light and then I woke up here."

"Ah, you found an old Fairy Circle in your realm," said the Fairy. "A Human shouldn't have been able to activate it but somehow you did. Chances are you have some Fae heritage somewhere in your lineage." She shrugged. "Was this the woman you wanted me to locate across realms?" She turned her attention to Tallyn.

"Yes it was. I have a psychic bond with her for whatever reason, and I could sense she was in danger and hurt. I was concerned." His voice was silky smooth as he spoke.

The Fairy leaned forward and looked into his eyes for a moment then did the same for me. "Ah, that makes sense." She looked back at Tallyn. "You two do share a special bond but she isn't awakened yet. She does indeed have Fae blood, but until it is activated the true nature of your link will remain as it is with no control."

Maerryn leaned close to the Fairy and whispered something in her ear. I felt Tallyn stiffen beside me. The Fairy looked back at us then back to Maerryn and nodded. Maerryn just offered us an amused look.

I interrupted the staring contest that was going on between Tallyn and everyone else. "So how do I go home?" I asked.

The Fairy looked flabbergasted that I would ask such a question. "I'm not sure how you activated the circle to get here but the Human realm is sealed. At the very least you will need to awaken before you will be able to return to your realm. Obviously, somehow you have broken the seal."

"How do I awaken then? I have a job and a life back there I need to return to." I was starting to get worked up at the thought of be trapped in a different dimension. Immediately, Tallyn took my hand, caressing it, trying to comfort me.

The Fairy considered me for a moment. "Awakening is different for everyone but normally it involves breaking down some barrier put in place to keep you from tapping into your magic. It is normally something big and life changing that starts it. Once it begins it can take months to fully awaken."

I processed her words but I didn't like her answer. Tallyn looked at me. "Don't worry, I'll help you get home." Something in his tone was so reassuring I couldn't help but believe him.

"Well, do you remember where you found me?" I asked him.

"I didn't so much find you, as you just appeared out of thin air." He stood. "Let's take a walk."

Tallyn pulled me to my feet and held my hand for lingering moment, running his thumb over its back. Then without a word he dropped his arms and walked away. I blinked at everyone around us, who looked just as confused as I was. I stared at the back of his head as he disappeared into the tree line.

With a shrug I chased after him, closing the distance as quickly as I could. We walked in silence the whole way. Finally we reached an alcove of trees. At the center of the alcove was a large white boulder. He stopped and turned back to look at me. "This is where you appeared." He motioned with his hand.

I walked past him and over to the boulder. I ran my hands over its surface. It was cool to the touch and smooth like a marble. Across it was a scrolling ornamental inscription. "Where hands of the lovers meet, so shall their hearts." I read it out loud. I wasn't sure without my phone but the markings looked the same as the ones I had found at the keep and on the boulder in the woods near my cottage. "Why can I read this now? Why can I understand and speak your language?" I turned to look at Tallyn.

"It's one of the Elven gifts. We call it *The Shared Tongue*. It allows us to impart any language we know to another Fae." He shifted uncomfortably and looked down at his feet.

"But I'm not a Fae," I retorted.

He shrugged. "The Fairy thinks you're at least part Fae, of some sort. Fae is a species and within it there are several races. Do Humans not have different races?"

"Yes, we do, but none of ours have magical abilities that allow us to kiss a language over to another person. That seems like a really helpful skill." There was awe in my voice.

Tallyn just shrugged. "The Fae have had a universal language we all use for a thousand years. We don't really need to pass it along anymore since very few people use any other. My brother and I both know ancient Elven and I can read some Fairy and Dwarven as well, but they are mostly dead languages now."

"I see, like Latin." He stared at me for a moment and I shook it off. I looked back at the boulder beside me. "So how do I make this thing work?"

"I don't know. I just sort of touched it last night and it started to glow." He shrugged.

"Same story with me." I tried running my hand across it like I had last night and nothing happened. I placed both hands on it. Still nothing. Tallyn walked over and tried as well. I stepped out of his way. Still, no response.

"Much of the old magic was linked to the moon and stars. We may need to wait until night to try again." He turned and leaned back against the rock to look at me.

"So what do we do until then?" As soon as the words left my mouth I regretted them.

His lips curled with a wicked grin. "Oh, I can think of a few things." He stepped close to me, his eyes burning into mine.

I blinked and lowered my head, taking a step back. I could feel a blush surfacing on my cheeks. "We could talk," I offered.

He reached out and pulled me against him. I could feel his heartbeat under my palm. With a gentle hand he tilted my head back so I would look at him. "We could test a theory I have and see if you can teach me your language?" He started to lower his head.

I cleared my throat and pulled back. "Or we could talk about ourselves."

With a grin and sigh he lifted his head but still didn't release me from where I was pressed against him. "You've been spying on me for a year, what questions could you have left?"

"It's not like I chose to spy on you. My dreams just sort of took me there." I considered what I was saying. My gaze slid to his ears. Without consideration I reached up and touched one. His body stiffened against mine and he held his breath. "They're real."

Taking a deep controlled breath, he reached up and captured my wrist in his grip. "They are real indeed. They are also an erogenous zone for my people. It's a very intimate gesture to touch them like that." I started to withdraw my hand when he said it, but he just continued to hold my wrist in his grip. "It's alright. You didn't know and I'm not upset. It is just a very intense feeling."

"I didn't mean to overstep my bounds or make you feel uncomfortable." I shuffled my feet. "I don't want to upset anything between you and your girlfriend...... wife...... boyfriend?" I said obviously phishing for information.

"Girlfriend? ... Oh, do you mean my lovers?" He was handsome, and I was not a fool. I knew he had lovers. I was crazy if I didn't think he had. I nodded. "The act is intimate. Someone you bed a few times would never touch you like that. A lover such as a wife or mate, yes, but not as something casual."

"Is it really that big a deal? We make out and nibble on each other's necks and ears fairly often in my world." I wondered if that made me sound like a slut.

"Would people think ill of you if you mated with many different Humans in a short amount of time?" I quirked a brow at the word mated.

"Yes, we try not to be judgmental, but it happens. Especially if you are a woman and you have sex with many partners in a short amount of time." I bit my lip.

"Here we understand that mating is a primal need. It's part of our base instincts. Until we are fortunate enough to find a mate, it is perfectly acceptable to be with as many others as you desire." He let go of my hand. "I suspected based on your reaction that was not the case in your realm."

"As many as you want? Do you use protection? What about disease? What about unwanted pregnancy?" If I was even going to consider doing anything with handsome here, I wanted a wrapper on it if he was going around with anyone he desired.

"I've heard that Humans had disease that could spread through mating but that isn't the case here. Pregnancy will not occur unless a couple goes through a binding ritual. Once bound only their mate can impregnate them. As for unwanted children, I can't imagine that really. Children are viewed as blessings. Elves live a very long time and because of that we don't reproduce all that often."

I stared at him in horror. "Considering that reaction I would guess this is not the case with Humans?" His words seemed very casual for such a subject.

"You can't get pregnant unless you are married?" I was flabbergasted.

"Married. Oh, you can. Marriage is just a legal binding. Being bound to a mate is deeper. It's done through blood. My parents were never married due to political and traditional reasons but they were still bound." I processed his words. He reached out and brushed a strand of hair from my face. "So mating is a very intimate interaction for you?"

I paused. "For me personally, yes. I have to have some sort of feelings for my partner, otherwise I feel bad about the action. When it is with someone I care about though, it is intimate and uniting. Does that make sense?" He just nodded.

Sensing my discomfort he changed the subject. "What do you do for fun, Lillian?"

I stuttered for a moment then blushed. "You're going to laugh at me if I tell you."

He smiled. "I promise I won't."

"I wear armor and sword fight. I like to go camping and wear traditional garb that Humans wore historically. I enjoy sewing, painting and dancing... Oh, and I love books!" I could feel the word NERD tattoo itself across my forehead.

"Why would I laugh at that? Those are all perfectly normal activities we enjoy here. Is that why you dress like a male?" His last question threw me for a loop. "The females on the royal guard also wear breeches and tunics when they are on duty. When they are not carrying a sword, they still enjoy their gowns."

"Ah, I understand. No, what I have on is typical fashion for women. While we do wear dresses many of us wear pants because we feel more comfortable in them." I suddenly was very aware of how I must look to him.

"Why are you not comfortable in a gown? Do you feel as beautiful in breeches as you do a gown?" His words were filled with double meaning.

"Not really. I don't feel unattractive in pants. I do feel prettier when I wear a dress but they get in the way, and I feel bad about sitting on anything that isn't a chair. I don't know." I shrugged.

"I've never worn a gown." He stopped and looked at me. "Never, no matter what Maerryn may tell you when we drink. It is my opinion that what someone wears daily should be something they are comfortable in. Yes, there will always be days where we must wear things that are fancy, but that is like a costume. If you feel prettier in a gown, wear a gown. I'm sure it must be a change if you always wear breeches. Gowns are made from the same fabric as breeches and tunics. They are no less durable." He looked down at my clothes and shrugged.

What he said made sense. "You're right."

"I know." There was an arrogance that was both annoying and a little sexy in his tone.

"Well, what do you do for fun?" I asked.

"Much of the same things you do. I like to camp with my friends. Work on my swordsmanship. I don't mind dancing and I can't really sew all that well but I enjoy riding my horse and practicing my archery. I even enjoy hunting from time to time." He turned, tucking my hand into the curve of his elbow so he could guide me as we walked. "Do any of those things sound particularly unusual?"

"No, not really. Swordsmanship is frequently a lost art where I'm from and on top of that, very few women are in the sport. When I mention it at home, I often get a lot of questions and funny looks." I rolled my eyes at the memories of my co-workers' reactions. "It tends to get me labeled an outcast."

"How do armies defend your land if nobody does swordplay anymore?" There was worry written on his face. "I think you should stay here for safety. I don't think your armies can protect you."

I tried not to laugh. "Our armies no longer use swords. We use mechanical weapons now."

He seemed to relax a little at that. "Mechanical weapons can still fail. They should still train with swords."

I smiled. "You're right again."

"I know. I do my best to be right as often as possible. The Dwarves to the north make mechanical weapons called guns. Even so, they still learn to fight with traditional weapons like swords and axes."

I shook my head. "We have guns as well, we just don't use bladed weapons very often. Just like the majority of people will never ride a horse."

His eyes widened with alarm. "How do you get from village to village quickly?"

I laughed. "We have cars and planes. They're sort of like motorized carts."

"You have great magic in your land. Our legends always told us that Humans didn't possess magic, but even in my dreams I saw you turn out all the lights with just a flip of your hand. Was that real or a dream?" His questions were filled with wonder.

"It's not magic at all, it was real, though." I smiled as we walked back toward the camp.

The silence between us was not uncomfortable. It felt ok to just be quiet and to be together. The cool autumn wind blew, causing his hair to dance in the light. I wanted to reach out and touch it. It looked so soft.

When he noticed I was staring at him he quickly started to speak to fill the silence and distract me. "Tell me about your family? Or about your work?"

"Ah, conversation." I grinned, realizing this was not his specialty. "Well, my parents are pretty normal I guess. Typical parents. They want me to be happy, healthy and successful at everything I do. They have no problem giving me advice, even when I don't want it. I have brothers that are loud but love to be in the company of their friends and family. One works for a large company and the other is a ranger for a forest." Tallyn nodded approval at their descriptions. "I'm a teacher. I teach literature to teenagers. I also do research on ancient texts in Western Europe."

"Western Europe is a kingdom?" I could tell he was trying to fit together how my world worked.

"It's a region made up of several countries or kingdoms." It was the easiest answer I could come up with and seemed to do the trick because he nodded in understanding.

We stepped through another row of trees. The ground was covered in a lush green grass that sloped down to a pool of water being fed by a large waterfall. Smooth gray and white rocks lined the outside edge of the pool. The water was so clear you could see to the bottom. My breath caught. "Where is this place? Is everything here is so perfect?" My words were more to myself but Tallyn grinned widely.

"We are at a far edge of a large Fairy Circle. It's a sacred land that is protected by strong ancient magic. Those who seek to do harm may not enter. There is a barrier they are unable to pass through. For that reason we must leave the circle to hunt, but while we are here we are safe. It has been a long time favorite of many of our people as a type of escape or vacation spot. There are several circles in this realm. You had to have been in one within your own realm to have traveled here."

"There was a circle of trees, tiny in comparison to this place. It's where I found the boulder. Something was chasing me but couldn't breach the barrier of the trees." I swallowed down the fear that rose inside me.

Tallyn stiffened. He turned to me and rubbed his hands up and down my arms. "You're safe here, I swear it. Nothing can harm you in here and outside of this circle I will not allow harm to come to you." His words were soothing and almost melodic.

"I didn't say I was scared. I'm alright." I pushed my shoulders back trying to look brave.

"You don't have to pretend with me. I can feel your emotions. It's part of the strange link we seem to have. Sort of like you being able to see me. I've always felt you, but lately I can feel your emotions when they are turbulent."

I blushed again. I didn't know how long he had been able to feel my emotions but it somehow seemed embarrassing. "How long has this been going on?"

"A few weeks. About a week ago I awoke with so much pain and sorrow I felt as if my heart was breaking. I couldn't imagine what would cause it. Then, you started appearing in my dreams and I was confused if you were real or just a dream. Somehow, I just knew you were real." Everything was so matter of fact and so honest with Tallyn. It was refreshing and scary because I had no doubt he would tell me the truth. I had put him on a pedestal as my dream for so long, that if he fell from the perfect pedestal I may be devastated.

He cupped my cheek in his palm and forced me to look up. "What's wrong?" His words were so soft they felt like a caress.

I shook my head free of his touch. "Nothing. I just overthink everything." I looked back at the pool of water. "Is it safe to drink?"

"Yes, but I would recommend the water from the fall that is cooler. The pool itself is fed by a hot spring and while clean, it doesn't really taste the best." He looked at the falls then took my hand and pulled me along beside him as he walked to the pool's edge.

He tested each rock before helping me step out onto it. Soon we were about a foot from the falls and the force of the falling water created a cool mist that clung to my skin. He helped me step around and then held my waist so I wouldn't lose my footing. I cupped my hands and reached into the falling water.

The water felt like ice on my hands but I was able to drink my fill with a few tries. It tasted clear, clean and refreshing. It washed down my throat and revived me.

The coolness of it pricked at my hands and felt wonderful as it soaked the bandages on my wrist, numbing the pain.

"Are you done?" he asked as I turned around. With a nod he led us back across the slick rock surface from which we had come. Once back on solid ground he looked at my bandaged wrist. "We will rewrap that when we get back to camp."

The walk back to camp was quick but cold. The front of my clothes were soaked from the waterfall and the October air was certainly too brisk to walk around wet in. By the time we arrived back at camp I was shivering and looking forward to my coat and the fire.

When we arrived back we noticed the Fairy was mounted on her horse saying her goodbyes. She turned to us after waving to the others. "Excellent, you've returned. I'm headed home to the village. If I leave now I should get back just a little after dark."

Tallyn looked up at her. "We are happy to extend our hospitality to you for the night. You can take my brother's tent and he and I can stay with the other guards." I ventured a peek at Maerryn who was silently reading but noticed his eyebrows had raised in interest at the notice he may lose his tent to a guest.

The Fairy waved away the idea. "I would rather my bed to the likes of a cot. Even a royal cot." She bowed her head. "Your concern and consideration touch me and I will surely pass along word to the Queen that I was well treated."

She looked at me, pursing her lips with consideration. "Lady Lillian, I am not sure how or why you are here. You must believe that fate has a path for you to walk that has led you here. It always has a reason, even if it doesn't match your own plans. Good luck to you. I have no doubt we will meet again." With one last wave she left, her horse moving at a fast pace through the woods and out of sight.

After she left all I wanted to do was get to the fire, curl up in my coat and get warm. I was shivering so hard I struggled to find where I had left my coat earlier in the day. When I finally found it I pulled it over my shoulders and sat almost dangerously close to the flames. One of the guardsmen stepped around the fire and leaned close, offering me a basket full of fruit, bread, and cheese.

"Are you hungry, My Lady?" I gladly accepted an apple, a hunk of white cheese and a small piece of dark brown bread from the basket. He smiled at me and disappeared back into the darker area of camp.

I took a bite of the apple. It was sweet at first and became tart as I chewed it. It tasted wonderful. The cheese was creamy and mild, and paired well with the chewiness of the bread. They were a perfect rustic compliment to one another. I munched happily, unaware of the world around me.

I was startled moments later when Tallyn dropped with a less than graceful thump beside me. Without a word he took my injured wrist and unwrapped it, disposing of the used bandages. He closely examined the injury. The color now was a nice pink, indicating healing.

Whatever the salve had done, it did it well. He reached into his bag and grabbed the bottle of salve again.

"I have a question," I announced.

With a slight smirk he continued examining my wrist. "And that would be?"

"Are Ithegas so common that you carry this medicine all the time, or is this like Elven Neosporin and it fixes everything?" I wasn't sure he would understand my Neosporin reference but I went with it anyway. Before I could protest he was rubbing it into the stitches. While it did burn, it was not nearly as painful as last time. He lowered his head over it and blew on my wrist.

I don't know why but it amused me and before I could stop myself I started to giggle. His head shot up, looking at me in question. That was all it took to grow my giggle to a full laugh. He began bandaging my cuts and allowed a scowl to crease his forehead. "I'm not sure why this is so funny to you!"

Catching my breath I offered my biggest smile, hoping it would take the sting out of my laughter which he seemed to have taken personally. He wouldn't look up.

"Tallyn, for a year now I have visited you in my dreams. I've seen you fight fiercely, train warriors, hunt, and I've even seen you sleep. I just never pictured you as the nurturing type. I'm sorry if that upset you but I promise I am glad that you are." I paused for a moment before pressing the issue. "So, about this miracle medicine, is it Itheaga specific?"

Tallyn sighed heavily, offering a martyred look my direction. "It's imbued with special herbs made to combat venom from dark creatures."

Maerryn snickered from behind his book. Tallyn's head shot up to give his brother an angry glare. "I'll have you know that I am very much a nurturer. My men get injured in practice and battle, and I help care for them. I take excellent care of my horse..." His words trailed off as he turned his glare on me. He stared, almost mesmerized by my grin.

"Are you comparing me to your horse?" I teased. He grunted at me and climbed to his feet. Smiling up at him I made it a point to call out, "Thank you!" to his back as he stepped into his tent.

When I leaned closer to the fire trying to get warm, Tallyn stuck his head out of his tent and called for me. I quickly stumbled to my feet and headed his way. I walked as close to the fire as I could passing through the camp.

When I stepped into his tent he pushed a pile of clothes into my arms. "You should change into dry clothes." I looked at him trying to decide how to respond.

"If you haven't noticed I'm built a little fuller than you." I looked at the clothes in my arms.

He waved away my concerns. "You should be alright. These are my riding breeches so they are roomier through the hips and thighs. I considered your body when I chose these." I really wasn't sure how to respond to the comment. He stepped outside and dropped the flap shut.

I quickly peeled out of my damp sweater and jeans. I pulled the pants up my thighs, doing the pants dance to get them over my hips. I held my breath as I pulled them up on my tummy. Yeah, he underestimated my size, but it still felt nice to be in dry clothes. I pulled on the shirt with its billowy sleeves that made me feel like a pirate. It had lacings that exposed my cleavage. If I tried to cinch it closed, it made the chest too snug.

"Clearly I am not built like an Elven male." Enjoying the feeling of being dry and warmer, I pulled on a doublet over the shirt, able to only close the lower half of the clasps.

I stepped back out into the cool air and sat back down by the fire. Another shiver ran through me but it didn't come from being cold. I looked up to realize everyone in camp was staring at me. Tallyn cleared his throat and suddenly everyone returned to what they were doing. In a fluid motion he pulled a heavy dark green wool cloak around my shoulders and motioned for me to have a seat by him in a chair.

"Warmer?" he asked.

I nodded and sank into the wooden chair by the fire. "Yes, much warmer. Thank you." Almost everyone seemed busy doing something: reading, cooking, working on some craft, or playing music on a guitar type instrument. "Is there anything I can help with? Or do? I don't like not being useful."

Tallyn showed me what he was working on. "Ever fletched an arrow? It may be difficult with your hand wrapped up but if you're bored and want to help, I can teach you." I shrugged and moved closer. I watched as he carefully split feathers and cut them, then wrapped them carefully on the shaft. He helped me with the first one or two but soon I was able to handle it on my own.

The sky was changing colors when one of the guardsmen brought over a bottle of wine and some goblets. Another brought a pile of bowls and a basket with breads, cheese and fruits. Tallyn filled the bowls with soup that had been cooking on the fire, handing one to each member of the group while Maerryn poured wine. They thanked each member for his help and soon we were gathered in a circle around the fire together.

Maerryn read poems from his book, while others told stories about some of their grandest adventures. I listened with delight. I watched with interest as their smiles and the light from the fire painted abstract shadows on their faces that looked like masks. I toasted with the group (Long Live the King) and enjoyed the jokes that followed. Before long the night was dark and the violet moon hung low in the sky.

Tallyn tightly held a bottle of wine in one hand as he helped me to my feet. "Ready to go home?" he asked.

The group grew silent and everyone exchanged looks. Taking a deep breath I realized he was right and I should at least try to go home. "Yeah, give me a moment, I'll go change. My clothes should be dry." Tallyn shook his head. "Don't worry about it. I'll grab your clothes. I would rather you stay dry and warm."

Moments later he handed me a bag which contained my coat, jeans and sweater. "Thank you," I said looking into the bag. I turned to smile and thank everyone for their hospitality.

Maerryn looked up. "You know, My Lady, if you can't return you are welcome to stay with us for as long as you are in our realm. If you don't wish to leave tonight, you don't have to."

I smiled at him. "Thank you, but Tallyn is right. I should go. It was wonderful meeting all of you." We said our goodbyes and Tallyn looped an arm around my waist and led me into the woods.

He took a drink of wine from the bottle he carried then handed it to me. "He's right you know. If you want to stay you are welcome. The plan was to return home tomorrow, but we can delay it. There's no hurry. You could even come with us." He paused a moment to consider his words. "I could show you what our realm looks like. Give you a tour of the castle. Maybe we could arrange for you to see the other three kingdoms," he offered.

I took a big gulp of wine. It was sweeter than anything I had ever had and I could feel it affecting me quickly. "I have work to do. Now that I can read the language, my project should be a breeze." He smiled uneasily. I took another sip of the wine.

The walk seemed to go much quicker than it had earlier. There, just past a line of trees, was the alcove that held the white boulder. I took one more sip of the wine and stepped out of Tallyn's grip. We walked side by side to the boulder. I paused a few feet away, turning to look at him.

"Thank you so much for your help and kindness. If we figure out how this works, you should come visit." I looked deep into his eyes. There were questions there that wanted to be answered but he wasn't going to ask them. "Of course, I hope I will still see you in my dreams."

He reached up and tucked a lock of hair behind my ear. My breath caught in my throat at the feel of his fingertips on my skin.

"Yes, I hope you can continue to haunt me." He looked almost sad. I tried to force a smile but suddenly felt the sadness of the moment squeeze my heart. I forced down the little lump that was building in my throat. It seemed so wrong to have met this stranger from my dreams and to part ways so soon, but I had my own life to think about.

Taking a shaky breath I stepped up to the rock and ran my fingers over the cool stone. The night became silent and the air grew thick. I touched the inscription as I had done the night before and the stone glowed a soft blue tone and the circle around me started to shimmer in the moonlight. I turned to give Tallyn one last look. Without warning there was a bright flash of light. I felt my phone vibrate in my bag just before the darkness consumed me.

Chapter Eight

I woke up when the first rays of sunlight started to brighten the sky. I was surrounded by his smell. At first I was excited because I thought it meant he would be there when I opened my eyes, but then I remembered I was wearing his clothes. I pulled his cloak tighter around me, as if clinging to it was proof I had actually journeyed to a distant realm. Ignoring the pain in my hand I sat up and opened my eyes.

It was then I realized that I was sitting on the cot, in Tallyn's tent. I blinked a few times processing that information. Shaking my head I dug into my bag and pulled out my phone. "Three emails and two missed calls." One was from Rose and the other from Mr. Dukes. It was then I realized I had three bars of service. "How the hell does that work?"

For shits and giggles I clicked on my uncle's number. A heavy male voice answered. "Hello?"

"Mr. Dukes?" I asked in disbelief.

"Lillian, is something wrong? Please call me Randall, dear." He seemed concerned.

Thinking quickly I came up with a tale I hoped would buy me some time to figure out what was going on.

"I went to the ruins Friday evening and found markings on the wall. I then realized that I had a lead, but it required more effort than I thought. I had to hop the channel. I may be gone for a couple weeks but I think I can crack the language because of it."

"That's excellent news! I guess then you won't be available for dinner tomorrow evening then?" he asked.

"No, I'm sorry. I also have a favor to ask. Can you let the professor know? I forgot my charger for this phone at the cottage and it takes some special type of adapter they only sell stateside. I'm not sure how easy I will be to get a hold of when the battery dies. I don't want him to think I'm flaking out."

"I understand. Please keep us updated the best you can, and be careful. There are lots of weirdoes out there." His fatherly warning made me smile.

"Thank you and I swear I'll be careful. Talk to you soon." I heard him mutter goodbye as I hung up. I then turned the phone off hoping to preserve the battery as long as I could.

The flap to the tent made a noise and Tallyn stepped inside. He came over and sat on the cot beside me then pulled off his boots.

"You must be in really good shape to keep carrying me back here." I commented and then offered a grin. "I'm sorry. Did I hurt your back?"

He gave me a look that said I was being ridiculous. "You're not heavy at all. I've been told that compared to Humans, Elves are much stronger. Maybe men of your realm are just weak if they can't carry you."

He reached out and cupped my cheek in his hand. "How are you feeling?"

I shook my head. "A little disoriented but alright. Sorry, I displaced you from your bed. How long have I been out?" I asked.

"About an hour or so." I blinked. That didn't make any sense, it was so bright out.

He read my confusion. "Oh, we have several large lanterns lit that illuminate the area well."

"Oh, I see." Was that all I could manage?

"I'm sorry the circle didn't take you home, but I meant it when I said you could stay and that I would help you get home. Please don't be sad." He stroked my cheek with his thumb.

"I was going to go take a bath in the hot spring. If I promise to behave like a gentleman, would you like to join me? I thought maybe the warm waters would help relax you."

I considered what he was saying with a certain amount of schoolgirl glee. The thought of seeing the gorgeous lines of his body in the moonlight sounded appealing.

"If you will behave yourself, like a gentleman, I will behave like a lady as well. After all, we're both adults."

I started to get up and felt my head spin a little. Immediately he was there with his arms around me keeping me safe. He steadied me and turned around for a moment.

Clearing his throat he pulled out another pile of clothes. "One of the others had these clothes from a Nymph friend of ours. She was more to your... proportions. They are washed and cleaned he assures me, but he thought they may be more comfortable for you." Tallyn pushed away the memories of the Nymphs from a few nights before.

I looked at the pile of clothes pushed into my hands. There appeared to be two chemises, a skirt and a bodice. I took one of the chemises and the towel that was being handed to me and followed him out of the tent.

Once outside I could see the three large lanterns hung in the trees illuminating the area. Tallyn stopped long enough to grab a few small unlit lanterns. He waved to the guards before taking my hand and leading me out of camp.

We stumbled our way down to the pool, out of the sight from the camp. Tallyn took a moment to lay out and light the small lanterns along one side of the pool. He then began to strip without any sign of modesty. The muted light illuminated his pale skin making it almost glow a soft silver. I realized I was staring and quickly turned around feeling the heat rise in my cheeks. A moment later I heard him slide into the water behind me.

With a deep breath I unclasped the cloak and pulled off his garments I had borrowed. The cold night air pricked at my skin causing me to suck in air in deep gasps. As soon as I was totally undressed I tiptoed into the water, hoping it was as warm as he had promised.

The water was perfect. Steam rose off of it and I quickly sank in, up to my shoulders. I pulled the elastic from my ponytail and allowed my hair to fall down around me. With a deep breath I dove below the surface of the water and pushed my hair back as I broke the surface again. I swam halfway out into the pool where I had to tread water before stopping.

I turned towards the waterfall where Tallyn was scrubbing away the day's dirt. I could see tiny bubbles from a cloth and noticed a golden bar of soap sitting on the nearby rock. Taking my courage in hand, I swam up beside him and noticed another washcloth. I tried to touch down and found I needed to stand on my tippy toes to keep my head above water.

Without warning, he turned and looked at me. Embarrassment flooded me and I sank down to flatfoot. It was then I realized just how much taller than me he really was. I only came to mid chest on him. His riding breeches, which had been flood pants on me, only came down to his knee. I pushed back up on my toes and attempted to sound confident. "I'm sorry if I startled you. I was hoping I could use the soap?"

He smiled and handed me the soap and other washcloth. I started to work up a lather on the cloth when he picked me up and sat me on a rock beside him. My feet didn't reach the pool's floor but my shoulders were out of the water and I could more easily scrub myself.

Once again I started to lather the cloth but the soap was taken out of my hands. Before I knew what was happening he was working a lather up and washing my hair. His fingers felt like magic on my scalp, massaging it as he went. He leaned close to my ear and I felt my spine stiffen with him so close.

"I thought you may want help rinsing the blood from your hair from last night's head injury." I had totally forgotten about it until he said something.

"Thank you," I whispered, leaning back against his chest and shoulder while he scrubbed.

"Hand me the cloth please." Before I could hand it to him he had reached around and plucked it from my grip. Seconds later he leaned me forward and began scrubbing down my back and over my shoulders, then along my arms.

Without thought or hesitation I turned under the cloth to face him. Adding more soap to the cloth he didn't even question my change of direction and ran his hands over my collarbone, then slid them down to my breasts. Soon the circular scrubbing motions turned to firm caresses. I sucked in my breath, biting my lower lip as he slid his thumbs over the pert points that were my nipples. They hardened under his touch and the softest moan escaped my lips.

"I'm sorry," he said, letting go of my breasts. "I promised to be a gentleman and I am not behaving as such. Please, forgive me?" He stepped back and as he did my whole body screamed in protest. He pressed the soap and cloth into my hand. "I'll wait for you on the rocks so you can finish in peace."

What had just happened? I wanted to cry for him to come back and finish what he had started but I didn't. I finished quickly and rinsed off before swimming to the edge of the pool. He offered me a hand getting out then wrapped a dry linen towel around me without so much as a glance at my bare skin. Once I was dry, I pulled the clean chemise over my head.

The fabric was so soft and so thin it felt like feathers against my skin. All it succeeded in doing was causing my breasts to tighten more. Before I could think he had the heavy wool cloak around my shoulders again. Gathering up our belongings he walked me back to camp in silence.

We arrived back at row of tents just as the last tall lantern was being extinguished. Maerryn glanced from me to Tallyn. The sparkle in his eyes said he could feel our discomfort. "Tallyn, I have spare bedding in my tent. You can bunk in there tonight and give the lady some privacy." Tallyn nodded.

I stepped into his tent and put the clothes beside the bag that held my actual clothing in it. He stepped in behind me and lit a small lantern beside the cot. "I just need to grab a few things and then I will be out of your way." I nodded in response to him and turned towards the cot. I suddenly realized my bandages were soaked again. Perhaps I could rewrap it myself.

I took the cloak off and turned to ask him about the dry bandages. "Do you have any more clean and dry bandages? I want to redress my wrist before I go to sleep."

I turned to look at him and as I did I watched his eyes widen and slide over my body. It was then I noticed you could see through the chemise I had on, and nothing was left to the imagination.

He took a deep shuddering breath and sat down on the cot, pulling me down beside him. To his credit he took my wrist into his lap and never let his gaze drift anywhere but my eyes and wrist as he redressed it. He finished with slightly shaky hands and got up to leave. I caught his hand with mine and pulled him down to sit beside me.

"I should go. I've crossed the line tonight and I don't want to cross it without your permission again. I want to respect your ways since they are different from ours." I put a finger over his lips.

"What happened in the pool back there, I wanted to happen. You didn't cross any lines. If I had been uncomfortable with your actions, I would have told you to stop." I reached up and ran my fingers through his hair. It was silky soft and poured through them like water.

Tallyn reached out and tilted my chin so he could more easily look into my eyes. "You don't have to do anything you don't want to do." He stroked his thumb over my lower lip. Instinctively my tongue lapped out and I took his thumb in my mouth sucking it lightly before I let it go.

"I know," I answered in a barely audible whisper. His hand slid back into my hair as he lowered his mouth to mine.

His lips were firm and demanding on mine. His tongue traced the shape of my lower lip before I opened my mouth to him. He sucked on my lip for a moment, giving it a playful nip before diving into the exploration of my mouth. I was timid at first but he was relentless in coaxing a response from me. He hungrily drank me in, encircling my waist with his other arm and pressing me tightly against his chest. My body responded to his instantly, my nipples tightening beneath the layers of fabric between us.

I moaned against his kiss, surrendering to the invasion that I so desperately wanted. He pulled back, releasing my mouth and I started to protest until I felt his lips press against the area just below my ear. My breathing became shallow as I buried both my hands into his hair pulling him closer.

He chuckled against my neck and ran his hot tongue down to the curve where my neck and shoulder met. A shudder full of need ran through my body. He lifted his head, his eyes smoldering with desire. "Ask me to stop," he said.

"I may kill you if you do. Stay here, with me tonight?" I pleaded.

"Thank goddess," he whispered before biting down on the sensitive area. A sound foreign to me escaped my lips.

He pulled away long enough to pull his shirt over his head and toss his pants to the floor. There in the soft glow of the lantern I could see every plane of his body. His hot thick manhood stood at attention. It was proudly telling me and the world he was aroused and all but aching to fulfill his need. He dropped to the cot beside me.

He slid his hands under the chemise and up along my body until he was pulling it off over my head and tossing it to the ground with his clothing. No sooner had it hit the floor then he had reclaimed my mouth. This time however, his hands slid along my sides, up over my ribs, claiming my breasts.

At first he timed the flicks of his thumbs with the flick of his tongue on mine, causing me to gasp a little with anticipation. Then his playful flicks became a masterful massage, rolling my aching peaks gently between his thumb and forefinger. I gasped as he lifted his mouth from mine and lowered me back onto the cot.

He positioned himself between my legs then lowered his head to one of my breasts. As he took possession of the first nipple between his lips, sucking on it with a bit more pressure, he slid a hand along my thigh until it pressed against the sensitive folds of my sex.

I bucked, rubbing myself against his hand. He pressed my hips down and allowed his fingers to go exploring. When he found the pearl that marked my center and entrance, he started making slow firm circles around it causing me to wiggle my hips in response. He increased the speed and pressure until I was gasping for air, teetering on a flood of ecstasy. He pushed me right up onto the edge and slid two fingers inside me. I gasped, tightening around him and crying out.

He switched to my other breast, this time suckling it in harder, and I bucked against the hand that held me as he slowly began to massage my core and heat in a maddening rhythm. Each time he picked up tempo until finally I exploded, tightening around his hand, gasping for breath. I cried out against the silence of the tent, arching my back and pressing myself hard against him.

It was then he finally urged my thighs apart and pressed his shaft to my opening. I was still riding the aftershocks of my first orgasm when he pushed into me. I was so tight I didn't think there was any way he could fit. He paused, allowing my muscles to relax and bid him to enter. He slowly stroked deeper into me and again a moan pierced the night air. Inch by inch he sank deeper into me until there was nowhere else to go.

With one last thrust he filled me completely and we lay there like that for a moment.

He leaned his mouth close to my ear. "Open your mind to me. Let me feel what you feel." Then without warning he withdrew and thrust into me hard. I cried out in pleasure and he shuddered for a moment. Suddenly, I was there sharing his feelings. I could feel the intense control he was using, afraid of hurting me. In response I bucked my hips up into him, causing him to moan as well. It was all the encouragement he needed.

He lowered his mouth to mine, laying claim to it in such a way as to let me know he was marking me as his. He thrust into me hard and fast repeatedly. Sharing our mutual pleasure the feeling and need for release grew so deep and overpowering I was begging him to tip me over the edge again and then it happened. All the colors behind my closed eyes exploded. With one more good hard thrust into my now painfully tightening nether regions he cried out his own release, my name on his lips as we experienced each other's pleasure.

My body rhythmically tightened around him, our foreheads touched, my nails dug deep into his back and I was riding not only my own waves of pleasure but his as well. I was so moved a tear of happiness ran over my cheek. I felt so totally complete and I could feel in his heart, he did too. Our breathing was shaky and our hearts were beating perfectly in time as we lay there.

"Is sex with an Elf always like this?" I asked gasping for air.

"No, mating has never been like this with anyone before." He leaned in, kissing my cheek. He moved himself to the cot beside me, then pulled me half on top of him before tugging the blankets up around us.

"I've never experienced anything like that before." My head was spinning as I nuzzled his chest.

He sighed deeply as if he knew something I didn't. "Good night, My Lady," he said pressing one last kiss to my forehead. With his arms wrapped tightly around me I sank into him and the blankets, quickly finding sleep. The dreams that came were peaceful and it was possibly one of the best night's sleep I had ever had.

I woke up slowly. I have never been someone who just wakes up and rolls out of bed easily. I stretched out and felt something tighten around me. My eyes flew open as I slid my hands over the beautiful pale skin of Tallyn's chest. He looked down at me, lazily running a hand down my back. "We need to get up," he said.

"No we don't. We can stay here all day." To prove my point I rested my head on his shoulder and closed my eyes again.

In a swift, fluid motion he rolled me on my back and pressed his body down heavily on me. I pushed against his chest but he was unmoving. I could feel his manhood resting against my abdomen, firm and aroused. With a dip of his head, he ran his tongue between my breasts, up my throat and then claimed my mouth with a kiss. My body responded to his touch and possession. Fire sprung to life within me.

Then, as quickly as he had come he was gone and standing beside the cot. "As much fun as it would be to stay in bed all day, we need to help pack up camp so we can leave. You don't need to help with the packing but it is hard to pack my tent and cot if you're still in them."

He gave me a flourished bow as I crawled off the cot, staggering to my feet. His eyes raked over me and suddenly flared. He turned around quickly.

Ah, well the mystery is gone now. He has seen me in the daylight and knows the truth. I thought to myself. I watched his back stiffen all the more as I stood there in thought.

I quickly pulled on my newly borrowed clothes. The skirt and chemise went on easy enough, but soon there was the bodice. I tugged and twisted at it to get it laced up the front on my own. With one last breath and tug, I was cinched into it. My breasts were served up on a shelf. Together with the low cut chemise it only amplified the attention to my cleavage. I cringed. Tallyn had been correct though, these garments did fit me better, although I liked breathing more than these clothes allowed for comfortably.

When next I looked up, Tallyn was breaking down the bedding and tent, and packing things down tightly. To my amazement, everything we had used for six men fit on one very tiny cart. The morning sun was just cresting over the hills when everything was finished.

I felt a soft tap on my shoulder and I turned to find a member of the guard. "My Lady, you may ride my horse and I will sit on the cart with my friend." As if to prove his intention he handed me the reins to a beautiful horse that towered over me, his brown body the color of a Hershey bar with a pink nose.

I reached out cautiously to pet him. "Hello there, you're going to be nice to me, aren't you?" I asked in a baby voice. I grabbed a carrot off the cart to feed it to him trying to create a quick bond of friendship with the animal. When it had finished it bumped me with its head and sniffed me for any other snacks.

The others were mounting up as I looked around. I turned to the horse, slid my foot in the stirrup, grabbed the saddle and pulled as hard as I could trying to get up; then the horse moved and I came crashing down on my backside. To the horse's credit when I made a loud unladylike noise all he did was stare at me.

I climbed to my feet and dusted off my backside... and pride. I grabbed the saddle again, slid my foot into the stirrup but this time as I pulled a pair of hands lifted me at the waist, helping me stabilize and successfully get my leg over. I turned in the saddle expecting it was Tallyn to my rescue, but was instead surprised to see Maerryn grinning up at me. "My Lady, have you ever ridden before?"

"Once, at summer camp when I was nine," I answered back, hoping to look confident when I wasn't.

"I see." He called to the guard behind him and handed him the reigns of his horse. "Please slide as far forward as you can." He held the reins and steadied the horse while I slid forward until I was sitting uncomfortably at the front of the saddle. Then, with more grace than I had seen anyone have, he mounted directly behind me. "There we go," he said, reaching around and patting the horse.

I felt immediately awkward. It was made worse when Maerryn wrapped an arm around my waist and pulled me back against his chest and off the front edge of the saddle. I refused to lean back into him even though it would have offered me more comfort. He squeezed his legs and gave the slightest kick and we were off.

"I would have had Tallyn stay and sent a different member of the guard I had known you were new to riding. Not that I mind having a beautiful woman pressed against me while I ride." His voice had a joking quality to it.

"He's one of the fastest riders I know and I wanted to make sure we had a scout ahead of us. We ran into a set of bandits the night before we arrived."

"I know. I saw them." I was suddenly worried I had said something I shouldn't have.

"Ah, you're the one that was always watching over him. It makes more sense now. He said that already, but until now I think I just pictured it as a fantasy in his head." In a way that seemed almost brotherly he gave me a brief squeeze. "Thank you. I'm sure you saved us a lot of pain that night."

"I didn't do anything." I looked down at my bandaged wrist trying to distract myself.

Behind me Maerryn shrugged. "Somehow he knew because of you."

He paused as if considering his words carefully. "Tallyn is the second prince to our current King, our father. He refuses to acknowledge himself as such, even though our father has always claimed him and raised him as a prince. He always tries harder than anyone else, because he believes he must prove himself. If he seems cranky or difficult at times, please do not be angry at him."

"He hasn't really been cranky since I got here. Is he often angry?" I wasn't sure what I was asking.

"When he is in the company of just myself or with his friends, he is the Tallyn you see. When he is in front of the court and in front of our father, he is never at ease, and things that wouldn't otherwise bother him...." His words trailed off. "I believe that because you two share such a special bond that you can offer him a safety and acceptance he doesn't think he has at home."

"I'm not sure I understand, but I will do my best to keep my temper in check. I don't really get mad, or if I do, I am always far more upset with myself for becoming so upset." I thought about Tallyn getting angry and had a hard time imagining such a thing.

"I know you want to go home, but for now we don't really know how to get you there. Once we are back, I will use every resource at my disposal to help you get home. I have two requests while you are in the Kingdom." There was no question in his voice. He said request but meant order.

"Yes, what can I do?" I hoped it wasn't something horrible like stop talking to Tallyn or be open to the mating rituals of the Elven culture.

"One, for your safety you are Lady Lillian. You are noble born. Everyone in the camp believes it already and has no reason to doubt it. With Tallyn and myself claiming it as well, there will be no room to think otherwise. Even if my father asks, you are Lady Lillian. Do you understand?" His voice while warm, was still commanding. I nodded that I understood his order.

"Two, try to get through to my brother. He often says there is an emptiness inside him. He will be frightening and cold at times. He may yell, say things he doesn't really mean and even make threats. You've seen who he really is. Please help him see past all that."

"How bad can he be?" I asked.

Maerryn gave a low bitter laugh. "Oh, he is a tyrant and a monster sometimes. Many members of the court believe his heart is hardened and cold. Of course it isn't, but his actions do not help his reputation. There will be times that things may be difficult for you at court because you are not of this realm and you have the added 'benefit' of being associated with him. If anyone is unkind to you, please don't hesitate to let me know."

"I've never really been a tattletale. As far as being Lady Lillian, my realm doesn't really use titles much anymore but if it lessens your guilt, my family is English nobility. So who knows, five hundred years ago I may have been Lady Lillian?" I forced a smile hoping it would reach my voice. I hated to lie.

"Good, then no lies are being told and you have nothing to feel guilty about. I am the Prince and future King. I never feel guilty." His words were crisp. I almost laughed. Both he and Tallyn shared the same confident arrogance.

By late afternoon we were approaching the woods they had been in the night they were attacked. We stopped long enough to rest the horses and await Tallyn's arrival. When an hour passed and he wasn't back I began to worry.

Maerryn approached me as I was taking a drink of water. "Tallyn has not returned yet. We do need to press into the woods for safety and cover. While these are peaceful times there have been some rumors. We will move quicker if I can lead us. Will you be alright riding alone? You will have guards on either side of you."

I looked at the horses and shrugged. "I can figure it out. I may need a little help getting back on, but I should be alright once I'm up there."

He nodded his approval. "There is one last thing." He handed me a sword and dagger. "Keep the sword easily accessible on the horse. If we are attacked ride as fast and as hard as you can. Keep the dagger hidden on you in case of an emergency." I accepted the weapons, tucking the dagger inside my boot.

Not long after, I was back on the horse alone riding deeper and deeper into the woods. The sun began to sink into the sky when we finally stopped and the men broke camp. I sat by the fire hoping that Tallyn would show up soon. I could see the concern written on the faces of everyone around me but no one wanted to say anything.

I got up and unfastened the sword from the horse I had been riding. Taking advantage of the only tent setup at the time I changed into my sweater and jeans, belting the sword on my hip. When I stepped back out into camp I was met by sorrow filled eyes.

"What's wrong?" I asked Maerryn. It was then I noticed Mavba behind the group, one of the guards affectionately patting her. "Where's Tallyn?"

Maerryn's eyes met mine. "The horse came back without him."

I sank to the ground and wrapped my arms around myself. Closing my eyes I tried to push all other thoughts away and think about Tallyn. In my mind I was surrounded by darkness but I wasn't alone. Something dangerous was lurking there but I didn't have time to deal with that now. Focusing, I pushed my way through the darkness. Then, faintly, I could hear a heartbeat.

Tallyn? I called out. I felt him stir somewhere in the darkness. *Where are you? Are you ok?*

It was soft but I could hear him. *Riverbank, too dangerous.*

I tried to focus more when something in the darkness grabbed hold of me. I turned to see what it was, pain radiating in my shoulder. I looked up into glowing red eyes and fought the terror running through me. I cried out finally against the pain in my left shoulder, and forced my way out of the darkness and back into reality.

When I opened my eyes Maerryn was urging me to lay back pressing bandages to my shoulder. "Lillian, Lillian, wake up. What's going on?" I blinked at him and struggled to sit back up. I turned to look at my shoulder, blood staining my sweater.

"Help me up, we need to go save Tallyn. He's in danger." The guards held me in place despite my best attempts to get up. Maerryn reached out and ripped open the shoulder of my sweater.

Swearing under his breath he looked at the claw marks. "You have an Itheaga hunting you?" He turned, calling for first aid supplies. "You need stitches, these cuts are deep."

"I know about the damn shadow monster hunting me in the darkness. I don't have time for stitches right now. Do you love your brother? Do you want to save him?"

Maerryn sat back on his heels looking at me. "Then we need to go now!" As if to prove my point I grabbed a clean cloth and clumsily bandaged it around my shoulder. I staggered to my feet. "How far is the riverbank?"

One of the guards responded that it was within a half hour ride. Ignoring my injuries I made my way to Mavba. Using a nearby log I climbed on her back before anyone realized what I was doing. With a tug on the reins and a slight kick we were off. I could hear the men behind me cursing and calling for me to come back.

Moments later I could hear the sound of horses rapidly approaching me. Maerryn had quickly closed the distance and was trying to stop me. He reached out, grabbing hold of the reigns and pulling me to a halt.

"Do you have a death wish? Itheaga venom is poisonous unless treated," he spat angrily.

"Your brother is in trouble. Possibly dying. Will this venom kill me in the next twelve hours? Because it hadn't killed me in twenty four hours and that was two days ago." I held up my wrist as if to prove my point.

"Tallyn needs help right now more than I do." I kicked Mavba, pushing her forward and following my instincts and her lead. The others followed closely behind.

When I could hear the sound of running water I pulled Mavba to a quiet trot. I listened carefully for any sounds that might help me pinpoint the location we were looking for. I should have trusted the ears of an Elf more because all I heard was silence. One of the guards held a finger up to indicate quiet and pointed in a direction upstream. I nodded in understanding.

I followed the lead of the others and carefully guided Mavba upstream as quietly as possible. As we got closer, I thought I heard the sound of several men talking and shouting. Then there would be a roll of laughter. One guard slid off his horse and darted silently through the cover of trees. I held my breath.

Moments later he returned. "Nine Goblins," he whispered to the group. The Elves all dismounted without as much as a sound.

As I started to dismount, one of them stopped me and encouraged me to stay seated on the horse. "Like hell I am," I whispered angrily and kicked my leg over the other side, sliding off the saddle. I landed on my feet with as little sound as I could.

I watched as the Elven guard fanned out into the woods. When I looked around I was alone in the forest again and the panic of a few nights ago came flooding back. I pushed it away, telling myself I had better things to be worried about right now.

As quietly as possible I maneuvered myself through the trees until I saw the glow of firelight. I tucked myself low behind a bush to watch. Tallyn sat with his arms and legs tied. His body was bruised and bloodied. His shirt was torn away, revealed marks that looked like he had been whipped. Anger stirred deep within me.

His assailants danced around. They were short creatures that stood about four feet tall with slimy green skin and bright red hair on top of their heads. Their smiles were wide, showing rows of pointed teeth, and their dark beady eyes sparkled like glass in the firelight. There was a cracking noise to my left. A few of them looked in my direction. I sat frozen and silent, not even breathing.

Suddenly, five tall fierce Elves rushed in with a battle cry, weapons drawn. The Goblins sprang to life, the first three of them meeting their deaths early. All of the Elves were fighting against Tallyn's captors. Taking my courage in hand, I made a dash for where he sat helpless.

I reached his side without mishap and started to untie his feet. His eyes met mine. "Run," he whispered. "The others are here, I will be fine."

Behind me I heard the yelp of one of the Elves. I turned in time to see him stagger to his knees, a nasty gash to his side. At the same moment his assailant saw me and bounded my direction. I threw myself backwards, avoiding the sword he swung.

With my right hand and injured wrist I lifted my sword. The Goblin laughed, baring his teeth again. "It's been a couple hundred years since I last saw a Human. I wonder if you will taste as good as he did?" I gulped and with trained reaction deflected his next blow. He thrust and nicked my already injured shoulder.

"This isn't a game, this is real, Lily. Pull it together," I told myself.

I twisted out of the way of the next shot and fell into a stance I had used a million times in practice. As he rushed forward, I lunged in and punched my sword past him. At the last moment I tightened my grip and snapped the sword with my aching wrist. White-hot pain shot up my arm as the blade buried itself into the back of the Goblins neck. I twisted and pulled it free. He stood frozen, looking at me. Blood gushed down his back and onto the ground below. He let out a gurgled scream.

I took a deep breath and watched as the Goblins fighting turned to look at us and I suddenly understood. Quickly I slashed out with my arm and watched as his head tumbled off his shoulders. The surrounding Elves and their Goblin foes all stood frozen. I lunged at the next closest Goblin, burying my sword in his chest. The moment of awe was over and the Elf behind him removed his head. Moments later they had all been dispatched.

I felt light headed but staggered back to Tallyn. Dropping to my knees I struggled to untie him. He looked at me with alarm. "Doesn't that hurt?" he asked.

"My shoulder and wrist are killing me but we needed to save you. I'll be ok." I tried to climb to my feet but my body refused to move.

"I was actually talking about the dagger in your leg." I looked down and realized the reason everyone had stopped and gaped was because a dagger was plunged to the hilt in my thigh and blood was oozing out.

"Dammit! These were my favorite jeans." Without warning, tears started flowing down my face.

An hour later, injured, exhausted and dirty we had made our way back to camp. I allowed one of the guards to help me off the horse and to the campfire area. Soon the flames were blazing again. Tallyn sat on one side of me and the Elf that had been injured by my assailant sat on the other side.

Tallyn had insisted that the guard and I receive first aid before him. Maerryn worked in some of the salve that had been used on my wrist on my shoulder. Too tired to fight the pain I screamed in agony as it burned into the wound. He made short work of cleaning it up and stitching it closed. He then worked more salve into it before bandaging it.

While I sat gasping for air Maerryn looked at my wrist. Cursing me for tearing out far better stitches than he could do, he put me back together as best he could. Beside me the injured Elf struggled as he was wrapped up.

Maerryn sat looking down at my leg. "This is a very serious injury. If your anatomy is anything like ours you have a major artery that runs through here. If it isn't nicked already it could be accidentally when I remove the blade. I must carefully remove the dagger so as not to disrupt and damage it." He turned and asked that an iron be put into the fire. "I'm really sorry, but you may hate me for what I have to do."

Taking his belt he wrapped it as tightly as he could around my upper thigh. Tallyn leaned close, throwing his injured body across my chest. I felt the leg of my jeans cut away. Quickly and with precision, the dagger was pulled free and a cloth was pressed hard onto my leg. Nothing could have prepared me for what came next, though.

Tallyn whispered. "Look at me, look at me," and I was drawn to look in his eyes. The hot iron was pressed into the wound and held there. The pain was so intense I wished I would have blacked out but all I could see was stinging white light.

Chapter Nine

Due to injuries it took another two days to get back to the Elven Kingdom. After one night's sleep, Tallyn had proved himself healed enough to ride. The Elf who had sustained an injury to his side was put on the cart and I sat cradled against Maerryn. Tallyn had argued that I should be allowed to ride with him but with his recovering injuries and the severity of my own, coupled with my inexperience, it was ultimately decided I would ride with Maerryn.

My whole body ached and I could feel I had a fever behind my eyes. As we approached the great castle I thought how excited I would have been if I hadn't been coming in broken and weak. As we passed through the outer gates and made our way to the front steps I noticed people rushing forward happily to welcome their Princes home.

At the steps of the great keep servants and guards rushed forward to help the princes and the injured guard, Cylan. Tallyn looked at the people around us. "Take Lady Lillian to my chambers and call the royal physician immediately." Dozens of helpful hands lifted and supported me.

I was taken to a large room that had three other rooms off of it. I was laid down on a large, overly stuffed couch. Tallyn entered shortly behind me. He dragged a chair over beside me and sank down on it. He gave directions to the servants that flitted in and out of the room. Without a word to me, he took my injured right hand in his and soothingly caressed the back of it.

Soon an old Elf rushed in with two younger lads behind him. He unwrapped the bandages on my leg and inspected the wound. He sighed in relief. He then checked my shoulder, which he seemed less happy with, and my wrist. Finally he touched my forehead and withdrew his hand quickly. He turned and looked at Tallyn.

"Her leg wound is completely closed and healing nicely. The magic of the land seems to like her. She shouldn't suffer any lasting effects other than a scar. Her shoulder and wrist, because of the nature of the creature who caused the injury, will take longer. Her body is fighting hard against the venom. If she had only sustained the one injury her body wouldn't be struggling so much but with them both and her leg..." He just shook his head.

"Get her cleaned up and in bed. She needs medicine, food and rest. Has she been able to keep anything down since the injury?" he questioned Tallyn.

I struggled but found my voice. "I haven't felt like eating," I commented.

The Elf looked at me. "Oh, you do speak our language. I was curious. How did all this happen?" he asked me while he turned to look over the back of the couch at Tallyn.

"He was captured. I went to save him." I ventured a look at Tallyn who considered me with eyes filled with mixed emotions.

"That was very brave of you," the older Elf said.

"It was foolish and she could have died," Tallyn bit out angrily. "Don't encourage her, Grelyem."

Grelyem rolled his eyes. "I am rather impressed that a high-born Lady would be as selfless as to risk her life for an ungrateful whelp like you."

Tallyn looked back over at me, giving my hand a squeeze. "I didn't say I was ungrateful, only that she was foolish for putting her life in danger for me."

I tried for a smile and failed. With a soft whisper, the last of my strength fading, I said, "Some things are worth fighting and being foolish for."

"By getting yourself killed? What would that have done?" His voice was barely a growl now. I had never seen Tallyn angry, but I now understood why his brother had felt the need to warn me. If I hadn't known it came from a place of concern I would be annoyed.

Grelyem chuckled. "Oh, I can see the two of you are going to be good company for one another. Good for you, Sire." He clapped a hand on Tallyn's shoulder causing him to wince a little.

He rummaged through his bag and handed Tallyn two jars and a bottle. "Have her take a shot of the anti-venom every four hours until her fever breaks. The other two jars are for your injuries and her bandages. Think you can manage?" He tossed a look my way. "I can send a female nurse and move you out of these dark quarters if you like, My Lady."

"I think I can manage. Thank you for your help and concern." My voice was hoarse.

Tallyn bid the physician goodbye and waited for the door to close. He moved beside me, gently helping me sit up. There was a knock from one of the far chambers. He stood and walked over to the door. I heard him speak with someone and watched as a young maid excused herself.

Tallyn came back and sat on the couch beside me. He considered me for a moment, then grabbed a dagger and cut into my sweater and jeans. Carefully he pulled them away. He considered my bra for a moment and reached out with the dagger.

"Stop! Not my bra. It's the only one I have here." He rolled his eyes and carefully cut away the straps and through the front center. When he had removed it, he set it off to the side.

"Don't worry, I'll have more made for you. As many as you need or want." Then, in a fluid motion that scared me, he lifted me off the couch and cradled me against his chest, carrying me into the other room.

Looking around I saw it housed a large tub that would make the one in the Savoy seem small and cozy. I could see steam hovering above the surface of the water. He lowered me into the tub.

The water made my injuries sting but relaxed the muscles that ached from three days of riding. I watched as Tallyn quickly shed his own clothes and joined me. He slid in behind me. His long legs framed each side of my thighs. He urged me to lean back against him. As soon as our skin touched I felt like I was melting into him.

With gentle hands he washed me and himself. Finally he stood and helped me get to my feet. He pulled down on a lever and warm water fell like rain on us, rinsing away the remnants of dirt, blood and soap.

Cautiously he stepped out, taking care to make sure the floor wasn't wet so he wouldn't slip. He wrapped a towel around himself, then one around me. Without the tiniest sign of effort he lifted me from the bath and cradled me in his arms again, this time ducking into one of the other rooms.

This room had a fireplace against the wall shared with the bathroom. A warm fire was burning in it now. On the opposite wall was a huge bed. It looked like it was made of twisted branches that reached up to the ceiling. Curtains made of a light gossamer hung from an invisible canopy, draping the bed. A large stained glass window that glowed with the light of the sun and the moon sat above the headboard. The third wall was made up of a long row of windows that overlooked the inner bailey below. Lanterns that appeared to be made from lotus blossoms gave light to the dark room.

Tallyn lowered me to the bed. Untucking the towel that covered me, he looked at my body carefully.

"I know there is a lot of me to love and now with the addition of the hack job it's not pretty to look at. I understand that the other day was a one-time thing. The ladies of your castle are no doubt..." He cut me off, pressing his lips to mine.

"The ladies of this castle cannot hold a candle to your beauty or courage. You are soft and womanly. Exactly what any man would want. If you say or think anything otherwise, ask me and I will tell you again. As for any emotional attachment, the only one I have is sitting here with me now." I started to open my mouth to protest. He pressed a finger to it so as to stifle my speech.

Silently, he worked the salve into my wounds then re-bandaged me. From a nearby chair he pulled a soft blue chemise. He helped me into it then insisted that he tuck me into bed. Once settled he handed me a cup with a small amount of the anti-venom in it. I gagged a little and happily accepted the spoonful of soup he pushed into my mouth.

"I'm not a baby bird you know, I can feed myself."
He pushed another spoonful of soup in my mouth.

"No you can't. Not until you heal more. I'm not
letting you do anything for yourself that I can help you
with." I swallowed and he had another bite waiting.

Once I finished eating he put the dishes by the door
in the main room then crawled into bed beside me. He
helped me lay back into the pillows. I shifted slightly
and rested my head against his shoulder where he lay
beside me.

"How are you feeling?" I asked.

"Better now that I know you will live." He took my
hand in his.

"I'm pretty stubborn and hard to kill." I was
becoming drowsy.

"I noticed. You even use a sword. That's pretty
exciting for an Elf like me," he joked. "Never do that
again!" The latter part was an order and not a joke.

"No promises. Stay uncaptured and I shouldn't
have to." He turned his head and pressed a kiss to the
top of my head.

"I didn't think you would have running water." I
made the comment out of the blue.

"Why? Because we don't have motorized carts or
war machines?" He chuckled. "Humans in our realm
are often painted as the technologically inferior race. I
know you're not now, but the folklore we have about
you doesn't paint the best representation."

I laughed and snuggled in against him, falling asleep feeling warm and protected.

Throughout the night I was awoken and fed more anti-venom on multiple occasions. When finally I awoke the next day it was to heavy pounding from outside the bedchamber. Tallyn shifted under me, easing me back onto the pillows before going to investigate. I watched with curiosity when he opened the door and it was pushed wide with force.

A tall Elf with broad shoulders and dark hair pushed passed Tallyn. He was dressed in fine silks. The thin gold band about his head proclaimed his importance.

"You've been home a day and still haven't come to see me," he accused Tallyn with wrath-filled eyes. "Now I hear you found a Human while you were out gallivanting around causing problems with the Goblins."

"It's good to see you too, father." Tallyn's tone was flat.

"You could have been killed," his father accused.

"But he wasn't," I piped up. I kicked my feet over the edge of the bed and slid to the floor. I forced myself to stand up as straight as I could and pushed my way between the King and his son. "Your Majesty, your son shows great bravery and practices restraint in all he does. This was not an act of defiance or youthful miscalculation. He was ambushed by nine Goblins."

Both the King and Tallyn stared down at me in disbelief. "Dear maiden, I bid you return to your duties while I speak with my son. This is a family matter." With what was meant to be a light touch to turn me towards the door, the King closed his hand over my left shoulder and turned me abruptly to face it.

"Father, stop!" I heard Tallyn say with force.

My shoulder filled with white hot pain, the torqueing motion of the turn caused my leg to buckle, and I crumpled to the floor. Tears made up of a mixture of frustration and pain ran down my face. I tried to right myself but I couldn't put pressure on my right wrist or left shoulder. My leg refused to respond the way I wanted it to. A soft sob was the only noise I made, and before I could struggle again Tallyn was there kneeling beside and lifting me into his arms.

"She's badly injured and shouldn't be out of bed." Tallyn paced the few steps back to the bed and deposited me on it.

"You, stay!" he commanded me.

Turning on his heel he resumed his position facing his father. "When I arrived home yesterday it was unclear if Lady Lillian was going to survive the night. I was also recovering from my own injuries." He motioned in my direction.

The King's gaze slid to me, his eyes apologetic. "My Lady, I apologize. I didn't recognize you or know of your fragile state."

"There is no need for an apology, Your Majesty. I have been well cared for since my arrival. You didn't know." I bowed my head.

Turning his attention back to his son he said, "And what about the Human that was found? Humans from the other realm have a history of being untrustworthy and foul." I bit my lower lip at the description. No wonder the portal had been sealed if that was the stereotype we had.

"That Human saved my life!" Tallyn countered. He straightened to his full height, looking the King in his eyes, motioning in my direction. "She almost died doing it. She has proven herself more than trustworthy."

The King turned his glare back on me. This time I was being scrutinized. "She is a Halfling, not a Human. Child, what is your family name?" There wasn't the slightest ounce of softness in his voice.

"My mother's family is English nobility, Craven of Essex. Our family was titled and landed by his Majesty Henry I, son of England in the year 1109. We rose in rank and ascended because of the support given during a difficult period with Normandy." I took a deep breath and thanked my mother silently.

"I see. And are you a Lady of the Court or a Lady of Leisure?" I had a sneaky feeling I was being tested by this question.

"Neither, Your Majesty. I am a scholar and teacher. I teach the literature of my ancestors to our youth." I was going to let him chew on that for a moment.

To my surprise he nodded his approval, looking back to Tallyn. "She is absolutely a Halfling, I can see it in her eyes, but it is evident she was raised within that realm. I remember it and the era well." He turned and looked back at me.

"I'm glad to see that with time the Human race moved beyond being barbarians. You are a Lady, Scholar and Warrior. You will have a place within my court for as long as you like."

The King turned his attention back to his son. "I'll have a nurse found for her and a chamber made up."

"That won't be necessary. She will be remaining with me." All the air rushed out of my lungs when I heard Tallyn's words. "She is my lover. Her place is here."

The King stopped and looked back at me again, his facial features softening. This time there was a twinkle in his eye I hadn't seen before. "My dear, perhaps you are confused. I have another son with a far more pleasant temperament. I know they look a great deal alike, but maybe I should show you to his chambers instead?"

Was the King teasing me? "That won't be necessary. I think I like this one," I said, offering a smile. I watched as Tallyn's jaw tightened.

The King turned back to his son with a smile this time. "See me to the door." The King gave the slightest head bow and exited the bedroom. Through the open door I saw the King and Tallyn exchange words. There was motioning in my direction from both participants. Finally the King embraced his son in a hug, kissing his forehead. With that he was gone.

Tallyn closed both doors including the one to the inner bed chamber. He climbed back on the bed, pulling me back into the many layers of blankets and pillows. Stretching out beside me he pulled the covers up around us. He touched my forehead and looked relieved. "Your fever is gone. You should still get plenty of rest though."

He pressed a kiss to my forehead. "In the future, please try to avoid correcting the King. If you were to do that in court it could prove problematic." I nodded agreement.

"So I'm your lover now? Does that make me more than a one night mating partner?" I wasn't sure how to feel about the most recent title.

"Yes. You said that you were unable to fulfill your sexual needs with noncommittal partner. You said you needed an emotional bond. We have a deep connection and you were willing to die for me. I think that all qualifies. What's more, I refuse to share you with anyone else. Since I rather dislike duels, or killing innocent men, I have decided you are my lover. As simple as that." He rolled over onto his side and propped his head up.

"Does that mean I can do this, whenever I want?" I pressed a kiss to his lips. He smiled and softly kissed me back.

"I guess I'm alright with that," he mumbled.

"What about this?" I lifted my head and nipped lightly at his neck. His whole body went rigid.

"I think I can live with that, as well." His voice was hoarse.

"Oh, then one last question. How about this?" I leaned up and flicked my tongue across his ear before sucking on it for a moment and giving it a nibble.

His whole body shook and he moaned loudly. With no thought to my injuries he grabbed and rolled on top of me. I winced a little but wasn't about to complain. "Oh, I may have to command as a prince of the realm that you do that again, and often."

I laughed. "That good?"

He captured my mouth with his, forcing my lips apart and drinking me in until I thought he would consume me heart and soul. He shifted his head, pressing kisses to my neck and shoulder. I moaned when he pulled the neckline of my chemise down exposing one of my breasts. Deliberately slow, he captured my rosy nipple in his mouth. He lightly grazed his teeth over it then suckled at it. My back arched and I gasped for air. He then rolled off of me and I moaned in protest.

He looked at me with a rather smug grin on his face. "Heal more, then we can play this game." He pressed one more kiss to my mouth, slid my chemise back up and slid off the bed.

"Are you hungry?" he asked me.

"For you? Or for food?" I wasn't sure how to respond. I knew I should eat something, but he seemed far more appetizing at the moment.

"For food. The evening feast will happen soon and if you are hungry I can slip downstairs and get us some hot fresh delicacies. With my brother having returned home yesterday, I'm sure there will be some less common delights. The kitchen maids rather fancy him."

I smiled at that. Having spent time with both of the brothers I could understand why the kitchen maids liked Maerryn. He was handsome, charming and a flirt. I still liked the younger, grumpier brother better, but I hadn't yet really seen the grumpy personality people were talking about.

Before I could decide one way or another Tallyn slipped out of the chambers with a vow to return soon. I made a slow journey to the bathroom, but before I could return to the bed there was a knock on the outer chamber door.

"Come in!" I called. I paused in the doorway and watched as two maids came in.

"Excuse me, My Lady. We're sorry for the intrusion, but Prince Maerryn said that your garments were destroyed in the process of saving Captain Tallyn and Cylan. We're two of the seamstresses of the castle. We wanted to come get some measurements and ask about colors so we could replace your clothing for you. It would be our honor. It has been a very long time since we've had the pleasure of sewing for a Lady."

I picked up my bra from the couch. "I would be greatly in your debt. I also have another challenge for you. In treating my injuries my favorite undergarment was destroyed. If possible, I was hoping you could repair it, or make me a few replacements?" I laid out my bra on a table, explaining how it would normally come together and work.

The ladies looked at it and packed it into their bags. They measured me, taking extra care to make sure I didn't jostle my injuries too much. "My Lady, your favorite colors? Any styles you would like?"

"I like most colors, though blues and purples have always been my favorites. As for styles, I've never attended court... here," I quickly added, remembering that I was supposed to maintain a certain level of appearances. "You two ladies would know better than I would. Please feel free to be as creative as you would like. Color really doesn't matter."

The women exchanged looks with one another. Pursing their lips they looked over me. "Most ladies of the court are highly demanding. We want to make sure we meet your expectations."

I waved it away. "Honestly I would be perfectly happy with some leggings and tunics." They considered me with raised brows. "I promise. I will gladly accept anything you ladies make me. Dress me in kitchen rags and it's better off than I am now."

The younger of the two dropped her jaw and leaned over to the other. They whispered back and forth. They looked back at me. "Will you allow us to make you a wardrobe set, fine enough for a queen?"

I started to protest that they shouldn't trouble themselves but the door clicked open. In came Tallyn followed by a lad carrying a large platter filled with food and a maid with her arms full. Tallyn set down a pitcher with goblets and a smaller platter with bread and cheese on it. The others followed his example.

He smiled warmly at the maids. "Dear ladies, Lady Lillian needs to eat, bathe and rest so she can see our fair kingdom in good health."

The older woman stood and looked at Tallyn. "She needs clothing if she is ever to be seen or even venture outside of this room. Also, we would be happy to serve as the Lady's maids while she is here. We can have her set up in her own quarters tonight if you like, Sire."

I watched him wince at the title but he kept the smile in place. "The Lady is my lover and so will stay here. I do agree that when she heals and I return to my duties, she will be in need of maids to keep her out of trouble. Since you have generously offered, she accepts." I stared at him slack-jawed and had to remind myself I was supposed to be a lady.

"Thank you for your concern, but I'm not accustomed to being watched over. I'm a scholar and teacher in my realm so I'm used to being the one watching." I smiled warmly.

The older woman took one look at me, then turned her attention back to Tallyn. Obviously, I didn't know what I was talking about anymore. "Sire, about her wardrobe. The lady seems uncertain about her tastes. We have some information from her but we would welcome your input."

"I owe her my life for certain and as I have said I am keeping her here as my guest, so please make sure she has the finest we can offer. If she says it is too extravagant, make it more so. If she says there are too many, make twice as many. She likes to underestimate herself or think that she is less deserving than she is. Don't believe her under any circumstances, when it comes to such things." He lifted me into his arms and turned, sitting me down on a chair at the table. "Oh, and if there are any concerns about cost, come see me."

"It would seem that all the men of your family have the same opinion, as both your brother and father made the same offers." The women gathered the rest of their belongings and left.

Tallyn saw everyone out and closed the door behind them all. I waited for him to have a seat at the table beside me. Sliding into a chair, he started putting food on the plate in front of me. He pointed at a thick brown mixture that had the consistency of mashed potatoes.

"This is my favorite dish. My mother used to make it for me when I was a child. It is famous within this realm." He added meat, veggies, and warm bread with soft butter and cheese on it.

"That's enough. I'm not sure I can eat all this." I looked at my very full plate.

"You've hardly eaten since you arrived in this realm. You need your strength if you're going to heal." He began putting food on his own plate. "Do you need help eating? Or cutting anything?"

I felt like a small child at dinner. "No, I'll be alright. Thank you." Quietly I sat and ate little bites of food. The brown mush was quite good. It was a blend of sweet potato and pumpkin that had been spiced with flavors I wasn't familiar with. Dried fruits and nuts were mixed through it, giving little bits of chewy texture.

"How is the food?" His words seemed anxious.

"It's delicious. Thank you." I was struggling to not comment on the incident with the maids.

He sighed. Turning toward me he took my hands gently so I would face him. "You're not saying something. I live in a world where people around me don't say things. I want your honesty."

I shook my head. "Be careful what you wish for."

He gave me a questioning look. "The maids earlier. I don't like being fussed over. It makes me uncomfortable."

He started to say something, then his features softened. "At first I was going to say that's how the world works here and tell you to accept it, but I really don't like being fussed over either." He sighed and ran his hand back through his hair.

"Having maids is something that is needed as much for protection as for assistance. Women's court gowns, while beautiful, are often cumbersome and require assistance. Also, court ladies are vicious. Having maids there to help navigate court life, at least in the beginning, will prove valuable."

"That makes sense - but the business about the clothes. Simple, comfortable and practical are all I need. Glamorous isn't something I'm used to. I recently purchased this blue ball gown. It is by far the fanciest thing I have ever worn, but I don't feel like me when I have it on." I sat quietly reflecting on my purchase. I doubted if I would be there in time to wear it.

He shifted closer. "I will let them know you don't particularly like courtly activities. I will try to get you out with me for at least archery or something daily to give you a break. There is an amazing library here you may be able to utilize texts from, for your research. We will also make arrangements to go see the Fairies and Dwarves. Perhaps their experts can shed some light so we can get you back to your own world, but you need to heal first."

"I dislike that you are right. I know I need to heal first, but I'm starting to go a little stir crazy. I'm in this amazing castle and haven't seen anything beyond your chambers." I leaned back against the chair.

He reached out, stroking the hair from my face. "Let's see how you feel tomorrow and if we can, we will join the great hall for meals. Keep in mind though, that who I am in here and who I am out there sometimes must be different people."

I waved away his concerns. "In here I get to be Lily, Goblin slayer and Human. Out there I am Lady Lillian... Halfling?" I thought about that word. "The whole Halfling thing is strange to me. My parents are both Human."

"Centuries ago the portals between our realms were wide open. We traveled between them freely. Humans occasionally would even enter our realms. Then your world made more demands on the other races. Eventually, fearing for the safety of our people, my father and the other rulers demanded the portals sealed. Many of our people chose to stay in your realm just as some Humans chose to stay in this realm. We do still have portals that open to other places that are safer. One you may have heard of in your storybooks is Avalon. A very famous King from your realm settled there." He watched me carefully during the story.

"It all sounds so fantastic. Until I came here I didn't believe in Elves, Fairies, Goblins or anything of the sort. So you're saying that one of my ancestors was from this realm?" I was trying to process it all.

"Ancestors, yes definitely. Most likely multiple ancestors. One of your parents is pure blood. They may have thought they were human because the portal has been sealed their entire lives, but you are half from this realm. My father has never been wrong about such a thing." He sounded so sure.

"You said your father had the portal sealed centuries ago. Just how old is he?" I was afraid of the answers I was going to get to the rest of my questions.

"Around eleven hundred years. He took the throne fairly early," he said with a shrug, like people lived to those ages all the time.

"How old are you?" I couldn't decide if I wanted to know or not.

"Does it matter that much?" he retorted. "I'm young but I know what I want out of life and who I am."

"I do like the confidence, but yes it does matter," I poked.

He thought about it for a moment. "Three hundred and twenty two." He paused, seeming to count again. "Yes. Three hundred and twenty two. My birthday isn't until closer to Yule."

Despite my best try I gaped at him. "Wow."

"Age doesn't really matter. The whole maturity-around-four-hundred-thing shouldn't worry you. At the time our numbers were running amuck in our adolescences between their thirties to mid two hundreds. It really isn't the case anymore." Was he really trying to convince me he was all man? "How old are you?"

"How old do you think I am?" I asked.

He scrunched his eyes and considered me for a moment. "You're fairly impulsive and don't take orders so you must still be fairly young, but you're a scholar and teacher in your realm. You must be a fairly young one. Two seventy-five to three hundred?"

I started laughing. It made my shoulder hurt but the laughter felt so good because of how ridiculous the answer was. "That's crazy. You are so far off..."

His smile turned dark and I realized I had just insulted him. I turned up the wattage on my own smile. At least I now understood part of the warnings were because he was still young by Elven standards. "Thirty-two," I said.

"Thirty-two what?" he asked with a mild annoyance.

"I'm thirty-two years old." I watched the play of emotions on his face. It ranged from disbelief, to confusion, to disgust and finally back to confusion. "Most Humans live less than one hundred years."

"I'm sorry. If you were an Elf you would be little more than a child. An adolescent. I had heard that because the Human realm was so devoid of magic the earth aged its people faster, stealing their magic and life. It is partially why the King I spoke of left for Avalon. Being here, should refill you. Look how fast you are healing. You belong here and the land knows it. It wants to make you strong again." His annoyance was gone as quickly as it had come.

He stood up abruptly and left the table, entering the bathroom. I could hear the sound of running water, and he emerged shortly thereafter. "I'm running a bath now."

"Is that a hint I smell bad?" I teased.

He gestured to the bathroom. After offering a playful smile I made my way to the tub, but not before Tallyn removed my clothes and checked all of my injuries. Then we enjoyed our bath and turned in for the night.

Chapter Ten

Since I arrived in this realm my dreams had been distant and disconnected. The only time they felt real was when I was trying to connect with Tallyn. The last time I had done that, I had managed to get myself attacked again by a shadow monster. Why it only came for me when I was trying to reach Tallyn, I didn't know. Nor did I understand how it existed in my dreams, but could injure me in reality. It seemed like for each new discovery, there were two new questions.

The next morning when I awoke I was delighted to see that I had awakened before the Princely Party Pooper. I was beginning to go stir crazy trapped in this room, and if he was asleep maybe I could at least get out of bed and check out the chambers a bit more.

As quietly as possible I slid from the large bed and out of the bedroom. There were three chambers off the main room and I knew what two of them were, but the third one had eluded me. Ignoring the coldness of the floor on my bare feet, I slid through the doorway and across the main room. I bit my lower lip as I tried to edge open the door of the unknown room, hoping to avoid being caught while I snooped around. When the door gave way silently, I slid in and closed it behind me.

The room was completely blanketed in heavy darkness and the air seemed suffocating. I ran my hands along the walls trying to find a lantern to illuminate the contents. I didn't find any. The longer I stayed in the room the heavier my body felt. As quickly as my injuries allowed, I felt my way back to the door. Relief washed over me.

I turned the handle and pulled. The door didn't open. I tried again with a little more force behind it and nothing happened. When I came in it had easily opened without any difficulties. From across the darkness, I heard the sound of scratching. The sound would get closer and stop, then just as I thought it was over, it would begin again. A cold chill ran down my spine. Once again I jiggled the handle, this time pulling with all my might, but the door held firm.

I could now hear heavy breathing coming closer. I ventured a glance over my shoulder, not expecting to see anything thanks to the darkness. What I found were two glowing red eyes slowly coming closer to me. Panic taking full possession of my body, I began to pound on the door and scream, "Tallyn!!! Tallyn!!! Anyone!?!?" The darkness seemed to consume all sounds.

I turned to face whatever was making its way towards me. Still calling for help, I jumped, startled when something soft and furry brushed against my leg, and I let out a shriek. I peered down and two small yellow cat eyes looked up at me. I could feel it paw at me like it wanted up. Instinctively I leaned down and scooped it up into my arms, noticing it was rather large and heavy.

The red eyes paused, seeming to float in the middle of the room. A low growl was coming from whatever it was. The cat in my arms cuddled against me, purring loudly, rubbing its head under my chin. The red eyes began to come closer again. This time I heard a hiss coming from the cat in my arms. Without warning the red-eyed beast charged at me.

With a scream, the cat leapt from my arms in the direction of the beast. I heard a menacing screech from the beast and a warning growl from the cat. As quickly as the red eyes appeared, they vanished. I sank to the floor so terrified I was shaking. A familiar fuzzy form pressed against me again where I sat, purring affectionately. I reached out and stroked the cat a few times, feeling myself relax and begin breathing normally again.

Just then the door was flung open, almost hitting me, and the room was illuminated. A red-faced Tallyn stood over me. Fear and panic gripped his handsome face. He sank to the floor beside me. "Are you alright? Did you fall? Are you hurt... more?"

He paused and looked around the room. "Why are you in the closet?"

I leaned forward and clung to him. While my breathing was normal again, I was still shaking. I looked around the room. No windows, no other doors, nothing. All around me trunks of clothes, racks of weapons and piles of randomness littered the space.

He wrapped his arms around me protectively, stroking my hair. "Everything is okay. Are you hurt at all? I came as soon as I heard you yelling. It was difficult to tell where the screams were coming from."

"Something was in here with me." My voice still as shaky as the rest of me. "If the cat hadn't been here I don't know what would have happened." I looked around, but the cat was nowhere to be found.

Confusion creased his brow. "This is a sealed room. Nothing can come in or out of it. Even a cat." He seemed to spit the last word out.

"Oh, not a cat man. Got it!" I made a quick mental note not to request a kitten to keep me company if I stayed for a prolonged period of time.

"No there was something in here, I swear it." I tried to defend my sanity, even though it hadn't been called into question. He studied my face closely.

"Alright, I will check it out a bit more. But in the meantime let's sit down, have some breakfast and let your nerves calm down." I allowed myself to be swept into his arms and carried out of the room.

Breakfast tasted wonderful. A bread loaf had been sliced into a grid, then between its many layers the kitchen staff had stuffed a soft brie-like cheese and slices of fruit throughout, then baked it again. Had I been left to my own devices and not had to share, I was confident I could have eaten the entire loaf.

Tallyn smiled at me approvingly. "What is it?" I asked, shoving another bite into my mouth.

"It's good to see you eating so whole-heartedly. It means you're healing." His face was so soft. It was hard to believe that there was a hardened warrior in there. I swallowed my last bite just in time for a knock on the door. "Enter," he called out.

In shuffled the two seamstresses. Both had their arms full of clothes. "We have some clothing to get you started, My Lady." They began neatly laying them out across the sofa to display their handiwork.

"As in done?" I asked. When I had seen the cloth I figured they were just bringing me samples to look at. Never in a million years did I think I would now be looking at a selection of clothing. Wincing only slightly from pain, I stood up and walked over to review the display of garments.

There were four dresses of various colors, two sets of tunics and leggings, and a pile of undergarments. The older lady held up a bra that looked like it was made from red silk. The fabric was so thin I could see through it. Instead of snaps it had two rows of eyelets with a heavy-looking cord running through them to cinch it closed in the back. "We made you two of these, My Lady. You will have to try them and let us know how we did. Once we get some feedback we can alter them to better meet your needs."

I smiled broadly unable to conceal how happy I was. "I can't believe all these are for me. They're beautiful. Thank you." I reached forward and hugged both of the women. The older one patted me on the back, unsure, and the other just giggled.

"We will make you more clothing once we better understand your tastes and needs. In the meantime these should get you through the next few days." Her voice was warm but stern and reminded me of every British nanny I had ever met. "Now, if you would like, I can change your bandages and help you dress."

I tossed a look over my shoulder to Tallyn who could only shrug. I looked back at the women. "Before we begin, may I know your names?"

The older one stepped forward. "I'm Beni and this is Jess." She motioned to the other girl. "We are happy and honored to serve you."

Tallyn stood up and offered a bow. "I'm going to get dressed and head out before you ladies take over my chambers fully. May I have a five minute head start?" He flashed them both a broad smile.

"Of course, Sire" Not wasting a minute he plunged into his closet and only moments later reemerged in leather pants that left little to the imagination, a white billowy shirt that made me think of gothic poets, a gray jerkin emblazoned with the royal seal on the back and holding a pair of tall black boots.

He tugged the boots on as he crossed the room to stand before me. "I need to go check on my men. I need to make sure the castle is secure and see what has gone on in my absence. You will take it easy and allow these women to assist you. Do you understand?" He pinned me with a gaze that said he was serious.

I rolled my eyes but gave a nod. "You worry too much, you know that?"

Wrapping an arm tightly around my waist he pulled me against him and pressed a fierce, take-charge kiss to my lips. Before I could respond he was gone. I swayed for a moment and stared after him.

"Alright, My Lady, do you have a preference for your clothing for the day?" I blinked a few times before turning back to look at Beni.

I looked down at the selection of clothes before me and chose a blue dress. With a nod she picked up a fitted red chemise, a bra and replacement undies, then led me to the door of the bedroom. I didn't object as Jess stepped forward and helped me out of the chemise I had been sleeping in at night. She then quickly cleaned and redressed my wounds. "They appear to be healing nicely, My Lady. You should be like new soon enough."

I thanked her and then with her and Beni's help, I donned my new undergarments. The lacing on the bra made it hug my ribcage comfortably and I felt well supported even without all the usual elastic and clips. The undies were cut like snug fitting shorts and at first

I thought they would be restrictive, but they seemed to stretch and conform to my body like a second skin quickly. The chemise was very tight through the arms and upper body. It felt too small but didn't seem to restrict my movement at all. Finally came the deep blue gown. It was also snug through the upper body, but the sleeves belled and nearly touched the ground when my arms were relaxed at my sides. It laced up the back and made me feel like a princess.

I turned and looked in the mirror. The gown had been designed to show glimpses of the red underdress at the low neckline. To finish off the dress, a gold chain girdle was hung around my waist.

"Please have a seat and I will fix your hair," Jess beamed at me.

Not wanting to cause trouble, I sat and watched as my hair was brushed and twisted into braids then neatly arranged around my head. The final touch was a narrow gold circlet with a single blue drop on my forehead. "Lady Lillian, would you like to wear a veil today?"

"Ummm, no thank you. I think you both did a beautiful job. If you wouldn't mind, could you call me Lily instead of Lillian?" I added a smile for an extra measure, ignoring the fact that I felt like their personal Barbie doll.

Beni considered me for a moment, her expression flat. Finally with a slight sigh she agreed. "As you wish."

"Thank you," was all I got out before she cut in again.

"Today we will take you for a tour of the castle and the grounds, then we will have tea with the other ladies of the court. After that I will take you to the library, and then it is back here to get you ready for dinner and court." She gathered a few things into a bag while Jess finished putting away my new clothes into the closet that I guessed I was now sharing with Tallyn.

I walked quietly and slowly alongside Beni and Jess. Occasionally, we would stop and I would be introduced to various people. When we stepped outside and into the inner bailey, the air was cool but I didn't let it stop me. I followed along as I was directed to where the various artisans were. We passed through a gate and into the outer bailey where the stables were and the royal guard was practicing. My eyes searched the crowd for Tallyn.

When I finally found him I sighed a little. I doubted it would be appropriate to interrupt him when he looked so busy. *I wish I could join in.* He straightened as I watched and shifted his gaze to meet mine.

You're not well enough to join in. I blinked, startled, and stared at him from across the field.

You can hear my thoughts? I pushed the question out into the air with my mind.

Of course, we're bound to each other. Why aren't you wearing a cloak? I looked around, noticing that

Beni and Jess had continued to wander on while I just stood there. Before I could react and follow them, I heard him again. *Stay there!* There was definite command in his voice. As I watched he strolled across the field, heading my direction.

Just as he arrived I felt someone take my hand. "My Lady, I turned around and you were no longer with us. Are you tired? Do you need to rest…" Beni's words died off as Tallyn was suddenly beside me. "Sire, I apologize, it wasn't our intention to interrupt you."

He waved away her apology. "Please, don't call me Sire." His eyes never left mine as he unclasped the cloak around his shoulders then wrapped it around mine. "Stay warm, get rest and don't give your maids a hard time. I don't have time to rescue you right now." I pursed my lips trying to decide if I wanted him to knock off the orders, kiss him senseless for being thoughtful or give the reminder him I saved him.

Ultimately I went with, "Thank you!" which I called after him. I tugged the cloak around me a little tighter, then turned to follow Beni and Jess for the rest of the tour.

The castle was huge and as we made our way back into the great hall, I was glad that I would soon be sitting down to rest. I never would have thought two hours on my feet would wear me out so quickly. The three fireplaces of the great hall were unlit, but a round table was set up in front of the one beside the dais.

Kitchen maids had set four silver place settings and eight simple settings, two between each of the silver plates. There were a number of fruits and cakes spread around the table along with breads, cheeses and cool chunks of meat, probably from last night's dinner.

Three beautifully dressed ladies approached the table, all of them coming to a halt when they saw me. Their gowns were elaborate with beading and jewels. They ran their eyes over me, trying to gauge my status. Beni patted my arm then left to speak with one of the older maids. The other maid looked shocked, turned to stare at me, and then went back to speaking with Beni.

Finally the sound of chatter stopped and a pretty blonde Elf dressed in a flowing pink gown that made her look like she was floating stepped forward. Her smile was inviting but her eyes were filled with something else.

"Lady Lillian, it is an honor to have you join us here. Please come have a seat so we can get to know you." She motioned to the table. I waited until the ladies had each chosen a seat then sat down with the help of Jess.

Having attended school in Britain the idea of tea wasn't new to me, but I still watched closely to try to avoid any faux pas. Once tea had been poured and maids had prepared the silver plates for the ladies, the blonde Elf turned to me.

"Lady Lillian, please allow me to make introductions. I am Gabriella." She motioned to another Elf who had dark hair like Tallyn, "This is

Rowena, and this is Fairwynn." The final lady was a Dwarf with shining coppery red hair that had been braided into a long thick braid that ran down her back. Her green eyes sparkled at me and her smile seemed genuinely welcoming. "Please tell us about yourself." Gabriella's words seemed disinterested before I had even began.

I took a deep breath and forced myself to think of red tag shoe sales so I would smile. "Well, I'm here visiting while I do some research. I'm my realm I'm a scholar, so I look forward to learning many new things during my stay. My hobbies include reading, sewing, archery and swordplay." The Dwarf smiled approvingly while the two Elves and their maids all exchanged looks.

"You fight and get dirty?" asked Rowena.

"Yes, it's a great deal of fun. If I hadn't, I'm not sure what would have happened with the Goblins." I started to really ponder it before pushing away images I didn't want to think about.

"Oh yes, I heard about it," said Fairwynn. "Maerryn talked about it a great deal your first night back, but he said you had been seriously injured. Are you feeling better so soon?"

"I was injured and it seems like it might have been pretty severe. Grelyem says the realm likes me and I am healing quickly." I took a sip of tea. Its flavor danced through my senses, tingling my taste buds with a mixture that seemed like vanilla and cinnamon.

All three ladies and a few of the maids gasped. Surveying the quiet maids it would seem they had already heard the gossip. Gabriella blinked innocently at me. "You were seen by the royal physician? You must have been deathly injured. Grelyem only cares for members of the royal family."

"Then I am lucky indeed." I tried hard to feign interest in the conversations that followed after that. Gabriella turned the conversation back to herself and the latest challenge in her needlepoint. Everyone seemed interested but me. *Will she ever shut up?* I wondered to myself.

Who? I could hear Tallyn in my head.

Lady Gabriella. She is regaling us with the hardships of needlepoint and her battle with double threading. I fought to keep myself sitting straight and my attention focused.

I could hear his soft chuckle. Her father brought her here in hopes that Maerryn or I would enjoy her company. Now imagine me hearing about her needlework adventures. There is a reason I avoid court. How many ladies do we have in court right now?

Three besides myself. Gabriella, Rowena and Fairwynn. The Dwarven Lady Fairwynn seems nice enough. I nodded my head at the appropriate time when Gabriella directed a question to me, asking if I had ever done needlework. *Do I have to do this every day?*

Yes. His answer was to the point.

Whyyyyyy? I couldn't help but whine a little.

Because you are a Lady while you are here, otherwise things become even more complicated between us. As it is I can't be seen being too soft towards you. Right now, Father is negotiating trade agreements that all three of those ladies could affect. Maerryn and I must not appear to show too much favoritism to any one of them.

And that matters to me why? I really wanted to be outside with him and watching the men practice.

He sighed into my head. I didn't even know that was possible. *Each of their guardians must believe there is a chance that his daughter could marry a prince. If there is a question about who you are to me I will answer it, but I also will not deliberately flaunt it in front of the court.* His answer made perfect sense but it still sucked.

Finally the tea ended and Beni looked at my plate and the food that had been untouched. "Do you not care for the food, My Lady?" she asked quietly.

"Oh, no. The food here is excellent. I just haven't gotten much of my appetite back yet. I'm sorry. If you take it to chambers I'll munch on it later," I whispered back.

Her eyes narrowed at me for a moment and then she handed the plate to Jess whispering directions. Helping me to my feet, I leaned into Beni a little and pulled the cloak around me again. I felt a bit of a draft and was quickly becoming tired.

Suddenly I heard a shriek behind me. I turned to see Gabriella rushing towards me. "His cloak. You're wearing the Prince's cloak!" she said jabbing a finger in my direction.

I looked down at it for a moment. "Yes, and?"

"Why? Why are you wearing it? It was a gift given to him from my family. Both the Princes were gifted with such cloaks. It's meant for royalty." Gabriella stamped her foot angrily at me.

"Well, when Tallyn wrapped it around my shoulders I'm sure he only meant to loan it to me." I started to turn again and walk away.

"Tallyn!?!?! Tallyn? You are too familiar with him. He may well be my husband in the near future and I will not have you use his name so openly. You will address him by his title." She crossed her arms and tossed a look back over her shoulder to the other Ladies. Fairwynn looked concerned and Rowenna just raised a brow.

I took a slow calming breath. "He is not Prince of my realm. I will be respectful towards him always, but please do not assume that just because I use a familiar name, given to me to use, by him directly, that I am being too forward. Perhaps he is just overly considerate." At Beni's urging I turned and followed.

The library was huge and overwhelming. Hundreds of thousands of books lay before me and I hadn't read any of them as far as I knew. It was a literature geek's wet dream. Books hundreds, even thousands of years old, well cared for and easily accessed.

I wandered up and down the rows of shelves periodically stopping to examine different tomes. When I finally found one I couldn't put off reading another moment, I collected it under my arm and went in search of a place to tuck myself away and read.

I found a large dark brown leather chair. The seat was deep and the arms high. I sank into it, basking in the natural light from the window above. The more I read the heavier my eyelids became and soon I was fighting off my body's call for sleep.

Beni shook me and I awoke, startled. "We can take this book back to the Prince's chamber. You should eat something and get some rest before dinner."

Too tired to disagree, I allowed myself to be led back to Tallyn's personal quarters. The maids helped me out of my outer gown and circlet. I snatched a few pieces of cheese of the plate on the table then crawled onto the bed. Within moments I was asleep again.

Dreams returned to me for the first time since I arrived in this realm. I pictured my mother at home making cookies. She was surrounded by baking supplies and the counters were covered. She only ever baked like this when she was upset. My father came into the kitchen, popped a cookie into his mouth, and then wrapped his arms around my mother, hugging her close lovingly. One of my biggest hopes is to one day have a love like theirs, one that can weather any storm.

As I lay there peacefully in my dream-like state, I could almost feel my father's hug. Strong arms encircled me, making me feel safe and warm. Reassuring me that everything was going to be alright. A featherweight kiss was pressed to my forehead. And in the distance I could hear my name being called.

"Lillian..." It was soft and seemed distant. "Lily, wake up." I slowly blinked myself back into reality, watching the dream of my parents fade into nothingness and then into a bedchamber. I looked up into two dark green eyes tinted by the slightest bit of worry and then flooded with relief. "How are you feeling?" His words were like silk on my skin.

"I'm feeling alright. I was just very tired." I captured Tallyn's hand in my own and held it there.

He leaned down and captured my mouth with his. His kiss was hungry and filled with unanswered desire. He slid his hand over my hip, lifting me more into him. He broke the kiss gasping for air.

"We don't have time for this. Dinner is in half an hour and you need to redress. Your maids are waiting in the main room." He helped me stand and shuffled uncomfortably under the desire that had already turned him hard.

I made my way into the main room. Beni gave me a knowing smirk while Jess surveyed my clothes. "My Lady, you've ruined your hair. Let's get you dressed so we can address it quickly." I was helped out of my red chemise and peeled from my undergarments. A gold silk chemise was dragged over my head. It was so thin you could see right through it. The bodice was so tight there was nowhere for my breasts to shift to, so they were held firmly in place, threatening to burst out the top of the neckline.

I looked at my reflection in the mirror, stunned. The chemise only accented my curves and made me look like I wore a gown of star dust. The Prince stopped, staring at my form in the mirror from behind. His gaze ran over me like intimate caresses. "We could stay here for dinner tonight. My brother can handle things."

He started to reach out to run a hand along me when Beni slapped it away. "Sire, you are needed downstairs. Eating up here isn't an option for you. I promise to make sure the Lady enjoys her dinner." He turned and left without another word.

To my relief a heavy purple surcoat was pulled over my head. Its sides laced up but didn't close. An elaborate swirl of golden ivy wrapped around all of the edges. The gold belt from earlier was placed on my hips, and this time they also added a gold ivy necklace and earrings.

Jess had unbraided my hair and it now fell in soft waves down my back. She stood back and looked at it for a moment before braiding two small braids and tying them back, leaving the rest of the hair to fall in waves around me. Once again I wore the circlet. She started to put a veil on me but then opted not to. "I think you're ready, Lady Lily."

With a nod I was led out the door. Beni directed me to walk ahead of them and that she would help me be seated when we arrived in the great hall. I walked quietly with the two women just steps behind me. I was relieved to find that I could remember my way to the Great Hall.

Inside, the long tables had been set up, each seating at least twelve on each side. They were covered in food from one end to the other. On the dais was the King's table, with five gleaming gold place settings. Two of the fireplaces now glowed with a warm fire in them and large, high-backed chairs around them.

I felt Beni's hand on my arm and allowed her to lead me to one of the three tables in front of the dais. I was set at a silver place setting similar to the ones that had been used at lunch. Across from me sat Fairwynn and a gentleman who wasn't much taller than me, with large blue eyes, copper hair and short well-trimmed matching copper facial hair.

Fairwynn looked at me with a smile. "Lady Lillian, this is my brother James." The gentleman shifted uncomfortably in his seat but gave me a warm, welcoming smile.

"I hope the two of you forgive me for saying so, but I always thought Dwarves were shorter and had long, thick beards not short, well-kept goatees?" My question was rewarded with a soft chuckle from both of the siblings.

"Many outsiders have confused us with Gnomes over the years, which are quite short. While Dwarves are shorter than Elves and tend to be thicker, as you can see we are not little people. As for the beard, I am still young and feel like rebelling a bit against the old ideas of fashion, but you are correct - normally our beards are much longer. Even some of our older women grow them."

My gaze shifted to Fairwynn who laughed again and shook her head to say that she didn't grow one. "Also, since we are frequent visitors to the Elven lands I tend to stay neatly shaven because the Elven maids prefer it." With his last words James gave me a mischievous wink that spoke volumes.

There was a sudden sound of music and we all stood. The King entered with what I presumed was usual fanfare. Moments later Maerryn and Tallyn joined him at the high table, taking seats on either side of the King. Then like clockwork Rowena and Gabriella came in to take their seats by the Princes. I couldn't help but raise a brow when Gabriella placed her hand on Tallyn's arm and leaned into him. We all sat back down. I listened half-heartedly as the King gave a welcoming speech, my eyes never leaving Gabriella and Tallyn.

As everyone around me sank back into their seats, I resisted the urge to swear and turned back to Fairwynn and James. James eyed me closely then looked up at the dais.

"You're better off here anyway, My Lady. I assure you I am far better at conversation." I blushed at having been caught staring. I laughed quietly at his comment then smiled brightly at the siblings. Fairwynn grinned and James seemed dazzled. "So rumor has it that you're a Halfling? I can't say I'm surprised. You have the grace of an Elf but are built more like a Dwarven Maid. Much taller, of course. You stand nearly as tall as I do and I am tall among my people. I'm really more surprised that you don't know more about Dwarves because of it." James words were playful and enchanting, begging me to open the conversation.

I shook my head. "I'm from a different realm where there are very few Dwarves. I'm half Human." I accepted my plate back once Beni had finished shoveling a selection of food on it. I tried to ignore the stares from James and the others surrounding us that had just overheard my statement.

"We haven't had any new Humans in this realm in nearly two hundred years. What brought you here, Lady?" Fairwynn's voice cut in.

"Ah, well I'm a scholar in my realm and we recently found some ancient Elven ruins. I was visiting them to help with translation research, and I ended up here. I guess now it is also part of my research." I took a bite of the meat on my plate. It was both sweet and salty at the same time. I had never tried anything quite like it.

"Interesting, beautiful and intelligent. I also heard that you saved the Prince's life from Goblins and were badly injured in the process. Where did a Lady and a Scholar learn to handle a sword?" It occurred to me that I had officially become public interest number one for my table and possibly the entire Kingdom.

"I've spent the last several years learning from a number of Knights in my realm. It's a bit of a hobby for me. That's all." I took another bite.

James let out a thundering joyful laugh that drew the attention of almost everyone in the hall. "Goblins are not weaklings or characters you play with. They are fairly fierce, My Lady. I fear that you underestimate your skills if you consider yourself a hobbyist. If you ever become a serious warrior I pray I do not find myself at the wrong end of your sword." He took a big bite of food.

The meal progressed slowly. I finished about a third of the food on my plate. Every time I looked up to find Gabriella wrapped around Tallyn, part of my appetite would disappear. When finally the meal was over, I rose to take leave but a hand on my wrist stopped me. I turned and found James smiling warmly. "Surely you wouldn't deny me just one dance, Lady Lillian?"

I shuffled uncomfortably, not because of who had asked me, but because... "I'm sorry, but I'm not a very good dancer, and with my injuries I'm not sure I should."

James gave me a soft tug. "Well, you're in luck. Dancing is one of the three things I do best." I followed him onto the floor, ignoring the glare I was getting from Tallyn while he held Gabriella in his arms.

I looked back at James. "What are the other two?" I asked.

"If you're lucky, maybe someday I'll show you!" With that he wrapped an arm around me and led me across the dance floor. It didn't take long for me to catch on. Soon thoughts of Gabriella and Tallyn left my mind and I simply enjoyed the moment.

Three dances later the pain in my leg and shoulder had grown enough to leave me out of breath and wincing.

"I'm sorry but I think I may need to leave you to entertain the other ladies and maids." I began to hobble out of his reach.

"Are you unwell, My Lady?" Concern laced his words.

"I may have overdone it a bit." I smiled. "Don't worry, a little rest and I'm sure I will be up for another twirl around the hall another evening." I didn't argue as Jess appeared at my side and gave me a hand and an arm to lean on. We made our way across the hall, doing our best to avoid other dancers.

Suddenly, a couple bounced into us, sending me to the floor. I winced and gasped as I connected with the hard stone beneath my feet. Without looking up I muttered an apology.

"What was that? Was that your best apology for a Prince of the land and his Lady?" I looked up at Gabriella as she stood over me.

I started to get up but her foot bumped my knee and knocked me back again. I looked up and glared at her. "My apology, Sire." I bit my words out the best I could, leveling a gaze with Tallyn that I hoped levied my discontent.

"How dare you make eye contact with him? Your insolence knows no bounds. You act far too familiar with him." Gabriella tightened her grip on Tallyn's arm.

Suddenly a strong pair of hands encircled my waist and helped me to my feet. When I looked up I found James pulling me against his side to steady me. "I'm sure Lady Lillian meant no great offense. She was leaving for the evening as her injuries are were ailing her greatly. I hope the Prince can forgive her misstep since the injuries were received in the defense of his person?"

Tallyn searched my eyes. There was a look of disinterest on his face, but his eyes were filled with rage. He started to open his mouth when Maerryn appeared at his side. "Of course she is forgiven. She is a most honored guest in this court. If the Lady isn't feeling well we should get her to bed. I will accompany her."

James, unable to deny the crown Prince his "honor", released his hold on me as Maerryn wrapped an arm around me and led me to the stairs. I whispered a word of thanks to James before leaving and he shook it off with a smile. Once out of the hall and down the corridor Maerryn paused and swept me into his arms to carry me. "You're shaking. You really shouldn't push yourself too hard."

We arrived at the door to Tallyn's chamber and Maerryn pushed the door open. "Thank you," I breathed as he sat me down on the floor. My legs felt shaky under me. Jess had followed closely behind and joined me in the room. I bid Maerryn good night while closing the door.

"My Lady, how are you feeling? You barely ate at dinner and now you are very pale. Perhaps you should go to bed?" I allowed her to undress me without argument but when she held out the chemise I had been wearing to bed I shook my head.

"Could you run me a hot bath, please?"

She guided me to the bathroom and left me to lean against a large stone table while she had the tub filled. When she was done I slid into the hot caress of water with her help and let it soothe away the pain and soreness of the day.

Jess washed my hair for me and helped me out of the bath. I dressed for bed and didn't argue when she braided my hair down my back and then helped me to bed. "Lady Lillian, please relax for a moment. I want to go get you something to eat before bed. I would feel better if you ate something."

I tried to argue but to no avail. Instead, I leaned against the pillows at my back and ate the soft cheese and pear slices she brought to me. Once I had consumed enough that she felt I wouldn't starve all night I sank under the covers. Sleep came quickly.

Chapter Eleven

I awoke to an empty bedchamber the next morning. From the look of the far side of the bed, Tallyn had never come back from the night before. The thought of him sleeping somewhere else was rather upsetting. We had never said we were exclusive so I didn't really have a leg to stand on with this. Even so, when I pictured him in Gabriella's arms my blood ran cold. Trying to force my mind off the subject, I slid my feet off the bed.

Everything ached. My leg and shoulder throbbed, my stomach growled in hungry protest and I was stiffer then frozen firewood. Cursing myself for dancing the night before, I forced myself to stretch. The nerves in my body screamed their displeasure.

I stumbled from the bedroom into the bathroom, where I ran a hot bath in hopes of soothing my rebellious muscles. They trembled as I pulled myself over the ledge into the warm water. Sitting in the room with no distractions I found myself missing my eReader desperately. Hot baths were a favorite of mine for some light reading. Instead I sat twisting my family's crest ring around my finger, thinking about all the reasons Tallyn might not have come back to his chambers last night.

"I'm sure there was a perfectly good reason why he didn't come back. Maybe it was his turn to do guard duty, or Maerryn got sick or he slept with..." my words trailed off. Shaking my head to clear the thoughts I struggled to my feet and climbed out of the tub, narrowly catching myself before I fell when my foot slid.

I toweled myself off and did my best to redress my wounds which were closed and in need of having the stitches removed. I limped to the closet, flinging the doors wide and quickly lighting the lantern within. I grabbed a dagger from a nearby shelf before venturing in deeper.

I tugged out a tunic, leather leggings and undergarments before dousing the lantern and dressing in the main seating area. I wasn't about to spend excessive time in that closet.

The leggings were so tight that not a single curve was left to the imagination. I eyed my backside in the full length mirror with a smirk. These were going to get some attention, of that I had little doubt. I tugged a dark green silk tunic over my head and was happy to find it didn't cling to me as tightly as other clothing had so far. I battled with getting my boots on but finally won out and successfully tugged them up to my knees.

I surveyed myself again in the mirror and decided I should for sake of appearances do something with my hair. Picking up the carved wooden comb that sat on the table, I managed to tug most of the tangles out of it. I braided it and wrapped it into a high bun on top of my head and secured it with some hairpins Jess had used the day before. While not elegant, it did look neat and tidy and that was the most important part to me.

With a slight limp I made my way down the corridor and stairs to meet the bustling breakfast crowd of the great hall. By the looks of things most had already finished breakfast and were on their way to tackle the worries of the day. I saw James and Fairwynn on the far side of the hall, engaged in conversation with a young maid.

I had just finished filling a plate for myself when Tallyn made his way into the hall. He stood on the stairs looking around the room. When his eyes found me he glided in my direction. Watching him cross the hall made me realize how graceful and toned he was. His clothes hugged him perfectly to compliment his masculine build and reveal all the power there. As he drew closer he looked me over carefully. I did a little turn to show off the leather leggings. His eyes were dark and unreadable.

"Good morning. Are you feeling better?" he asked.

"I am, thank you, so yes, it is a good morning. How are you, my lord?" I avoided using his name so as not to be tagged too familiar and to be respectful.

He seemed to consider me carefully. "You slept well, then?" he asked, but this time I could sense he was asking more.

"While the bed was warm and big, I found it rather lonely for my taste. Perhaps I should consider moving to a smaller chamber that's a bit cozier if I'm going to spend so much time alone?" I finished the barb with a big smile. Tallyn ran his hands forcefully through his hair. I winced for his scalp. "How about yourself?"

He grinned wickedly at me. "I was busy last night, so alas, I couldn't enjoy my large warm bed." His comment made my blood boil.

"I see. Then I will not take up further space in the bed. I will let Beni know immediately that I am to move into a different chamber." I was clenching my fists tighter and tighter, my fingernails digging into my palms.

"And then who will keep you warm on the coolest of autumn nights?" He reached out, running his hands down my upper arms, causing me to suck in a deep breath.

"Your highness is too kind worrying over me, but do not fret. I am excellent at keeping my bed warm when I so choose. Just because I need to have an emotional attachment doesn't mean I can't form one easily enough." I watched his jaw tighten as he considered the full meaning behind my words.

I decided to go for the jugular. "I'm rather exotic here. I should have no problems making new friends.

James was very nice and very handsome." I looked over my shoulder and found the Dwarven Lord making his way over.

I turned to greet him. James smiled warmly in my direction and then at Tallyn. "Good morning Prince Tallyn, I hope the night was kind to you and you slept well."

Tallyn narrowed his eyes and in a flat tone responded with, "Yes it was, and you?"

James chuckled. "Thank you, yes. My morning is already off to a wonderful start with the sight of this fair lady here." James turned, capturing my hand and bowing over it to place a kiss. "Good morning, Lady Lillian. My sister and I look forward to you joining us at our table to break our fast this morning. AND, might I add, that on you those leggings have been elevated to high fashion. Beautiful enough to stir any man's heart."

"Or loins," Tallyn commented under his breath. I blushed and shot Tallyn a glare. Mumbling something about talking to his brother and the guard he excused himself and left.

James, still holding my hand, turned and tucked it into the curve of his elbow and led me towards the table. When we arrived Fairwynn was already seated and filling her plate. I took a seat beside her and James sat across from us.

"How are you feeling this morning? I hope there are no ill effects from my brother dancing on your toes last night?" Fairwynn's gentle smile was filled with a bit of lighthearted teasing.

"I'm afraid the limping is a remnant of injuries from my dealings with the Goblins. James was an excellent dancer and avoiding stepping on me... mostly." I joined in the teasing, offering a wicked grin and an eyelash flutter.

James and Fairwynn both laughed and the mood was considerably lighter. We chatted about our plans for the day, our bets on what was for dinner and discussed local politics. I also learned that while James and Fairwynn were here now discussing trade between the kingdoms, that they had both lived and trained here in their youth. They were both close in age to the princes and the four had grown up together.

"What were Tallyn and Maerryn like as youths?" I couldn't pass up the opportunity to find out more about life here growing up.

James cleared his throat. "Maerryn has always been lighthearted and good with the ladies. He was older than both Tallyn and I but was always a good sport about things. He loved to play practical jokes on his father and brother. Tallyn was a serious child. The weight of the crown and title has always weighed heavily on him, like he had to prove he belonged."

Fairwynn laughed. "Tallyn, despite his hard exterior, is a good man. He was a good lad as well." Her smile brightened as she replayed a memory in her head.

"I loved honey cakes when I was younger. Once, Chef Seya had made a large platter of them for the Lady's High Tea but when I asked for some she told me they were for the adult ladies. I was so mad that when she wasn't looking, I took the platter and hid with them. I ate every last one of them." She glanced in Tallyn's direction before looking back.

"When Chef Seya couldn't find them she knew I was the likely culprit, so she told my uncle Kenthur I had taken them. The punishment would have been a walloping I never would have forgotten but Tallyn lied and said he had eaten them. He got a belt on his backside but never told a soul. He didn't cry or even get mad at me."

James snorted. "You would have benefitted from that walloping. You were sick to your stomach all night from eating that many sweets. Maybe the crying would have helped you consume all the sugar in your system?"

Fairwynn shrugged. "Then James told Aunt Ethba a few days later and I went to bed without dinner. Still an easier punishment then what Tallyn endured."

I turned and looked over my shoulder at Tallyn. His frown deepened when I smiled at him. Gabriella noticed and made a loud noise to draw his attention back to her. When I looked back at my companions I realized I had been caught very obviously staring.

James broke the silence. "She's a real rotten piece of work. Her father had her up sniffing around the

Dwarven Keep after me. They have their sights set on a royal tie and they don't really care who it is with."

"Shhhh," Fairwynn hushed him. "Like her or not, this is a delicate time for the Elves. Her family has purchased away land from three of the King's vassals. They now control the lion's share of the Elven farming land which provides a lot of the food for the Kingdom."

"It's the Kings land, right?" I wanted to understand why she had so much power.

"It is," answered James. "But, they control whom they sell to. They could sell to the Fairies or to the Were, and while the King could raise taxes to penalize them, really it just ends up hurting the farmers."

"Then why not remove Gabriella's family from power?" I asked

"It's not how our laws work. To strip a Noble of their title and rank they would need to commit an act of treason against the crown or threaten one of the King's allies." Fairwynn's explanation made a lot of sense. It also explained why Gabriella paraded around like a princess. She knew nobody would challenge her for fear of what may happen to the farmers under her father's power.

"Well I, for one, don't like her," I declared in an intense whisper. Both James and Fairwynn were quick to voice their agreement with my assessment.

"So you won't be joining us today?" asked Fairwynn.

"I'm afraid not. I want to find Grelyem and get these stitches removed, then I was going to go outside and explore the baileys. I'm going stir crazy inside and doubt I could handle another day where my only highlights were gossip about out-of-style gowns and needlepoint." Fairwynn giggled and nodded.

James chimed in. "Well, be careful not to push yourself too hard, Lady Lily. It would be a shame if you found yourself unable to fend off my advances due to injury." Gathering his things he left the table with a nod.

"Don't worry too much about my brother. He has his eye on someone already, not that I wouldn't like you for a sister-in-law." She smiled warmly. "Come on, I'll give you a hand with your plates. We bus our own dishes in the morning."

I followed slowly behind Fairwynn as she led me into the busy kitchen where we surrendered our dirty dishes. She introduced me briefly to Chef Seya before excusing herself. I poked around the kitchen, watching as the preparations for tonight's dinner were already underway.

I located Jess and Beni whom seemed to be looking for me. Squaring my shoulders back I looked at them both. "Please make arrangements to move me to my own chambers. The prince deserves to have his privacy back in the near future."

The two maids exchanged looks with one another before looking back at me. Beni smacked her lips together for a moment. "Has My Lady spoken with the Prince about her intentions to leave his generous accommodations?"

"Briefly, yes." I answered.

"It will take a few days to make the needed arrangements because we have a few extra guests at the moment, but we will see to it." I thanked her and refused the recommendation to join the other ladies for some light sewing.

After asking a few members of the Castle staff I managed to get directions on where to find Graylem. Outside of the castle but within the walls of the inner bailey stood a gray stone two story building. A large arched wooden door greeted guests. I knocked with purpose and stood quietly waiting. It didn't take long for the door to creak open.

A young woman with dark skin, soft eyes and blue hair stood in the doorway. She had a number of tribal markings much like Graylem's and ears that stood taller than most. "Can I help you?" she asked in a pleasant tone.

"I'm looking for Graylem. I'm Lady Lily, and I was hoping he could take a look at my stitches." I winced a little when I rolled my shoulders back.

"Are you the Lady that defended Prince Tallyn against the Goblins?" she asked, blinking.

"I am," I answered, not sure what else I could say.

She moved out of the doorway. "I'll go get my father. Please have a seat and he'll be with you in just a moment." I nodded and hobbled into the home. The room I entered was a large kitchen that doubled as an apothecary for Graylem. Every available inch of wall was covered in shelves housing all manners of ingredients and medicines. I took a seat on a large wooden bench that faced away from a work table.

Moments later the Elven woman and Graylem entered the room. I started to stand but he motioned for me to stay seated. "Lady Lillian, allow me to introduce my daughter Gretta. She's visiting for a few days before returning to the Dark Elves' lands with her mother."

I nodded towards Gretta. "It's a pleasure, but why does she not live here with you?"

Graylem smiled warmly. "My wife is a midwife in the Fairy court. The Dark Elves land lies within the Fairy Kingdom. While my daughter is young I believe it is wise for her to be with her mother."

"Then why don't you live there?" Gretta rolled her eyes as I asked the question. Evidently I had hit a nerve.

"I made a promise to King Naelym a number of centuries ago to serve him and his family. The arrangement isn't ideal, but I see my family often enough." Something about the words often enough didn't sit well with me. I had used those words about my own family and knew it was a cop-out.

"Ah well, I won't keep you long. I was hoping you could check my stitches and possibly remove them?" He nodded and took a seat beside me on the bench.

He poked at my shoulder a few times and looked closely at it. "I'll get you some salve to dissolve them."

"You don't cut and remove them?" I asked, more than a little shocked.

"I can if there is a reason for it, but normally we just dissolve them, which does less damage to the surrounding and healing flesh." He walked around the room and pulled down a small green jar. He packed it with another large vial in a small sack. "I'm also giving you something for the pain that should help you relax a bit more and hopefully move easier. Just don't push yourself too hard."

It seemed like that was everyone's advice to me. I accepted the pouch and thanked him for his time. I hobbled for the door departing quietly.

The air outside hadn't really warmed up any and I found myself wishing I had thought to grab a cloak. I made my way out towards the wall. With a little effort I climbed up on the wall and found a place where I could watch the guard practice.

Tallyn's hair danced in the breeze behind him. He walked through the lines adjusting stances, fixing strikes and demonstrating defensive maneuvers. I found myself smiling in spite of myself. He turned and instantly narrowed his gaze on where I stood on the wall.

Why aren't you inside where it is warm? Even telepathically he sounded annoyed.

I went to see Graylem, he checked my stitches.

And? Did he saying anything else? Some of his men were starting to notice he was randomly staring up at the wall behind them.

He gave me a dissolvent and pain relievers. Shouldn't you be paying attention to your men? They are starting to stare at you.

I don't give a damn if they are staring. Are you still in pain? His tone softened a little bit when he asked the last question.

Yes, a bit.

Then you should go back inside and rest. Why are you standing up on the wall watching?

Because I didn't see you last night, I didn't really see you much this morning and I don't know... I just wanted to see you.

He shifted back and forth uncomfortably for a moment and called one of his men over. They spoke for a moment and he dashed towards me. Moments later he stood beside me, overlooking the castle grounds. When he arrived he wrapped his cloak around my shoulders again.

The cloak was warm and it wrapped me in his scent. "Why didn't you come back last night?" I hadn't meant for my voice to sound so pitiful.

He pulled me against his chest and encircled me with his arms. "Gabriella had a meltdown about your lack of respect last night. I spent the better part of the night calming her down. When I finally got her to go to bed I was informed it was Cylan's turn on duty. I didn't want him out on guard duty while he was still injured so I took his place."

I heaved a sigh of relief. "I was afraid you spent the night with Gabriella."

He pulled back and looked down at me with concern. "She's not my type. Besides, while you're here I have decided I will abide by the rules of conduct from your realm. I will not bed any others but you." He paused for a moment. "Please do the same."

I smiled. "Were you concerned?"

"Not at first, but now that I realize how upset you have been about all this." He stopped talking and squeezed me tightly again. "Let's just say I don't fancy the idea of sharing you."

"I should give you back the cloak and head back inside." I started to pull away.

"Keep the cloak, I'll be alright without it," he offered.

"Oh no! If Gabriella sees me in it again, I'll never hear the end of it." I shrugged out of the cloak and handed it to him.

"Did she say something to you about it yesterday?" Concern was laced through his voice.

"Of course she did." I smiled.

Tallyn swore under his breath and wrapped the cloak around me again. "I'll walk you back. She won't dare say anything with me there."

"I don't need you to rush in and save me from the angry blonde goose."

"Goose?" he asked.

"Yeah, it's a large ugly bird that squawks a lot and gets angry easily," I explained.

"Oh, we have geese, but until you explained it I didn't understand the reference. Now that you mention it though." He smiled.

He helped me down the stairs and walked beside me as I hobbled. After a few moments of my slower pace he swept me up into his arms and decided it was better to carry me. "You don't have to do this. I'm capable of walking. Besides, this is bound to draw unwanted attention."

"I'll take the back entrance if you are really concerned. I told Rin that I was going to check on my guest and see to her wellbeing. I was up all night, so I am without a doubt welcome to leave practice and get some rest." He ducked around the back side of the kitchen, through a door and up a row of steps I hadn't known was there. When we reached the landing at the top I realized we were at the end of the corridor his door was on.

He set me down and opened the door to his chambers. With a quick look inside he tugged me in behind him, then closed the door and latched it shut so no one could enter. Without a word, Tallyn scooped me back up and carried me into the bedroom.

With the skill of a master he undressed me and urged me into the bed. "Get under the covers, I'm going to build a fire. When I get back I will apply the salve and we can rest together."

I questioned how much resting we would actually be doing if we were both without clothes but I didn't argue. When he finally slid into bed beside me, I was already imagining the feel of his hands caressing my skin.

After the salve was worked in and he convinced me to take some of the pain medicine he made love to me until we fell asleep in a tangle of limbs buried beneath the warm blankets of the bed.

The next few days went without mishap. Tallyn returned to me each night and I split my afternoons between walks outside and needlepoint with the ladies. I found that I could sit by the fire and appear to be deeply focused and Gabriella would leave me alone.

Fairwynn and I would quietly chat in our lucky moments when Gabriella wasn't around, and I learned that Rowena, while quiet, was rather pleasant. She and Gabriella had grown up together, having the same tutor. She advised it was best just to be quiet and let Gabriella have her way rather than engage with her antics.

On the afternoon of the third day Beni approached me. She leaned close to whisper in my ear. "We'll have a chamber available for you tomorrow after dinner. Do you still want us to relocate you?"

I nodded yes then leaned back and whispered back in hushed tones, "I think with things being so delicate right now between the Kingdom and Gabriella's family, the sooner I can be seen going to my own quarters the better."

She leaned back and stared at me, considering me for a moment before glancing around the group. She nodded and departed without another word.

Chapter Twelve

Cautiously I tugged the chemise off over my head. I felt... good. The pain was gone. The only stiffness I encountered was from sleeping in the same position for a prolonged period of time. I sat on the edge of the bed and removed the bandages on my shoulder and leg with the intention of redressing them both. When I removed the strips of cloth though, the injuries were gone. Only raised red scars remained, and even those were smaller than I thought they would be. Shrugging I rubbed some salve on them just for good measure and walked naked through the chambers.

Taking a deep breath I opened the closet door wide and made sure to keep it open while I looked for the light. Tallyn chuckled softly from where he sat reading on the couch. "I told you I checked the closet. It's perfectly free of Itheagas and stray cats.

I glared at him before I stepped in to select clothing for the day. There were piles and piles of clothes for Tallyn along the left-hand wall. I noticed there was a small rack on the wall opposite me. Eight gowns and their matching chemises hung there. I recognized some of them as the dresses the maids had brought me. The rest were new, but lovely. I also noticed my boots, leggings and tunics there. I gathered what I needed and left the closet, still not feeling totally safe within it.

Dressed in boots, leggings, tunic and jerkin I quickly pulled on a sword belt that looked plain enough to be common. "Do you mind if I borrow this today?"

Tallyn looked up long enough to notice I had a sword belt slung across my hips. He shrugged. "I don't mind. You can wear whatever of mine you like. You can even wear me," he teased as he tugged on the belt, pulling me down onto his lap. I blushed as he kissed my neck and struggled to pull my hair up. With one last quick kiss I slipped from his lap and headed out for breakfast.

When I arrived, the hall was busy with bustling staff preparing for the morning meal. I noticed the tables were already set up but that maids were bringing in trays of food. I went to lend a hand, asking what to grab and put where. Soon I had learned how to properly set the high table on the dais and what dishes the King and Princes expected on the table in the morning. Tallyn was happy as long as it was warm, Maerryn had to have eggs and fresh bread and King Naelym wanted a selection of meats, breads and sweet butter.

Fairwynn eyed my choice of attire carefully as she approached me with James at her side. "What do you have planned today, Lady? Dressed up like a man but still looking so womanly."

I smiled. "I was thinking of going for a ride, maybe shooting some archery and playing with a sword I haven't picked up in several days. There is also a castle ruin near the beach I want to check out. I read about it in a book from the library." I snagged a few bits of steak and some fruit, along with part of a loaf of bread which I shared with Fairwynn.

"A lady shouldn't ride out alone. It's not safe." Fairwynn and James exchanged looks. "The Prince wouldn't like it," she added, hoping that would deter me.

"I won't be alone if one or both of you were to come with me?" I turned on my thousand-watt smile and watched James melt. Fairwynn laughed and agreed, as long as she could change first. The rest of the meal was spent making plans for our adventure for the day. I could feel Tallyn's gaze drilling into the back of my head.

His voice crept in while we conversed. *What are you plotting?*

Nothing.

I don't believe you, he responded. *You're smiling far too much to be up to nothing.*

I turned and glared playfully at him. He flashed a smile in my direction while Gabriella was busy speaking with the king.

After the meal I found Beni. "Good morning, Beni. Whom do I see about packing a picnic lunch for three?"

"Check with the chef, she can put together a lunch basket. I will have your things moved. Please come find me before bed tonight so I can show you where your new chamber will be." I didn't stick around much longer. I gave the maid a quick squeeze and set out to be productive.

When I arrived at the stable, James had already seen to getting three horses saddled and ready to go. "There you are." He handed me a bow and quiver. I looped them both over my head with a thanks.

"I have one other thing for you." Fairwynn slid in the doorway and stood next to me with a smile. James handed me a bundle.

I carefully folded back the cloth and marveled at the contents. Inside was a sword and dagger set. They were the color of brass but the shine on the edge told me they were steel. An old runic-looking language I didn't know wrapped around the blade. "They're beautiful. I'll make sure to give them back at the end of the day. Thank you."

Fairwynn wrapped an arm about my waist. "No, they are a gift. You should keep them. It is a thank you for saving the Prince. All of our peoples would have felt the blow if something had happened to either of the Princes."

"Oh, but there were others that did more. These are too nice for me. I am only a novice at best..." I kept trying to find reasons why I couldn't accept such a generous gift.

"You should take them so as not to insult us. Besides, Dwarves make the best blades in any realm and you don't have a sword of your own here, do you?" James narrowed his eyes at me, giving me a mischievous grin.

"No, I guess you're right. I don't have a sword or dagger here," I agreed with a laugh as he waggled his eyebrows at me.

"It seems to me a great injustice to the world when a warrior doesn't have a blade of their own." He took the bag of food for lunch I had slung over my shoulder and tied it to the saddle of the horse I was going to be riding.

I slid the sword into my belt and the dagger into my boot, then with a little boost I mounted up. We rode out into the sunshine. A cool burst of wind lifted my ponytail, causing it to swirl haphazardly behind me. We consulted the directions I had taken from the book and headed out riding southwest.

The ride took longer than I expected. When we finally reached the coast all three of us were ready for a break and food. The horses seemed happy for the rest as well. Spreading out a woolen blanket on the ground we unpacked the lunch Chef Seya had been kind enough to prepare for us.

"What is the Lady Lillian hoping to find at the ruins?" James asked playfully.

"There is a Fairy Circle there that is linked to my realm. Last time I was near one I was able to use my cell phone to speak with my family across the realm. I want to try again before the battery dies and I have no way to power it up." I took another bite of chicken.

"The Fairy Circles were all closed to your realm centuries ago. Do you really think it will work? I mean the communication device you have." James sounded interested but doubtful.

I shrugged. "Worth a shot. I had a dream that makes me think my family is really worried about me. Even if I can't get back, just letting them know I'm alright may help. This circle is much closer than the one I came through."

"What type of power supply does your device need that it is running low on? Many of the races here have the ability to imbue things with power. Dwarves can imbue metal and mechanical items. When it runs out we can see what we can do to help." I considered his words and doubted magic would work, but it was something to keep in mind.

It only took another hour or so of riding to get to the old ruins. The castle looked almost identical to the one near my cottage. We wandered around a bit, but with Fairwynn's tracking skill it didn't take us long to find the circle.

The circle was lined with closely set trees. The grass was spongy there and almost a blue color, and like the other places I had seen, at the center sat a large white boulder. I walked over to it and ran my hand along the inscription reading it out loud. The air around us seemed to hum to life and it smelled like lightning.

I pulled out my cell phone and turned it on. Suddenly it began to vibrate violently. Sixteen missed calls, one hundred and twenty-one messages. Wow, I had missed something. Most were from my mom.

I dialed her first, not wanting to postpone the lecture any longer.

"Hello? Lily? Is that you?" Panic and relief filled her voice. "Where are you? Where have you been? We've been worried sick. Why didn't you tell me you were speaking with your Uncle Randall? Sweetheart, there are things you should know." I rolled my eyes knowing I wasn't going to get a word in edgewise.

"I'm fine but I'm not entirely sure how to get back. Or how to explain where I am." I looked at James and Fairwynn where they watched me and shrugged. They looked as clueless as I felt.

"Did you end up going through the Fairy Circle? When I saw the GPS coordinates for your phone I just knew!" she sounded annoyed.

"Ummm, yeah but how did you know what it was?" I had a sneaky feeling I was about to have my mind blown.

My mother sighed heavily. "Because I'm a Halfling. My parents were an Elf and a Fairy." She paused, allowing the words to sink in.

"When they married the clans weren't happy about the races mixing so they left the UK to come to the States. You would think they would have been more open to me marrying your father because of their background, but they threw a fit knowing I was going to marry a Human. They haven't spoken to me since. I only found out, when your Uncle Randall called asking if I had heard from you, that the family had forgiven the folks years ago and it was their own stubbornness that has kept us separated so long from the rest of the family."

I was silent. I couldn't think of a single word to say. "Lillian, are you still there?"

"Uh, yeah mom. Still here." I took a deep breath and tried to process the information. "So you couldn't have mentioned this to me before now?" I asked.

"You never asked," she said matter-of-factly.

"You mean to say that in thirty plus years of life you never thought to mention it?" I was starting to get upset.

"I'm so glad you're ok. Wait, how are you calling?" She totally sidestepped the question.

"I have no clue why it works but it does. If I get close enough to activate a stone I can use my cell phone. Let's get back to the question at hand. My brothers and I are only half Human. Your life span is ten times longer than Dad's. Don't you think he would notice?"

"Don't be ridiculous, of course I didn't tell your father. I'll let him think I got plastic surgery or something. He already thinks I get botox." I rolled my eyes. "How did you know to call?"

"I had a dream that you were really upset and baking so I figured I should try to let you know I'm alright. You were baking, right?" I was trying to keep this call on track. I still needed to call the professor and my uncle.

"Of course I was baking. Thanksgiving was a week ago." She has always had this way of making my questions and concerns seem invalid.

"Wait, what? No, the Halloween ball isn't for another week. I've only been here a week." I was very confused.

"Oh, I guess you wouldn't know. None of us born in the last several hundred years would know for sure, but time moves differently in the realms. You've been missing for almost seven weeks dear." Reality hit me hard.

"Mom, I gotta go. I need to call Uncle Randall while I still have phone battery. I love you and Dad and the stinky brothers. Happy Holidays if I don't talk to you soon." I listened as she passed along her love, and ended the call. I looked at the phone. I had enough juice for one more call.

When Uncle Randall picked up I concentrated on giving him a huge amount of information. "Fell through a Fairy Circle. We are working on this side to get me out. I can totally read Fae now and want to help but my phone battery is dying. Don't worry and please keep my stuff sorry and thanks." I sucked in a deep breath.

There was a soft chuckle on the other end of the line. "Your mother called me an hour ago to tell me. Worry about getting home. I will take care of things here." An hour? The time difference really is weird. Last time I called him, this realm was ahead of his.

I thanked him while I could, then ended the call. I sank back against the stone and closed my eyes. Talk about information overload. Well at least I knew about my Fae lineage. That should help make things easier. I let out a slow, controlled breath before opening my eyes again.

James and Fairwynn were in heavy conversation, pointing at one of the trees. I pushed off the rock and strolled over to them. "Hey you two, what's going on? I'm all set." I grinned widely as I approached. I felt like a huge burden had been lifted by letting my family know I was safe.

"Stay back from the edge!" James commanded.

It was then I followed their gaze to the darkness of the tree surrounding us. Two large, glowing red eyes stared back at us. They dared us to step out of the safety the circle provided.

"Oh no! What do we do?" I asked James.

"It's an Itheaga, I don't know what to do. They don't do well up north with all the mountains and snow. They say they have to be summoned by someone in trade for part of their soul, and then they

~ 225 ~

can hunt their prey even in their dreams." He swallowed hard, looking at the glowing red eyes.

"Wait, someone summoned that thing? Why would they do that?" If what he was saying was true, the Itheaga had followed me across realms. I was its prey. Someone hated me that much. I thought about everyone I knew but nothing seemed to make sense. "I think it wants me." Both Dwarves turned and looked at me in shock.

"Why?" Fairwynn asked.

"No clue, but it attacked me in my last realm too." My whole body was trembling in fear as I realized I was now face to face with the beast. I closed my eyes and opened my mind. *Tallyn? Are you there?*

I could sense his hesitation. *Yes, what's wrong?*

Can I kill an Itheaga? How do I kill an Itheaga? I could feel rage followed by fear, and then panic filled me, but they were not my own emotions.

Where are you? His tone was sharp.

Four hours southwest, at the old castle ruins. I went to the Fairy Circle to see if I could contact my family.

I could hear a slur of curses running through my head. *Stay there, don't leave the circle. I will grab some of my men and come to you. Don't panic!* I started to point out he was far more panicked then I was but thought better of it.

James and Fairwynn are here too. Just tell me how to kill it?!?! I was starting to feel a little lightheaded. Communication at this distance seemed to be taxing.

WHAT!?!? Are you mad? They are niece and nephew to the Queen and King of the Dwarves. If anything happens to them, then it could mean war. All the panic slipped away and all I could feel was his rage.

So if you are four hours away how about telling me how to kill this thing in case it decides it doesn't want to wait that long to try and kill me. All I met was silence.

Remove its head as a last resort, but I will be there soon. Just stay in the circle. The last part was certainly an order.

At that moment Fairwynn screamed. I looked up to see a blue and black claw pushing against the magical barrier surrounding the circle. There was a horrible noise that sounded like a screech and the walls of the circle shimmered. I looked at James and Fairwynn. "Stay here. Tallyn is on his way with his men."

James looked at me in shock. "You can't mean to actually do battle with that thing, My Lady?"

"We have two choices. Let it breach this barrier because it's hunted me for weeks and still hasn't killed me, or let me lead it away. I'm going to head for the castle ruins. I'll have better footing there." I checked that the dagger and sword were in place. I pulled my bow from my back and then checked the quiver.

"It's suicide My Lady. If one of us must go, let it be me. I'm the m-" I didn't stick around to hear the end of his sexist statement. I pushed out through the barrier and forced my legs to pump as hard as they could towards the ruins.

Soon I could hear the sounds of something speeding along behind me. There was a terrible screech but I refused to look back to see how close it had gotten. The noise continued to get louder the closer to the tree break I got. As I finally burst through the trees and into the blue skies I stumbled. I quickly caught my footing and sneaked a peak over my shoulder. Sure enough, a large shadowy creature was leaving the woods behind me.

I ducked behind an ancient wall, drawing an arrow from the quiver. I quickly drew and took a shot through a small break in the stones. There was a painful shriek when my arrow hit its mark. I drew another and made a dash for another set of rubble. Diving behind it I leaned up enough to take aim and let loose another arrow. The creature ducked into safety as my arrow whizzed by, but it was getting closer. I stood up to take one last shot. The creature came to a stop as we made eye contact with one another. I had my arrow nocked and held at the ready.

The creature's red eyes pinned me as I examined the rest of it. It had a long serpent-like neck with a scaled face, two legs that were thick but as long as an ostriches and two arms held razor sharp claws that waited at the end. Its scales turned into feathers across its back and body, and a black glowing aura of shadow surrounded it. It was truly a thing of nightmares.

"Itheaga," I whispered.

Its mouth opened, revealing double rows of large, sharp teeth. It seemed to smile at me. Then I heard it. It was as if the voice surrounded me, coming from no one place. It started with a roll of laughter. "So brave. Even now when I can taste your fear you are still so brave."

I almost blinked. "You can talk?"

"But of course, child. How else would I conduct trades if I couldn't talk?" The voice boomed around me, full of menace.

"What kind of trades?" Curiosity was getting the better of me. I kept my arrow aimed and ready to fly.

"I trade vengeance for souls dear. It's nothing personal, but you are the first hunt in a thousand years to give me so much trouble. The witch and her pet have kept a close eye on you. Making it hard for me to reach you in that realm. This realm, however, was much easier. Luckily claws grow back." The air was filled with a chuckle again. Chills ran down my spine.

"Who sent you after me?" It was the last question. If I was to die I wanted to know why.

"I can't tell you that, but I can tell you - your only crime is being a Soul Mate." I didn't understand what the creature meant but it was done talking and charged at me. I let the arrow loose. It tried to dodge but the arrow sank deep into its neck. It roared angrily.

It closed the rest of the distance in a few steps. The monster slashed at me with a claw but I raised the bow as protection, allowing it to take the hit rather than me.

I used my free hand to draw my sword. The beast swung at me again. I dove for a nearby wall, rolling behind it. The beast followed. This time when it struck out at me I was ready. I brought my sword up and across its body.

There was a scream of pain and I quickly backed up a few steps as the blood sprayed everywhere. Angrily it swung at me with its other arm. I allowed myself to be pushed back. Doing my best I countered and parried every strike of claws. When the moment was right, I stepped in and took its other arm. The fury it roared at me almost made me wet myself. The first severed limb had already begun to grow back. It was now or never.

I leapt forward, swinging my sword with both hands. The creature was caught off guard and when my blade connected, I continued to draw it through. The head separated from the neck and there was a shower of red and black blood. The creature's body dropped to the ground. One last agonizing shriek filled the air around me.

Trembling I sank to the ground. I watched the beast's body, carefully making sure that it wasn't like the Hydra in Greek mythology where two heads would grow back. I sat there gasping for air.

I rested there for what seemed like hours until James and Fairwynn found me and sank to the ground on either side of me. James wrapped his cloak around me in an effort to help me stop trembling.

"You killed the Itheaga?" Fairwynn whispered. Her voice was filled with disbelief. "Who are you really, My Lady Lillian?"

"I don't really know." I whispered.

At some point Tallyn and a dozen men showed up. They found us at the ruins. Sunset was nearly here. Somehow we had managed to build a fire. We sat around eating as Tallyn and his men approached. The soldiers seemed unnerved by the dead Itheaga.

"James?" Tallyn asked, looking at the severed head.

"Nay your Highness, credit for this goes entirely to the Lady Lillian." Tallyn looked at me where I sat watching the fire. I hadn't eaten any of the food that had been pressed into my hands. I was covered in blood. The smell was almost nauseating. The only thing I could think about was that I was being hunted for being a Soul Mate. Someone hated me without even knowing me. Someone hated me enough to sell their soul to see me dead.

Tallyn reached out a hand to me. "Let's go get you cleaned up. We'll make camp for the night and ride home tomorrow." The men around him set to work putting up a simple camp. Fairwynn and James both got to their feet to help. I placed my hand in Tallyn's and allowed him to drag me to my feet and away from camp towards the shore.

Once we had made our way down the rock path and were standing on the shore, Tallyn broke the silence. "Do I need to tell you how foolish and dangerous it was of you to go after the Itheaga on your own?" I shook my head. "It has been known to take out entire towns."

I shrugged. "I was scared, but it didn't seem that hard." He stopped, grabbing hold of my hand again and turned me to face him. His face was cold and angry.

Suddenly I was pulled against his chest and his lips were on mine. They were demanding and angry. They pushed their way past my own and bid me make ready for his tongue. At first I was too shocked to respond but then I leaned into his kiss, opening up my mouth to him further. Letting him possess it and all but taking ownership of me. His other hand pressed my hips hard against his so I could feel his need pressed against me. When he broke the kiss we were both gasping for air.

"NEVER do anything that foolish again. Wait for me. I will not let anything happen to you." He tucked my head under his chin and just held me against him. We stood like that until the sun set and the violet moon rose high in the night sky.

The water was icy cold and the night air had grown much cooler. I stripped out of my jerkin and tunic and rinsed them in salt water. Tallyn handed me his spare tunic when I had finished rinsing the blood from my upper body. I pulled it over my head, happy that it was of a thicker material that was warm. I shrugged James's cloak back over my shoulders and allowed Tallyn to take my hand and lead me back to camp.

We both sank to the ground around the fire. The rest of the night was spent debating if minstrels would sing songs of my heroism and strength for defeating the Itheaga, or if it would come from having saved a prince.

Chapter Thirteen

The ride back the next day passed quickly. I had adjusted to riding a horse easily enough that now, as long as I followed the group, I could autopilot. I had so many questions about my Elf and Fae roots I wasn't sure what to think or where to start. It was as if my whole world had been turned upside down. What did that mean for me? Would I be more welcome here? If I was a Seelie, was my blood noble enough to date the Prince? Did Elves date?

I heard a call at the front of our group and looked up. Stretched before us stood the towers of the castle. We rode through the outer walls of the bailey and made our way to the stables. Once there I found all I could really do was sit atop the horse. Nothing seemed to motivate me to move. I was startled when someone grabbed and shook my knee. I looked down at Tallyn.

"Come on, we need to go present the carcass of the dead Itheaga to the King. He will want to celebrate you as a Hero tonight at the feast." I groaned inwardly but accepted his help as I slid from the horse's back.

It took four of the guards to bring the monster into the castle. As we approached the throne room, Gabriella rushed forward, encircling Tallyn in her arms. "I was so frightened for you. I heard you had ridden off to help the Lady Lillian with an Itheaga."

She turned her glare on me. "How selfish are you, calling on the prince for help? He could have been killed. I'm glad to see he wasn't injured while taking care of it for you." She turned and dragged Tallyn by the wrist into the throne room. "Let's go see the King so you can be rewarded for your heroism."

The doors were opened and I stepped into the throne room, following Tallyn and Gabriella. King Naelym was standing at a nearby table, looking over documents for the court. When he looked up he smiled warmly at us all. "Back in one piece I see. Excellent. I'm glad to know the Itheaga wasn't too much for you and your men." He clapped a hand on his son's shoulder with pride.

"When I arrived the monster had already been slain." Tallyn shifted uncomfortably under his father's grip.

"Did you reward the parties responsible for its demise?" The King looked over his shoulder at the guard and the wrapped carcass.

"No, I brought the Hero to you, and she in turn brought you the carcass for a bounty." Tallyn turned to look at me. "Lady Lillian slew the beast by her hand, and her hand alone."

Gabriella's head shot up. Her eyes burned with a gaze full of hellfire. The King was slack jawed, but to his credit, only for a moment. "You, My Lady, are full of surprises. Do you know the reason the beast was there?"

I shuffled uncomfortably. "I do, Your Majesty. It was after me. While it wouldn't tell me who summoned it for my demise, it did tell me that the attack was nothing personal, that I just had the misfortune of being a Soul Mate." Without meaning to, I heaved a heavy sigh realizing I had again endangered my friends. "It tracked me through the realms, and then without meaning to I put Lady Fairwynn and Lord James in harm's way." I dropped to my knee and lowered my head. "I am truly sorry if my actions have caused any harm."

From behind me I heard James speak. "Your Majesty, let it be known that my sister and I gladly set out on this adventure with Lady Lillian. If there are any repercussions, which I doubt, I will gladly bear the brunt of it. She, without consideration for her own safety, led the monster away from the circle and took to battle without us in an effort to keep us safe. She deserves not criticism, but accolades."

"I'm inclined to agree with you. She has saved my son, slain a monster, and healed from the point of nearly dead all in a week's time. She is the type of Heroine that stories are written about." The King turned his attention to me once again, striding towards me fluidly. Taking my hand in his, he raised it to his lips and pressed a kiss against it.

"My Lady, you are from this day forward, and always, a Lady of my court. Tonight we will feast in your honor." He turned to those standing around. "See to the feast, and hang that monster where travelers may see it and the villages may rejoice."

People dispersed from the room quickly going about their business. "Lady Lillian, one more moment of your time please." I turned at the sound of my name and approached the thrones.

The King slid out a chair at the table he had been working at. "Please have a seat." I nodded and sat down. He ran his gaze from Tallyn to me. "How did my son know you were in trouble? I was told you were down at the far southern coast."

I shifted uncomfortably in my seat. "I called to him, Your Majesty."

"Called to him?" he asked, raising a brow and looking back at his son.

"We share a psychic link," Tallyn filled in. Gabriella gasped loudly, turning all attention to where she still clung to Tallyn's arm.

"I see," said the King, considering the ramifications of this information.

"She's a witch! She has bewitched your son." Gabriella pointed at me in an accusatory statement.

Anger bubbled within me but I stayed seated and leveled my gaze at her. "I am no more a witch than you are a virgin," I said flatly.

From somewhere behind me I heard a deep laugh. Maerryn strolled into the room from some side entrance. "Then I can attest if that is the case, then Lady Lillian is by no means a witch." He sent a pointed glare in Gabriella's direction before dropping into a seat beside me. Smiling broadly he looked at me. "I came to congratulate the Kingdom's newest Heroine. You will save me a dance tonight, correct?"

I blinked, not knowing what to do or say anymore. Tallyn patted the back of Lady Gabriella's hand. "I think you should go get ready for the feast tonight and leave affairs of the state to us. I look forward to seeing what high fashion you will delight us all with tonight." He smiled warmly at her. She all but melted under his touch then disappeared down a hall.

The King and Tallyn both settled into chairs at the table. "My Lady, what was the reason for your adventure?" The King's words were soft.

"I realized that my family didn't know where I was and that they were probably worried. Before we left the other Fairy Circle I had been able to use a communication device I have to reach people in my own realm. I thought maybe if I got close enough to another circle I may be able to contact them and tell them not to worry." I bit my lower lip and resisted my urge to fidget.

"I see. That is an excellent reason. If either of my sons disappeared without a trace I would mourn their loss greatly. Were you able to contact your family?"

He considered me carefully, as if I was a small child speaking in front of a large audience for the first time.

"Yes, Your Majesty, I was."

"And?" he asked.

"My mother knew I had somehow tripped through a Fairy Circle. As it turns out, everyone is correct. I am a Halfling." I grimaced as I said it, still trying to figure out exactly what that meant.

"Of course you are, child. I know a Halfling when I see one. Your heart pulses with the land." The King shifted his gaze to Tallyn. "Do you plan to bond?"

"Father, we aren't sure that she is my Soul Mate. Moreover, I understand what my obligations are." Tallyn's face was fixed in a very determined glare.

"What more proof do you need? She skipped realms when they are locked from passage and she speaks to you without words. These things can only happen when your souls are tied together. These are the type of unions that are written by the fates. Obligation means nothing when compared to the forces of magic and destiny." I was trying to process the King's words fully. Did he think I was Tallyn's Soul Mate?

Maerryn captured my hand in his. "Claim her or I will," he warned Tallyn.

I shook my head and pushed to my feet. "I'm sorry if this seems rude, but nobody can claim me." I pulled my hand free of Maerryn's and turned a glare on Tallyn. "I have no desire to be with someone who feels

that I am a duty, an obligation, or a prize to be won."
At the last bit I turned to glare at Maerryn before
returning my attention to the King. "Your Majesty is
an excellent host. I have had my maids relocate me to
a private chamber so as to no longer burden the Prince.
I look forward to the feast tonight, but I would rather
not show up dirty, so if you will excuse me I will take
my leave." The King nodded. I made haste to leave the
throne room and headed for the Hall where I hoped to
find Beni or Jess.

I heard running behind me. I didn't bother to turn
to look at who it was. I knew even before his fingers
closed around my arm. "Lady Lillian, stop." With that
I swung around to face Tallyn. "What do you mean
you have moved to a private chamber? You haven't
seen your maids since we returned."

"I saw to it a few days ago." I started to turn to leave,
but his fingers dug in painfully.

He stepped in front of me. "Why would you leave?
I have opened up my private sanctuary to you. Is it not
fine enough? Do you feel it is below your station?"

I let out a bitter laugh. "The reason I left is because
it is *your* chamber. You deserve to have peace and
solitude without fear of who may be watching. I
shouldn't have made it my home."

"You made it your home?" he asked with the hint
of a smile.

"No, of course not. I was just a guest." I muttered
the words and looked down at his feet.

His finger reached out and lifted my chin. "What if I want you there?" he asked. His voice was as soft as a whisper.

"Tallyn, I can't separate my feelings and actions like you do. You have made it clear that you have a duty right now towards Lady Gabriella. The longer I share your bed and chambers the harder it will be for you to fulfill your obligations. Especially now that she knows we have some sort of connection." I turned and left without hearing anything else he had to say. He let me go.

I quickly found Jess by the fireplace embroidering a blue velvet gown. All the trim was a silvery gray with silver embroidery. "There you are, My Lady. I heard the news. There is a feast in your honor tonight. I'm just finishing this up, if you would like to wear it?"

I ran my fingers over the soft fabric. "It's beautiful. I would very much like that. Also, could you show me to my new chamber?" She stood, taking my hand, and led me through the hall. We mounted the stairs on the other side and turned to the left at the top of the stairs instead of right towards the Prince's chambers. Half a dozen doors down on the outside wall we arrived.

When she opened the door I smiled brightly. "I prepared the room for you myself. It's not as big as what you have been used to, but I hope you like it."

The room itself was rather large. On the far right wall stood a large bed with pale blue curtains and many large pillows and blankets of the same color. The back wall had a row of three windows, each with a small alcove that had a bench in it. The far left wall had a big fireplace that already had a small fire burning. Beside it was a large screen that blocked off a bathroom area with a small tub and the Elven equivalent of a toilet. Past the fireplace was an armoire that I was sure my clothes had been fit into. The center of the room had a small sofa, a square table and two wooden chairs. The stone floor even had soft rugs to keep the cold from my feet.

"It's perfect!" I said.

"I even put some books that may interest you on the bedside table." She gave me a smile. "Shall I run you a hot bath?"

I nodded as I still took in the room. Every detail had been thought of. Dishes, water to drink and fresh towels took up little corners here and there. I peeled out of my dirty clothes and folded them, placing them in a basket by the armoire. When Jess called I sank into the steaming hot water. I didn't even argue when she began scrubbing my hair. I just relaxed back into the side of the tub.

As I approached the Hall I was stopped. "You should wait. You are the guest of honor and will be announced as such." I looked at the Elf in front of me. He was one of the guards that had been in the group when I first arrived.

"And such a beautiful Lady should be escorted in. I hope you will do me the honor?" I turned to face King Naelym. I gave a curtsey which he immediately waved away.

"My dear, you are stunning. The color and style of that gown truly suit you. I am glad to know the seamstresses are taking your wardrobe so seriously. I heard you told them to dress you as they please?"

I blushed. "This may come as a surprise to you, but I tend to dress more like a male by Elven standards. Where I'm from I dress very feminine. This whole elaborate braided hair and gowns with several layers thing still overwhelms me."

The King chuckled as he took my hand and slid it into the curve of his elbow. "Are you ready to be the center of attention?"

"No," I answered honestly.

"It gets easier with time. I promise." With those words the doors swept open and everyone rose. I walked with the King to the high table where a member of the guard helped me with my chair so we could be seated.

Maerryn, who was seated to my right, leaned over. "You look amazing. I daresay you make the rest of us look shabby." He gave me a playful wink. The servers brought dish after dish to the table. I had so many choices I tried to take just a little of each.

During dinner his Majesty did his best to keep me engaged in conversation. I picked at my meal. It tasted wonderful but I wasn't really hungry despite not eating all day. As dinner came to an end the King stood, causing everyone to go silent.

"As all of you know, Lady Lillian has served this Kingdom not once but twice now. First by saving my son Tallyn, and then by defeating the Itheaga single-handedly. Both were acts of strength, courage and selflessness. That is why I have decided to recognize her not only as a Lady of my Court but also gift her this."

The King took a box from a servant beside him and opened it. Within was a necklace made of sapphire and amethyst gemstones laced together with black pearls. "This was a necklace I gave to my first wife, the late Queen. It was my intention to pass it on to a daughter, but I was never blessed with one. I now pass it on to you so you may pass it on to your own daughters someday." Then he unclasped it and placed it around my neck. The necklace sat heavy along my collarbone. "Now, let the festivities continue!" There was a cheer from the crowd and I sank back into my seat.

"Your Majesty, this gift is too kind. It is too much and I am undeserving of such a treasure." I reached up to remove it and give it back.

He stopped my hands. "Is not the life of my son worth a necklace? Are not the lives and safety of my people worth a title? I think you grossly underestimate your worth my dear."

I smiled. "Thank you. I will treasure it always."

He just nodded and patted the back of my hand.

Lady Gabriella stood and tugged on Tallyn's arm, saying "Let's dance," then dragged him to the dance floor.

Maerryn escorted Rowena to the floor and many other couples joined them. "Aren't you going to join them?" His Majesty asked.

I shook my head. "I would rather not. I would almost prefer to find a big chair in the Library and be enchanted by a book."

He laughed lightly. A tall member of the guard approached the high table. I recognized him as Cylan, the Elf that had been injured during our battle in the Goblin camp.

"My Lady, would you do me the honor?" He held out his hand. The King motioned me on. Resisting the urge to roll my eyes I accepted his hand and allowed him to escort me to the floor. From there the night was a blur. One dance turned into twenty, with many of the men of the court, the guards, and even Prince Maerryn coming to collect his turn with me.

"You know my brother is only placating her until she returns home, right?" Maerryn held me comfortably as we glided around the floor.

"I don't care who or what he does. It's his life and he has made it clear that I don't rank that high in priority." I pretended not to notice Maerryn was drawing me closer.

"Don't be too hard on him. His mother wasn't a Lady or a Soul Mate so father was never able to marry her. He was allowed to make the bond and claim her so as to have more children, but the poor dear died not long after Tallyn was born. He has always felt he had something to prove, but everybody has always seen him as a Prince of the Realm. He takes his duty very seriously. That is all Lady Gabriella is to him." The music changed but Maerryn didn't relinquish his hold on me and began to lead me through the next dance.

"She just makes me so angry with the way she treats people. Lady or not, trade agreement or not, I'm not sure why someone hasn't put her in her place." My tone was sharper than I would have liked. After all, I wasn't mad at Maerryn.

"I don't know either. I certainly would have chosen to come back to your arms and enjoy your company over hers." Maerryn turned me in his arms and as he did I could see Tallyn watching us very closely over Gabriella's shoulder.

"I don't care what the reasoning is. I just wish he would make up his mind. I can't keep up with the hot and cold treatment anymore." I swear even I could hear the whine in my voice.

"It is very common that unless a pair is bonded, they can spend nights with other lovers." He smiled at me with a shrug. I ignored his obvious flirtation.

"He wouldn't care if I spent the night with someone else? Ha, I highly doubt that. I just can't

behave like that with someone I care about that much."
I considered it for a moment. I was reminded of our
conversation a few days earlier.

"Oh, I believe he would be in great pain in it if he
thought you were in the arms of another. Even though
he won't admit it, he is absolutely smitten with you.
Lady Gabriella means nothing to him but a temporary
duty. She only clings to him because I turned down
her father's request for a betrothal to me. I have no
doubt she will beg her father to request Tallyn next if
he hasn't already. Make no mistake though, he has
eyes only for you and it scares him greatly." At this
point my body was pulled tightly against Maerryn's.
"Allow me to prove the point."

"What do you..?" My words were cut off when
Maerryn dropped his head and claimed my mouth
with his own. I pushed against his chest and struggled
against him. His lips were tender on mine but still
demanded entry. I tried to turn my head but he
released me.

I stumbled back and away from him pinning him in
place with my angriest glare. "I hope you forgive me
but I promise that was for your own good." His words
would have been easier to believe had he not been
grinning like the cat that ate the canary.

I was so mad I could have socked him and should
have. I turned and stormed away up the stairs and to
my chamber. When I arrived I slammed the door with
as much force as I could. I marched over to my bed,

climbed under the damned blankets and extinguished the bedside lantern that was burning.

Sometime later in the dark of night there was a soft tap on my door. With such a gentle touch I figured one of the maids had come to check on me.

"Come in," I called to the door. I heard it open and then click shut. What surprised me was the sound of heavy footsteps on the floor. I pulled back the curtain from the bed to look at the shadowy figure that stood there. I watched as the figured wobbled, pulling off boots, and swore when he hit a shin on a chair. He pulled off the rest of his clothes as he stumbled to the bed. Soon I was pushed towards the wall and a familiar shadow slid under the blankets. He reached out an arm to pull me towards him and paused.

"Are you still wearing your dress?" Tallyn whispered.

"Yes," I replied sleepily.

"Why?" Alcohol and confusion slurred his speech slightly.

"Because I was so mad at your brother I just wanted to hide. I was afraid if I stayed I would have said something really inappropriate." Just thinking about it raised my anger.

"That still doesn't explain why you are still wearing your gown." He rolled over and fumbled with the lantern by the bed. It glowed to life. "Come here, let me help you get out of it." I didn't fight him when he pulled me across his body and sat me on the edge of the bed where he began unlacing the dress. Soon he had peeled away all but the final layer. A thin shift. I hadn't even needed a bra because the dress supported me so well. I then climbed back into the bed and rolled over so I was close to the wall.

When he reached me again I pulled away. "Why are you here?"

"Because this is where you are." He yawned a little as he spoke.

"What about Lady Gabriella? Don't you need to go do your duty with her?" I was so mad I smacked the stone wall through the curtain on the far side of the bed. It caused my hand to sting.

Tallyn rolled me over to face him despite my struggle. "I hated seeing my brother hold you and kiss you. I hated that you could tease me with James so coldly. I don't want another man to touch you or even be near you. Goddess help me, I was even mildly aggravated that my father took up so much of your attention at dinner."

"You still didn't answer my question," I pointed out again.

"Lady Gabriella's father has asked if I would marry his daughter, but that was before I met you. I had held off answering because I have no interest in the girl but still had to act like I did until negotiations were finalized. After tonight, I don't think it will be an issue any longer." He paused and ran a hand down my arm.

"Why, is she leaving?" I asked, angry at the news he had almost been engaged.

"She is now. Her father was just dragging out negotiations until a decision on the betrothal could be made. I made a decision this evening. A very loud and obvious decision." He wasn't saying something. He captured my hand and lifted it to his lips pressing a kiss to the palm. "I punched my brother, in front of everyone, after I saw him kiss you. I was just so angry that I couldn't help it."

"You what?" I choked back the urge to giggle since that had been the first thought that crossed my mind as I had left the hall.

"I was so distraught that my brother was kissing you while I was standing there that I punched him. He, of course, played dumb, asking why I had done it and I, like an idiot, declared in front of the entire court that he knew why. That it was a low blow to try and take your brother's woman." He sighed heavily.

"Lady Gabriella ran from the hall in tears. Father and I went to try and make amends with her family, which went very poorly. Then I pissed the night half away trying to figure out how to make things right with you." He still held my hand in his.

"And how did you decide to make things right with me?" I asked. He was going to be damned if he thought he could just swoop in here and kiss away all my anger.

"Since you wouldn't come to me, I thought I would come to you. My bed is where you lay your head. My home is where you are. I hoped that if I came to you and asked for forgiveness you may forgive me." He stroked my hand with thumb and leaned forward kissing my fingertips.

"Ok, let's hear it," I said pointedly as I tried to ignore the tingling feeling in each fingertip.

"Hear what?" he asked between kisses.

"The apology?" I prompted.

He heaved a big sigh and reached out to run his hand through my hair. "I'm sorry that I was rude to you in court. I'm sorry I didn't consider your feelings in regards to Lady Gabriella. I'm sorry that I have been trying to deny what is in my heart and obvious to everyone but us. Our connection, our hearts, practically beat as one. Despite how hard I have tried to deny it, you are my Soul Mate."

I leaned my face into his palm. It was warm and gentle. "So what if I am?"

"I should claim you and bond with you." I froze and tried to scoot away.

He could feel the panic rushing through me. "What's wrong?" he asked, even as he captured me in his arms and drew me against his chest.

"This is too fast!" I exclaimed into his chest.

He stroked my hair. "Relax, shhhh, relax. If you don't mind letting me make a show of things we can push it off for a while."

"Where I'm from we date sometimes for years before we get married." I was trying to figure out how all this worked. Was this like the Fae version of Vegas?

"I can court you if that's what you wish. Bonding and marriage are very different. Marriage is a legal contract. Bonding is spiritual." I could tell he was doing his best to explain it. "Either way, I can court you if you prefer? If you want to venture back to the Fairy Circle I can contact your parents and ask permission. You tell me what I must do, just don't make me hurt like I did seeing you in another's arms." His plea gripped my heart, almost making me tear up.

I shook my head. "Then yes, I think you should court me and we can see where this goes."

He pushed me back into the covers and pressed his lips to mine. I tried to turn my head to evade his kiss. Tallyn, seeing his chance, changed tactics and attacked my ears. Knowing how intimate Elves felt about their ears I realized what he was doing. He nipped and sucked at the top edge and I can admit, I melted a little.

I pushed at his chest with my hands. "My ears? Aren't those super intimate?" I teased.

"I did just ask you to bond with me. I think we are at the point where I can touch your ears and welcome your touch openly on mine." There was a fire in his eyes that only grew larger the more he talked about the topic. I bit my lower lip to keep from giggling. The idea of ears being that secret sensitive place amused me when I thought about where those places were in my own realm. He read my grin and seized the opportunity to tease me.

"Oh excuse me, for thinking that we are at that level." He started to lower his head again. "If you are going to insist on biting that lip, I'll insist you let me do it for you."

Pressing his weight into me I was pinned against the pillows and him. He nibbled at my lip, running his tongue over the sensitive skin. My own tongue once again darted out to meet his, inviting him in. He worked a hand under the hem of my shift, pulling it up over my hips. The other tugged the neckline down, exposing my breasts and pinning my arms to my side. He moved both hands to my breasts, running his thumbs over each nipple, making them harden more under his touch. He rolled them between his fingers, causing an aching need that made my legs quiver and the mound between my legs to soften and become wet.

I moaned into his mouth and arched my body against his. I could feel the large swell of his erect manhood pressed against my thigh, urging me to buck under him more. I cried out when he broke our kiss and dropped his mouth's attention to my pebble-hard nipples. He lovingly licked and lapped at them. Caressing one with his hand, he pinched at the nipple as he sucked the other into his mouth. The hot, wet surge of his tongue caused another moan and I shrieked a little when he bit down. The slight pain receded and opened up a spectrum of colorful pressures behind my eyes.

Then unexpectedly he switched to the other breast, taking its hardened bud into his mouth. He nipped, bit and tugged at it as moan after moan rolled off of me. With each instinctive thrust of my hips I ached more and more to feel him within me. His mind was set to prolong my torture though, sliding his hand casually along the curve of my hip and the arch of my thigh, before urging me to spread my legs for his amusement. Alas, the pleasurable cruelty did not stop there. His fingers danced over my most sensitive bead, causing me to jerk frantically, spreading and hoping he would soon linger at my core.

Using just the tip of his finger he traced the lips of my wet opening. I bit my lip to keep from crying out when he slid his fingers deep within me. My muscles contracted around his hand as he continued to encircle my bead and massage my inner core. Quickly I fell in with rhythm and he pushed me higher and higher. Each time I would almost hit the point of release and ecstasy he would change his pace or motion.

"Look at me," he commanded, and I raised my lids and then just as I did he adjusted the speed, causing me to fall over the edge. A scream escaped me as waves of release washed over me. "Keep looking at me," he commanded as I allowed my head to fall back.

I pulled my thoughts together enough to focus on him as he quickly slid between my thighs and drove into me with his full weight. I bucked and cried out against him. My muscles were still tightening as he forced his way in, sending shock waves of pleasure through me. He withdrew and entered me again, hard and quick, and I could feel shoots of lightning running along my spine. There was no containing myself any more. I didn't fight it, as each deep hard thrust pushed me higher and higher to where it was hard to breath.

I watched in his eyes and felt his own overwhelming pleasure with each thrust, which made me feel like there was a fire burning deep within me, until finally in a blaze of emotion and release we climaxed, this time together. I wrapped my arms tightly around him and allowed him to lift me straddling his lap. He pressed his forehead to mine.

"I love you, stay with me here," he whispered as we sat gasping for air, his shaft still buried within me, my body hugging it tightly, refusing to let go.

He could have asked anything of me in that moment and I would have given it to him. All I could do was nod in agreement as he pressed me tightly to his chest.

Chapter Fourteen

The next day when we finally awoke and realized we were hungry for something other than each other, we dressed haphazardly and made our way down to the kitchen. The morning meal was well past and a table of midday snacks had been set up within the hall. Tallyn moved about with almost childish glee, greeting each person with a smile and filling my arms with fruit and fresh bread. When Jess rushed forward with a basket for me to unload my burden she stopped short, staring slack-jawed at Tallyn.

"My Lady, what did you do to him?" Her gaze swept from his head to his toes as he offered her a wide boyish smile and a slight bobbing bow.

I studied him for a moment before looking back and shrugging. "He is normally stoic, but I hardly think his giddy behavior is my fault. Maybe it was something in his wine last night?" I handed Tallyn the basket to finish filling it and walked with Jess to a corner.

"You heard about what happened last night?" Jess asked.

"Yes, he came to me afterwards."

"Did he spend the night with you?" she asked, her eyes flaring.

"Shhh, yes. Is that a problem?"

She shook her head. "Lady Gabriella and her father left this morning. They felt a great dishonor had been done and hold you responsible."

"Me?" I gasped. "I had no part of that."

"I know that, but she had her eye on having one of the Princes for a husband and last night made it look like both of them fancied you. She never really stood a chance with Maerryn because he will have to marry a Soul Mate or a member of a royal family, but Tallyn would have been a good match." She gripped my arm. "I'm afraid you have made a powerful enemy and will have much competition for him."

I rolled my eyes. After last night's declaration and impromptu agreement that went from bonding, to courting, to stay with me, I wasn't too concerned about the competition. "So be it. I didn't start out on the path trying to sabotage them. I can't help it that he likes me better."

"My Lady, this is a bigger problem than you know. She will use all sorts of trickery to make you miserable and separate you. Her family has provided a fair amount of the grain needed throughout all four of the Kingdoms. People are loyal to her name and would support her family in their quest for power." Jess was truly concerned about me.

"I'm his Soul Mate," I whispered.

She froze, and all color left her face. "Are you sure?"

"He is, and I am inclined to agree, all things considered. We share all our thoughts and emotions. We even feel each other's pain." I chewed the edge of my lip.

She blinked and threw her arms around me abruptly. "Does that mean you will stay and be bonded with him?" she asked in hushed excitement.

"Yes, I think so. He asked me to, but shhhhh. I'm not sure if there is an order to how this is supposed to be done. I don't know anything about these customs."

She considered me for a moment. "You run along, I'm sure he has plans for the two of you today. Ask him about the binding and if he doesn't tell you, then Beni and I will act as your maids and fill you in on the details, but they may sound less frightening coming from him." I blinked at her words, prepared to ask why it would be frightening, when she turned and bounced away.

What had I agreed to? I looked back towards Tallyn. The basket was full and he was headed in my direction. He wore a smile that seemed endless and it made him so handsome I felt my breath taken away and my knees go weak. When he was within an arm's reach he held out a hand to me.

"My Lady?" I placed my hand in his and followed as he led me through the hall and back towards the King's solar.

"What are we doing?" I asked nervously.

"Speaking to Father. We need to let him know, immediately. Then arrangements can start being made."

I processed the information slowly, not wanting to rush things along. "How long do arrangements take?"

He shrugged. "Hopefully as little time as possible. I would guess a few days maybe. We need time to send out invitations to all the Kingdoms and Realms we are allied with, so maybe even a few weeks."

Days? Weeks? I gulped. *Isn't that fast?*

He was there in my mind, reassuring me without hesitation. *I know it's overwhelming, but you are the one person in the entire universe made for me, and I for you. Ancient magic and time wasn't enough to keep us apart. I've waited hundreds of years for you, and if you truly wish I will wait hundreds more, but I know I'm right.* He set the basket on the corridor floor and wrapped his arms around me, hugging me close.

My doubts rushed away as quickly as they had come. I was left nervous only about the conversation before us when he raised his hand to knock on the door. "Father?" he called.

There was an immediate answer from within. With a hand to my lower back I was swept inside and the door closed behind us. Upon entering I curtseyed before the King until he waved it away and motioned to the chairs along a short table for four.

"Save it for court, have a seat. I assume this is to speak more about last night?"

Tallyn helped me into my seat before taking his own. "Partially, yes."

The King sank into his chair and motioned for him to continue.

"Lillian is my Soul Mate," he said excitedly.

"I know," the King responded matter-of-factly.

"Wait, what?" I blurted out. By the look on Tallyn's face he was thinking the same thing.

"I knew, your brother knew and even Grelyem knew. We've known since the night you woke half the castle. You and she were the ones that insisted you weren't." The King chuckled and I relaxed a bit.

"Don't misunderstand, I'm not unhappy that you found your Soul Mate. I have my concerns since someone sent an Itheaga after her, but I am not concerned about the pairing."

"I understand. It's part of why I would like to seek your permission to bond with her. Then any action against her would be one against the Kingdom. I hope it will be deterrent enough to settle whatever grudge someone has. Also the added benefit of my extended life will make her... sturdier." He glanced my way, clasping my hand with an affectionate squeeze.

The King considered his words carefully then turned his gaze on me. "Are you comfortable with the understanding that you may never go home? What if the reverse were true. What if Maerryn asked you both to leave and return to your own realm so he didn't have to fear his brother making a play for the crown?"

I shuddered at his words but thought carefully before adding my own. "I would miss my family, but I believe that the Dwarves may be able to imbue my communication device with magic enough to power it so I could still contact them from time to time."

"As for returning to my own realm, I would be fine with that as well. I've never had eyes for the weight of a crown. Honestly, I find it rather intimidating." Tallyn stroked the back of my hand with his thumb.

The King's gaze seemed heavy on both of us. "I will grant your request to be bound. We will begin the preparations." He nodded his head as if confirming the idea. He stood and lovingly embraced Tallyn. "Congratulations, my son."

He then turned and captured me in a bear hug. I heard parts of my back pop that hadn't in years. The King's last words on the subject were to Tallyn. "I would recommend telling your brother before someone else does."

❧

Maerryn hugged us both. His wink gave me hope that he wasn't angry about the prior night's events. After our conversation with Maerryn we headed to the stables, taking along our food basket. Before I realized what was going on, I was saddled and riding after Tallyn. He urged Mavba to her full speed. Still timid on horseback I did my best to keep up, but quickly fell behind.

Once he was out of sight I slowed to a more comfortable pace and watched the surrounding scenery. The leaves were now a palette of golds and reds, painting the forest and hillsides. Many had already fallen and you could easily see where the animals had prepared themselves for the winter ahead. I started to wonder what a winter without my electric blanket would be like. Would we get mostly icy rain here or would everything be covered in snow? I allowed my vision to blur as I tried to imagine the land covered in a thick blanket of white.

Something suddenly startled my horse because he reared, letting out an anxious noise. I threw myself forward to keep from falling, tossing my arms around his neck. He burst into a gallop and all I could do was hold on for dear life until I could get him calmed down. I peeked over my shoulder hoping to see what had caused his startling reaction, and watched as the glow of a fire grew smaller and smaller behind us. At some point Tallyn had doubled back to find me and was surprised as I rushed past.

I'm not sure if he caught my terror or the horse's but he gave chase, catching up with us quickly. In a feat of death-defying acrobatics he flung himself from Mavba to the back of my horse. He righted himself quickly, slowing the horse and taking the reins.

"Are you alright?"

I shook my head and leaned back against him, allowing some of his strength to travel through and reassure me. "Yes, we were just riding and then the horse took off. When I looked back there appeared to be a large fire burning. All I could do was hold on at that point."

"You're lucky you didn't fall off and get trampled." If his words were meant to be reassuring he missed the mark. "Let's get some place safe and quiet, have a picnic, and we can take a look on the way back. Alright?"

"You're not concerned about a fireball?" I asked.

"No, not really." I had a nagging feeling there was something he wasn't mentioning, but if he seemed confident there was no danger I would trust him.

We reached a small clearing within the woods where we finally stopped. Tallyn helped me off the horse, steadying me when I reached the ground, my legs still shaking a little. He pulled the basket and blanket free.

"Go unpack and I'll secure the horses." I accepted the basket and blankets while turning to survey the area.

I spread out two blankets on top of each other, hoping the added layer would help prevent the cold of the ground from seeping through. I sat and started unpacking our booty. Two soft loaves of bread, a pot of honey butter, a small roast bird, some soft creamy cheese, a couple apples and pears and a bottle of sweet wine.

"How did I do?" he asked as he dropped on the blanket beside me.

"A little overkill for a midday meal, don't you think?" I said picking a piece of bird free.

"Ah, but we slept late and used a lot of food last night in our lovemaking. I want you to have plenty of energy for tonight. Keeping an Elf satisfied is a tall order, especially for a half Human like yourself," he teased.

I reached for a pear. "Then perhaps I am the wrong girl for you. If I can't satisfy you perhaps I should return home and find a Human male." I bit into the pear to emphasize the last word and turned to look into the woods. Instantly I was on my back, his lips on mine. The taste of him mixed with the sweetness of the pear and aroused me. I arched, pressing my chest against his hands where they cupped my breasts through the fabric of my gown. I drank in his kiss as he deepened it, invading and possessing me. His need and desire flowed through me.

As quickly as I had found myself on my back I was jerked upright and shoved behind him. He reached for his sword, unsheathing it, the whole time his eyes never leaving the woods.

"Show yourself!" he commanded.

I focused on the darkness between the trees, watching for any slight movement, but didn't see anything. Then out of the trees a large serpent-like being with golden green skin moved forward. Sharp teeth were bared for us to see. A wisp of smoke was on its breath as it exhaled.

"State your business!" Tallyn demanded with deadly seriousness.

"A Dragon?" I asked, mostly in disbelief. Tallyn's nod confirmed my fear and awe.

I couldn't be sure but I thought I heard the Dragon chuckle. Before my eyes its scales rippled and there was an intense wave of heat. I watched in amazement as the Dragon took on a human form. His eyes were large and golden, short blonde hair spiked out in a careless way. His skin still seemed to shine like his scales and a large tattoo that looked like tribal flames covered his left arm and chest.

"Your Human is flattering me with her fear and awe. If she were a virgin I would consider keeping her for myself." He looked me over. Chills ran through me. "Or eat her." He shrugged, giving a handsome smile.

"What do you want?" Tallyn straightened still grasping his sword tightly.

"I am Lord Hudraer and I've been sent for the girl." His large eyes that gave him an almost innocent look had a wicked gleam to them. "At first I was thinking dead, but now that I see she is cute, perhaps I will keep her alive to play with for a while."

"You can't have her. I've claimed her as my own. Tell your master that she is spoken for." Tallyn stepped fully in front of me, blocking my view.

"You think claim is enough?" The Dragon was coming closer. I could feel his presence grow even if I couldn't see him.

"She is my Soul Mate and I am a Prince of the Realm. That should be more than enough. Even now the binding ceremony is being prepared. An attack on her is an attack on the crown." His words were filled with warning.

I could hear movement stop. I ventured a peek around Tallyn.

"I was unaware she was your Soul Mate. Our clan recognizes the title of Soul Mates as well. Very well, I will spare her. I wasn't told she was your one true mate. Be aware though, that there are those who do not live by our code and I am sure her enemy will send them." The Dragon turned to walk away.

Finding my voice I stepped from around Tallyn. "Tell me, who sent you?"

The Dragon paused, turning back to look at me. He studied me carefully, looking deeply into my eyes. "You are certainly his, My Lady, but as I honor the law of a Soul Mate I also honor my agreement with the person who hired me. While I will return and refuse the task, I will not betray them either. Do try and stay safe. Soul Mates are rare blessings that very few ever find."

I forced my shoulders back and raised my chin defiantly. "Then let your master know I slew the Itheaga with no more than a sword, a bow and my

Human hands. I wish for peace, but I will defend myself."

The Dragon looked from me to Tallyn. "She slew the Itheaga? By herself?"

Tallyn nodded.

Looking back at me the Dragon gave a bow. "You have done a great service to this Kingdom, My Lady. I look forward to seeing what else the future holds for you." With that he turned and parted ways with us, disappearing back into the darkness of the woods.

"Dragons? You couldn't have mentioned Dragons?" He kissed me as if that would make me forget about Dragons. I didn't forget, but it did distract me from caring.

"I think we should eat lunch then head back to the castle. As much as I would love to enjoy you and not just the food right now, I believe that the security of stone walls around you may be for the best until we get things sorted out." I wanted to moan and protest but he had a valid point.

Lunch was delicious and before we could get packed up I did convince Tallyn that a little heavy petting and making out wasn't out of line. He was resistant at first but a nibble to his ear was the undoing that made him see my side of things.

I rode back sitting in front of him on Mavba. The idea of another runaway horse incident was too fresh in my mind. The silence was almost unbearable. I began to fidget in front of him, wiggling more and more.

One of his hands pulled me back tightly against his groin and I stilled. "You are making it hard to concentrate."

"Oh, sorry. Are Dragons native to this realm?" I tried to start a conversation, anything to give me something to focus on.

"No, Dragons are not native. Believe it or not, they used to be native to your realm and I believe that many still live there." He paused. "Not that there have ever been many, but of the realms, yours probably still has the most. They have, of course, traveled and settled in other realms, like many other creatures. He may not even be from this realm. Just because the portals were closed to your realm, doesn't mean they were closed to all the others."

"I see." I had never seen a Dragon that I was aware of in my realm, but then, they obviously had human forms and I probably wouldn't have. "Tell me about the binding ceremony. The maids are under the impression it may scare me. They also said you should explain it to me."

It was his turn to fidget uncomfortably. "I think we should discuss the details a little later. We're almost home." Something about the way he said "we" and "home" made me melt a little. It told me that he really felt I belonged there with him.

I turned my attention to the castle that grew larger as we closed the distance between us and it. The towers seemed to reach the sky. Colorful banners stood out in stark contrast to its white walls. In the short time we had been gone there already appeared to be more decorations, more color and more life dwelling within. "Is it just me, or does the place look more vibrant than when we left?"

Tallyn shrugged. "It probably is. Preparations will have already begun for our upcoming binding ceremony. We tend to celebrate in a big way, for these types of events. People will come from all over the realm, and some from other realms, to attend this event or come offer congratulations."

"Don't get me wrong. It makes sense I guess, but I've never really been one for this much fanfare. There is no chance of a little binding ceremony with close friends and family, is there?" I tried to turn and look at him closer because it was always easier to convince him when we made eye contact.

"Calm down. The blood binding is fairly public but the branding is done with only a small group of witnesses." He ran a caressing hand over my hip.

"Branding!?!?" I yelped. I almost threw myself off the horse, prepared to take my chances with the Dragon. Mental link in place as strong as ever he tightened his grip on me.

"It will be alright. You'll be so distracted you won't notice it until afterwards, and then I promise we can kiss each other's pain away."

As we crossed the first drawbridge a sinking feeling came over me, like there wouldn't be an escape now. I tried to beat down the panic, and I had it mostly under control by the time we arrived back at the stable. I didn't even resist when Tallyn reached up, lifting me off the back of Mavba.

"I'm scared," I announced without warning.

"I promise you a long life full of happiness." He reached out, cupping my face in his hand.

"Oh, I'm less worried about the long life thing and more worried about the ceremony. Is all this really necessary? I know I was anti-wedding but really, I could do a wedding." I nodded my head enthusiastically.

He ran his thumb along my lower lip. "Seeing you enthusiastic for a wedding is both heartwarming and a relief but I'm afraid the binding ceremony is something I must insist on. Marriage is little more than a legal contract. It can be broken, as you well know. I want to know that you're mine forever. That we are truly bound to each other body, mind and soul." I shuddered a little bit. "Come, we will go inside, retreat to our chamber and discuss this all in more detail. I can see that you need reassurance." He captured my hand and led me back into the Keep.

It took us far longer than expected to cross the Hall, as at least a dozen people stopped us to ask questions and offer their congratulations. There were people asking about invitations, choices for the feast, colors and more. My head was spinning by the time we reached the stairs on the far side.

Tallyn's hand at the small of my back urged me up the stairs while the battle for civility raged in my head. I hated feeling like I was ignoring people. When we reached the top of the landing four people were hot on our heels as Tallyn rushed me through the corridor towards his chambers. With a gentle shove I was through the door but we hadn't successfully outrun the entourage. With a heavy sigh, he closed the door behind them.

"Lily, take a seat, we have decisions we need to make before we can be left in peace." He glared at the members of the castle staff that surrounded us. Realizing it may be a while I curled up on the small sofa leaving room for him to join me.

"Ok, one at a time," he said, as he all but collapsed on the sofa beside me.

The first to step forward was a thin, willowy man. His limbs looked like they would break under the slightest pressure. His eyes were a smoky gray color that seemed to add a kindly old man vibe to the way he carried himself. He laid four sets of invitations across the table in front of us.

The first was a heavy white linen paper with lacy black script and the royal seal embossed in the lower right. The next was a dark blue almost midnight color that looked like silk. The script was thicker and simpler in a light silver that stood out against the blue. The crest was at the top center and subtle. The third was a wash of colors and looked like old story book illumination. Characters that could appear in stained glass windows danced across the ivory paper. The fourth and final was on a gold fabric so light that if you held it up to the window it almost disappeared except for the slight shimmer. The script also in gold seemed to float above the paper.

Tallyn looked at me with question. I shrugged and looked back to study them again finally deciding on invitation number four because it was so different from anything I had seen before. I turned my attention to the man before me.

"I like the last one. It's very different from anything I have seen in my own realm."

The man nodded. "An excellent choice, My Lady. I will see that they are finished today and we will have them out on horseback tomorrow." He gave a quick bow and exited the chamber after gathering up his samples.

The next to step up was Chef Seya. I had seen and met with her several times before so I figured she had come with suggestions on food choices. I studied her carefully. She was very short and looked far more like what I had always pictured as a Dwarf. I had since learned she was a Gnome and very friendly, but a workaholic through and through.

"I'll be needing a list of both your and your lady's favorite dishes, Sire." Her words broke my concentration.

"You don't need to worry about me," I insisted. "You probably cannot get or prepare my favorite dishes. Please, just continue to make delicious food as you have since I arrived." I offered her a reassuring smile.

She pursed her lips together. "My Lady, do you know how to make the dishes from your own realm?" she asked.

"Yes, of course." I answered with some trepidation that I was going to be giving cooking lessons for the next two weeks leading up to the ceremony. Maybe it would take my mind off things, or maybe it would stress me out more.

"Good, then you will sit with me tomorrow morning after you break your fast and explain to me each of the dishes and how they are traditionally made." Her gaze pinned me in place, telling me this wasn't optional. I nodded agreement and she excused herself.

The third person to approach was an older Dark Elf I recognized almost immediately. Grelyem stood before us with his eyes slightly lowered, holding a large heavy book. The bindings on it appeared to be made of silver. He carefully placed it down on the table as if it were a tiny delicate infant. He opened its pages and turned the book towards us. "We must decide on your branding. I have brought the registry thinking since Lady Lillian has probably never seen them, she may appreciate gaining an understanding about what they look like and what is done."

Tallyn stiffened where he sat. He took a deep breath and considered Grelyem for a moment. "Old friend, would it be alright if we helped the last person behind you and then discussed this in private? The Lady is not yet familiar with this custom and I believe this is a discussion best done with as few as possible."

"But of course, Sire." Grelyem stood and moved away from the table, allowing the last member of the staff who had followed us to approach.

This man was tall with dark skin. His ears were much taller and more pointed than the Elves I was used to. Tribal tattoos wrapped around his wrist and neck before disappearing under his garments. He wore a pair of circular glasses that reminded me of a college professor I once had all prim and proper.

"Sire, I will not waste too much of your time since you have other matters to attend to." The man before us turned a warm smile in my direction that spoke volumes before meeting Tallyn's gaze once more.

"The Lady has maids to see to her personal needs and clothing for the ceremony. Please come find me tomorrow and we can make decisions for your own, based on the decisions your Lady will make today." I smiled as he left with little more than a quick bow.

Grelyem eased the door shut behind the tailor that had just left before turning his attention back to us. "So you haven't explained the ceremony to her yet?" he questioned.

Tallyn shook his head no and didn't meet my eyes. "Then I will leave you to explain all the details, but I need the two of you to make some decisions. If the Lady would like I can show her my own branding where I am bound to my wife."

The old Elf faced me and quickly pulled off his tunic. Running across one shoulder and down his side before disappearing into the fold of his breeches was a large gold marking. The design seemed organic in its shape, winding and twisting along his muscles. The color of the gold shimmered ever so lightly but seemed one with the skin. It was beautiful.

"My wife and I share the same marking, just as you and your Prince will share the same marking as one another. Each marking is unique to the couple and connects you fully with each other mind, body and soul. I know this can all seem very intimidating Lady Lillian, but as the royal physician I will be there on hand to make sure nothing goes wrong. The branding is done through a combination of fire and magic."

I swallowed. "Are they always so big?" I asked. I thought I may be able to handle something small but something that ran the length of my body seemed like it would be hard to get through even with the best of distractions.

"Usually, yes. I promise though, the Prince will do everything in his power to make sure you feel as little of the pain as possible. Usually, the worst of the pain is harnessed by the male but even he will be in a throe of pleasure deep enough he will not care."

Grelyem slid his tunic back on then redirected his attention to the book, explaining what different parts of the markings meant.

It took about two hours but finally we had an idea of what the brandings would look like. We wouldn't know for sure until the day of, but it did make it a little less scary even knowing the size just by understanding roughly what would be there afterwards. Also, knowing that the brands were partially done with magic and that a physician would be on hand did relieve some of my worries. When we finally finished Grelyem excused himself from the chambers.

Tallyn turned and captured my hands in his. "I need to tell you about the ceremony, but from what I know of your realm and customs it frightens me to tell you."

"Why does it frighten you?" I asked very curious. I didn't think I had ever gave the impression that I wouldn't be able to handle some strange customs and traditions.

"The first step will be an exchange of blood. This is normally done through a three part handfasting ritual, where a small cut is made in our palms, drops of blood are combined in a chalice that we both drink from, and finally our cut hands are bound together. Usually the person presiding over the ritual completes the wedding agreement at this time as well." I nodded

- so far everything seemed pretty straightforward. He stopped and poured a glass of wine and quickly gulped the whole thing down.

I started considering the size of the branding and realized that in order for the brand to cover that much skin we would need side-less clothes or lack thereof. "I'm not going to like the rest of this am I?"

He shook his head before taking my hands again. "After the blood binding we will be taken to a small private chamber with only a few witnesses where I will claim you. In the ultimate moment of ecstasy when we are least likely to feel much pain the brands will be applied." He grimaced as he finished what he was saying.

It took me a moment to process what he was saying. "People are going to watch us have sex and then when we finally climax we will be branded, which is an experience that is so painful it takes an orgasm to make it bearable?" I pinned him with my gaze. "What happens if I cannot get there because people are watching?" I was struggling not to scream I was so outraged.

"The brands will not be applied until you do, even if that means hours." He took a deep breath. "The brands are the ultimate connection between us. The consummation serves to make the final connection between us. It is witnessed to make sure the brands are matching and that the consummation is completed." He buried his face in his hands.

"Oh, public humiliation, extreme pain AND no more birth control. You're doing a great job selling this." I tried to stand up. I wanted to walk out, to run and hide. This was ridiculous.

"I know it is a lot to ask, but understand the reasons behind the ceremony. When our kind joins it can cross species, and even prove dangerous. It is the one time and then over with. Because I am a member of the royal family despite my own desire to carry the title, it is even more important because there is always the chance that we or one of our children could end up on the throne. People have to know that our markings are in fact the same and I was the one who claimed you."

"Is it possible for us to be branded and the markings not match?" I asked.

"Yes, and then it would mean that we are already bound to another person or have an unfound Soul Mate in this life. As we are Soul Mates it isn't possible for us to have non-matching markings, but equally it is just as important to prove they are truly identical and that we are true Soul Mates." I didn't like his words. I understood them and in a sick way they made sense, but I still really disliked them.

"Do you know how wrong all that sounds to me?" I asked him.

"I can imagine since you made it clear how you feel about having only one sexual partner at a time and always insisting on a private place." He reached up and caressed my cheek with a fingertip. "As we are bound mentally and emotionally I will share all of your fear, embarrassment and pain. Heap it upon me and I will give you my strength and love to see you through it." A single tear rolled down his face. He would gladly bear it all for me if it meant I would stay. It was in that moment I realized I would do anything for this Elf even if I really didn't want to.

Chapter Fifteen

Ceremony preparations were well underway by the time I woke up the next day. Invitations had been sent, gowns were being made, and the smell of food being prepared in the kitchen taunted my senses as I made my way there. I hardly had time to look around before I was pulled into a chair next to a large work table and made to begin dictating the preparation of my "favorite" foods.

Chef Seya nodded at me and took notes on each ingredient and instruction. "This is what you eat for celebrations in your world?"

"Not exactly, but I was told to explain my favorite foods. Not celebration food. Most of what I like wouldn't be described as party food, I guess." I paused to consider if mac and cheese and spicy tuna rolls were really what I wanted served. Then I remembered what-all the day would include and decided that chocolate cupcakes with buttermilk frosting would also be in order.

I spent the better part of the morning and early afternoon in the kitchen, tasting and helping to make dishes. When Chef Seya excused herself to begin preparations for dinner, I decided it was time to get some fresh air. I thanked her for her time and left to find my way to peace and quiet. I didn't get too far.

As I entered the hall Jess noticed me and made a beeline. I looked at the door that would lead to my freedom but resisted the urge to make a run for it. I plastered on my best enthusiastic smile. "Hello Jess," I said, hoping she would smile and pass me by.

"Hello Lady Lillian, is everything set for the feast?" Her voice was almost sing-songy. She was far more excited about this ceremony than I was.

"Yes, food is taken care of, I believe. If not, I'm sure someone will tell me. What can I help you with?" I asked her, trying to cut to the chase.

She took my arm and started leading me towards the stairs that would lead back up to the chambers. "We need to fit your gowns." She gave me an affectionate tug. "Let's go before dinner."

I sighed, resigning myself to my fate as I stared longingly over my shoulder at the doors leading outside to freedom. "Oh, sweet freedom. Wait for me," I mumbled.

"Did you say something, My Lady?" Jess asked as we mounted the first of the stairs.

"Oh no, sorry. I was just talking to myself." I shrugged and continued climbing the stairs. Before long I found myself back in "my" chamber where Beni was already laying out a number of fabrics and dress mock-ups.

As soon as the door shut behind us, Jess started unlacing me from my gown. In no time, I was stripped bare and my hair was piled on top of my head as the women draped layers of fabric over me, looking at colors, patterns and weights. I followed directions, lifting my arms, turning around, and standing up straight.

"What do you think of this color?" The fabric being held up to me looked like pale violet and blue stardust. You could see right through it, but it cast a slight shadow on the skin and made me look like I shimmered.

"It's pretty, but shouldn't it cover more?" I asked.

The two maids laughed. Jess finally spoke up. "It's for your undergarments and claiming gown. It's made more for your Prince than to be seen by the public." I relaxed a little knowing most people wouldn't see it. She then draped a bright blue velvet over it. "This is what I was thinking for your outer gown. If you like it?"

My eyes flared and I may have drooled a little. "I love it. It is the most beautiful color I have ever seen and it's velvet. I love velvet." I cuddled the cloth to me as both women continued to laugh.

"I will make sure there is enough of it for Lord Tallyn's garments and then order the rest put away for your use. It's the first time I have seen you really excited about any fabric since you arrived. I was beginning to worry you were more warrior than woman," the older maid teased lightly.

"What were you thinking for the outer dress?" I asked excitedly.

Beni held up the fabric as Jess explained. "We were thinking sleeveless, with a deep V in the front, showing off the Fae Stardust silk. Then have it lace from waist to armpit on either side, exposing the fabric underneath. Then, since there are no sleeves, make arm bands with layered sleeves attached that would tumble free behind the elbow. Of course, we will use the finest silver and gold threads to embellish it, and we still need to decide on your accessories."

I perked up. "I do love accessories. If possible, I would like to wear the necklace given to me by the King."

The women exchanged looks then nodded. "That should be alright. Most people choose to design something special for the day."

"Is there really anything that I could ever design that would be more meaningful than the gift given to me by my future father-in-law for defeating the Itheaga?" I looked at them in consideration.

Beni smiled warmly. "It's true, most women wouldn't have such a token in their collections. I think you honor your new family and Kingdom greatly by choosing to wear it. I'm sure that many will feel the same."

This was one of the few occasions I had gotten Beni to smile. I liked it. The smile brightened her face and made her appear younger than I had first thought she was. I held still as the women pinned, tucked, cut and pulled at the cloth around my body. As we were nearing the end of the process my stomach grumbled loudly. I blushed brightly as I stared at myself in the mirror.

"Well, let's get you out of this and dressed for dinner," Jess said through a giggle.

It didn't take long for me to dress but I was delayed by Jess insisting I do something with my hair. I made my way down to the hall just in time to help with the last of setup and lend a hand in bringing out dishes.

When dinner began I sat down across from Fairwynn and James. They both stared at me dumbfounded. "What's wrong?" I asked between bites.

"Shouldn't you be up there?" James motioned to the seat beside Tallyn who was staring daggers at me. He motioned for me to join him. When I took another bite of food he rolled his eyes before picking up his plate and goblet then meandering down to sit next to me. Room was immediately made for him beside me.

"Why are you sitting down here?" he asked, confused.

"Because I haven't seen my friends in days and wished to break bread and speak with them," I said pointedly, before turning back to look at Fairwynn. "So I was thinking of practicing some archery in the outer bailey tomorrow, would you like to join me?"

The Dwarven woman looked at me with a telling smile. Her eyes flashed from Tallyn to James before returning to me. "That sounds like fun. I don't think I can stand another day of needlework. Should we meet after we break our fast in the morning?"

"Sounds perfect, but you may need to rescue me." I took a bite of warm buttered bread, noticing that Tallyn was eating and had struck up conversation with James.

"Why?" she asked between bites.

"There are a million and one questions to answer with the binding preparations. When people see me they tend to slow me down and ask a lot of them." I took a sip of the sweet red wine.

"Ah, that's understandable. If need be, I will gladly come to your rescue." We laughed between ourselves throughout the rest of dinner.

As we were finishing up Fairwynn stopped me again. "Do you have your communication device handy? I would like to try and imbue it for you."

"Not with me tonight, but I'll bring it in the morning." The chance that I would have power to call home was exciting.

"Excellent, then I will see you in the morning," she said cheerfully. It was then I watched her make one last sly look at Maerryn. I smiled to myself, the gears in my head clicking away.

I waited for the crowds to thin and told Tallyn I would meet him in my chamber shortly. When the opportunity came up I tugged on Maerryn's elbow. He turned, giving me a hug. "It's my new favorite sister," he proclaimed, laughing.

"I'm not your sister yet, and I will set you on your backside if you try another stunt like the other night." To emphasize my point I held up my fist.

Snickering he urged me to put it down. "What can I do for you?" he asked.

"Tomorrow morning Fairwynn and I are going to practice archery in the outer bailey. Tallyn will be busy with his guard so I thought I might trouble you to come keep a couple ladies safe and help us with our targets." I grinned a big flirty smile for an extra measure.

Sure enough he chuckled and nodded in agreement. "I will gladly come along, though I fear it is you who would be protecting me, Lady Heroine of the Kingdom." He looked over at where Fairwynn stood speaking with a Dark Elf and smiled. "Tell me, if I come will I be subjected to listening to you and Lady Fairwynn talking about stitchery and steaming fish?"

I blinked at him. "No, why?"

"That's what Lady Rowena likes to discuss. May I ask what your topics tend to be?" He looked back, locking gazes with me.

"We talk about Dwarven Life, other realms, which squires have the nicest butts. You know, typical stuff I guess," I said with a shrug.

His eyes flared with surprise. A smile curved the outside edges of his lips. "And Lady Fairwynn enjoys these discussions?"

"As far as I know." I patted him on the shoulder, smiling to myself that I had read the signs correctly. "So, you'll meet us in the morning after you break your fast, right?" He nodded agreement then turned his attention back in Lady Fairwynn's direction.

When I returned to my chambers I found Tallyn seeing to the tub being filled with hot water. "You know the tub and shower are larger in my chamber," he commented looking at the tub.

"I know, but this way we just have to get cozy." He grinned knowingly at me before strolling over to assist me with the many laces on the bodice of my dress.

"So, have you decided on fabric for your gown?" he asked distractedly as I peeled off my shift to stand naked in the center of the room.

"I thought about wearing this." I motioned to myself, doing my best Vanna White impersonation.

"I approve." His voice grew huskier the closer he stepped.

"You would," I snorted before sauntering over to the tub and sliding in. He nudged me with his hand to move forward so he could join me. I sighed in pleasure as he began to run a soaped up cloth over my skin. "Love, immortality, wicked hot Elf... these were all great selling points, but really you had me at back rubs."

"I don't remember promising a life time of back rubs."

"Oh, I promise you did. You promised a life time of back rubs when you told me I would have to be branded and peeped on while we do the naughty, naughty."

He chuckled deep within his chest. "Glad to know you can be won over so easily."

I wiggled until I could turn around and face him. "So, once we are bound, and all the thank you cards are sent, then what? I mean, in my realm we go on a honeymoon where the couple pretends they are bunnies for a week or so and enjoys a vacation. Do you have a custom like that?"

"Yes," he said with a smile.

"What's it called?" I grinned.

"A honeymoon." His smile deepened.

I splashed water in his direction. "Well that was anticlimactic. A honeymoon, how lame!" I crossed my arms over my chest and pouted.

"You don't wish to go on vacation with me and have copious amounts of sex?" he shrugged. "What a shame," he said as he feigned heartbreak.

"Oh, no! That wasn't a complaint. I was just hoping you had a spiffy word for it here." I smiled widely and nodded vigorously. "Yes, I do want to have copious amounts of sex." I quickly added, "-with you."

He started to say something, but it turned into a round of deep, rolling laughter. The shock on my face just made him laugh harder. When he settled back down he wore a smile that made him seem boyish and carefree.

"I'm glad you clarified that you didn't want to go on a honeymoon and have copious amounts of sex with other people. It makes me feel much better. I was afraid there for a moment." He winked as he teased me.

"I'm sorry, I just thought the comment sounded weird without the clarification." I chewed my lower lip. "Has a day been chosen for the ceremony? I thought your father mentioned something about two weeks?" The anticipation was building within me. I was excited and nervous all at the same time.

He rubbed his chin for a moment. "I was thinking of ordering it kept a secret from you. Then you wouldn't know when it was coming and would worry less."

"That is a terrible idea." I started to jump up out of the tub in fury. Tallyn grabbed my wrist and tugged me back down onto his lap. "That would be like knowing I was going to be shot but wouldn't know when."

"Are you comparing being bound to me with an attempt on your life?" he asked, his smile slipping away.

"Yes, I mean no.... wait, is this a trick question? I want to be prepared for it." I hoped I hadn't offended him.

He sighed and pulled my head down for a kiss. My body responded to his instantly but before I could act on it the moment was over. "You have four days to worry and panic. After that, it will all be over."

I swallowed hard. "That doesn't leave much time," I whispered as I climbed out of the tub, accepting his hand to help steady me as I stepped over the edge. I contemplated customs and traditions from my own realm, because this was binding was planned quickly, I knew there were things I wanted to do to prepare for the ceremony. I wanted to complete a gift for Tallyn. I didn't have money but I knew I could complete some embroidery or something in time. After all, doesn't a groom deserve some small token of love?

I pulled a clean shift made of silk over my head and slid under the blankets on the bed. Tallyn, done drying himself, soon joined me. I turned my back to him but didn't struggle when he pulled me against him, holding me close. He quietly stroked my hip where his hand rested.

"What are you thinking about?" he asked.

Nothing.

He nuzzled the back of my neck. *Tell me, then I can make everything better.*

I rolled over to face him. "I will need some time to myself the next few days. Also, the night before, I want to sleep separately. I want to have some friends come over to enjoy being girls. Is that allowed?"

I paused for a moment. "Actually, can I use your chamber that night?" I smiled widely.

"You want me to sleep alone AND would deny me my own chamber?" He frowned at me.

"You can use this chamber. It will smell like me, and have all my stuff in it." I nibbled on my thumb.

He pulled my hand away from my mouth and kissed it. "Have you not figured out yet that I would do anything for you? Of course, you can use OUR chamber as you see fit. I will sleep here that night." He ran his thumb over the back of my fingers.

"Thank you," I whispered. Finally, the wear of the long day claimed us both and we fell asleep quickly.

The next morning came before I would have liked. Tallyn was already up and dressed when I opened my eyes to greet the day.

"I wondered how long you were going to sleep. If you hurry and dress we can break our fast together." Scrunching my nose I rolled out of the bed and began the frantic search for clothes.

When I finally stepped away from the water basin after washing the sleep from my eyes and dressing I found Tallyn waiting impatiently by the door. He started to say something but clamped his mouth shut as his gaze raked over me. He seemed less than thrilled to find me in leather leggings, a layered wool tunic and boots.

"I'm shooting archery with Fairwynn and your brother in the outer bailey today."

He shook his head and forced a smile. "I didn't say anything."

"You didn't have to, your eyes said it all. I can't be a pristine lady all the time." I grabbed my bow and quiver from beside the door, along with a woolen hood for added warmth, before stepping out into the stone corridor.

Tallyn rolled his eyes but smiled genuinely. "I want you to be yourself. I just would have thought so close to our ceremony you would be behaving a little more... I don't know, girly?"

"I'm hanging out with Fairwynn, she's a girl," I retorted.

He snickered. "As much as you are. When we were young, she would follow me around everywhere asking questions about Maerryn. She would fight alongside her brother and take her lumps right there with the squires if it meant I would tell her another story."

He slid an arm around my waist and pulled me against his side as we walked. "As long as you are staying within the bailey and have both Maerryn and Fairwynn with you, I won't worry and will let this go."

"I hope you aren't always going to try and be so controlling," I mumbled.

"Just until we are bound and you take on my immortality. After that, attacks should stop and you will be a bit sturdier. I will then have less to worry about." I resisted the urge to roll my eyes at the familiar lecture and didn't struggle when he kissed me on the head like an obedient child.

Maerryn, James, and Fairwynn were already seated at a table and eating when we finished descending the stairs into the great hall. My maids waved us over, two large plates already stacked full of more food than we could eat waiting on us.

"Morning!" I chimed when we approached the table. I was happy to see we were met with cheerful smiles.

"I heard Maerryn is going to do his best to help my sister improve her aim with that bow," James said with a playful grin. "I think she's past hope, but perhaps the Prince can perform a miracle."

His teasing didn't seem to stir Fairwynn at all. Instead she launched into a discussion with me about what to wear the night before the ceremony. We giggled like mad scientists, ignoring the perplexed looks on the men's faces.

Maerryn cut in. "You're having a party and not inviting your new brother?" He dramatically threw his hand to his forehead and pretended to fall from the bench. I couldn't help but laugh.

"I am having a women's-only party, it's true." I eyed Fairwynn. "But how did you know about it already? I just talked to Tallyn about it last night."

Maerryn's most wicked smile cleaved his face. "A women's-only party sounds perfect, as long as there is one Maerryn to keep them all company."

Fairwynn and I both exchanged looks, choosing to ignore the comment.

"Ah, you spoke to the chef about food for it. Her wife, the laundry mistress spoke with your maids. Your maids told my maids, who then told me. I knew before dinner last night." Fairwynn smiled. "Dwarves always know when and where a party is. I sent a request to our family attending to bring some of our special brew down for it." She winked at me. I wasn't sure if that was good or bad.

"I see. Well, good to know we will be well stocked. Thank you!" I said, taking a bite of the food before me.

"Gladly. When you finish up we'll get going. Oh, did you bring your communication device?" she asked.

"Yes, in my quiver." I quickly ate my fill, kissed Tallyn on the cheek and rushed out to the waiting world before I could be delayed further.

There was more of a chill in the air each day and I had no doubt that soon winter would be upon us. I started thinking about winters at home with my family. Depending on how time was moving I wondered if there was any way to take Tallyn home with me for the holidays. I was sure my folks would like to meet him.

The walk to the outer bailey was slower than I would have liked, and cold... very cold. It seemed the further out of the castle we got the cooler it became. By the time we reached the archery field I had my hood pulled up protecting my ears from the wind. The field was empty except for the three of us and I already understood why. The wind gusts were fairly fierce and would make shooting much harder. On the upside, if we could figure out how to shoot in this, we would be making some major improvements.

The morning wore on, chilling the three of us to the bone. Maerryn, to his credit, worked tirelessly with us, and by late afternoon we were hitting more targets in the wind than we were missing.

I smiled as he stood close to Fairwynn. She blushed brightly every time he leaned in close to help her with aim or posture. He grinned broadly while doing it. They made it very difficult for me not to play matchmaker when they both so obviously liked each other. I felt like I was in middle school all over again.

When the sun started sinking in the sky we made our way back to the keep, cold, tired and hungry. I wondered if I could convince Tallyn to have dinner in his chamber and run a giant steaming hot bath.

As if on cue I heard him purr in my mind. *That sounds wonderful, love. I'll see to the food and will meet you in my chamber.* I smiled, glad no one else could hear our thoughts and conversations. Sometimes they were rather risqué.

With a smile and a wave I parted ways with my comrades and headed straight up the stairs on the far side of the hall. Beni met me at the top of the stairs. "My Lady, I trust your archery went well today?"

I walked and spoke with her. "It did. We had a lot of fun and I became much more proficient at shooting in the wind."

"Shall I help you prepare and dress for dinner?" she asked.

"No, that won't be needed. Tallyn and I will be dining in his chambers tonight. I am frozen to the bone. I think a hot bath, a warm meal and early to bed is the better plan. I wouldn't want a cold for the ceremony."

She started to protest but seemed to think better of it. "Do Humans become sick easily?"

"Not always, but cold weather, tiredness, stress, and a chill mixed together are known to take down some of the strongest of us." I smiled. "Luckily, I am only half Human, but even so, why take a chance?" I gave her a wink. My argument seemed to placate her.

"I will send some hot tea up as well. Better to do preventative care," she agreed. She pushed open the door to Tallyn's chamber and immediately saw to getting a hot bath prepared. She helped me peel out of my layers before taking her leave.

The hot water steamed and swirled around me as I sat in the large stone tub. My muscles relaxed, my eyes closed and I leaned my head back against the side. The sound of the chamber door snapping shut brought my eyes open. Tallyn stood at the edge, staring down at me approvingly. His arms were heavily weighed down with food. Wasting no time, he pulled a small table tub-side before stripping and joining me in the bath.

"How was your day?" he asked, taking one of my feet in his hands and beginning to massage it.

"It was good. By the end of the day I was hitting targets consistently in the wind." He nodded his head in understanding.

"Did you know that Fairwynn and Maerryn like each other?" I grinned with childish delight.

"Of course, we all grew up together. We all like each other and are friends," he answered.

"No, I mean they REALLY like each other." I wiggled my eyebrows at him.

"I'm afraid I am not following your logic," he admitted.

"They have chemistry. They are interested in each other. They are crushing." He still stared blankly at me. "They are romantically interested in each other." The light bulb went on over his head.

"Oh! Really? Did they tell you?" Tallyn's sudden interest caused me to giggle.

"No, I can see it in their eyes. I just know." He stopped rubbing my foot as he sat there and pondered the possibility of a relationship for his brother.

"You know, if you are right, my father would probably support that union. James and Fairwynn are part of the Dwarven royal family. While not exactly a Prince or Princess they both have claim to the crown. I think it would be a fine match. You can help broker the binding contract." He leaned back, rubbing his chin.

"Whoa, slow down. Don't say anything to your father yet. Let's just help them naturally unfold the romance. It will be better for them if they think it's all their own doing." I added a smile for an extra measure.

Finally he agreed with a nod and moved beside me to rub my shoulders. He quickly found the knots created by a long day of shooting in the cold. His hands felt like heaven on me. I closed my eyes and moaned softly. He leaned forward to press a kiss to the back of my neck before reaching across me and grabbing a bowl of soup. He held it out for me to take then grabbed his own. "We should consume this before it gets cold." Sipping the soup sitting in a hot tub was definitely a new experience. Being warmed with liquid on the inside and outside was certainly unique and very pleasurable.

When the bath and soup were finished we donned warm bed clothes and continued our meal in front of the fireplace. "Who do you plan to invite to your all-women's party?" Tallyn asked between bites.

"Any Ladies of the court or who are here visiting and their maids. A few of the women here in the castle that I have had the pleasure of getting to know will also be invited." I started thinking about desserts, wine and party games I would teach them all.

"So there will be no men? All night?" I blinked at him.

"That's correct. Why are you worried?" He shifted uncomfortably.

"For one, Lady Gabriella and her father will be back for the ceremony. She is less than fond of you. Two, it is a custom here that the night before a couple are bound, eligible men will present themselves to the woman for one last night of... consideration." His choice of words caused me to laugh.

"And do the women do the same thing for the groom?" He nodded. The effect was a sobering one. "Can I ask you to promise not to consider another woman?"

He smiled warmly. "I wouldn't, even if you hadn't asked." I relaxed at his words. When a yawn escaped me he leaned down and captured my mouth in a loving kiss. *You should go to bed and rest.* His thoughts felt like a caress on my mind.

Breaking the kiss I grinned and headed for bed. "Ok, but you should join me soon. I was very cold today so I may need you to be my Elf blanket tonight." He almost tripped rushing to extinguish the lights.

Chapter Sixteen

The next few days were a blur of planning, tasting, fittings and welcoming guests. It was finally the morning of the day before the binding ceremony and everyone in the entire castle was busy. Tallyn and I awoke early to Beni and Jess pounding on the door. The first glimmer of a lighter sky was barely visible at the horizon. Tallyn looked at the maids through a single squinted eye that glared at them angrily.

"Get out!" he barked, his voice sounding deadly.

Jess took a step, back out of the doorway, while Beni just pursed her lips at us. If I hadn't know his bark was worse than his bite, my reaction would have been to retreat. Beni would not be intimidated by his grumpiness. She marched to the side of the bed and with a tug on our blankets she sent them scattering to the floor.

"Time to get up you two. There is much work to be done and you will have guests to greet and entertain today, many of which will be arriving later this morning. You need to bathe, and be dressed and fed before they start pouring in. Once they start arriving you may not get much of a break."

Tallyn growled and rolled over, wrapping his arms around me. "You should get up and enjoy the bath before me. You have all the hair, makeup and women's layers to put on."

I pushed off of his chest. "Is this just so they will leave you alone for another half hour or so to sleep?" My voice was flat and irritated.

"Would I do that?" he asked trying to look innocent. He followed up with, "I'm just thinking of you."

I climbed over him to get off the bed. I hadn't even made it to the tub, which was already full of steaming water, when I heard him snore again. Rolling my eyes I sank into the sweet lily-scented water and let it seep into my skin. I was so dazed I didn't object when the maids began washing my back and hair.

Within an hour I was clean with my hair braided intricately and a small circlet adorning my head. Jess fussed over my makeup while Beni laid out my gown and the accessories I would be wearing for the day. I had a different gown for tonight's party, and of course my outfits for tomorrow. The sky had lightened considerably when Tallyn finally crawled out of the bed.

"Good morning sunshine!" I called out to him in a mock cheerfulness that I could see made him cringe. I smiled to myself, taking a certain amount of joy in the moment. Mumbling something about outlawing mornings if he was ever king he climbed into the steaming hot tub. I listened as the sound of the water lapping at the sides pierced the quiet of the room.

With my hair and makeup in order, I was shoved into a skintight shift with a skintight chemise laced over the top of it. Its color was a shimmering golden ivory. The silk felt like a fine lotion or oil against my skin - smooth and soft, clinging to my every curve. The outer dress was a deep burgundy trimmed in a thin gold braid. Its neckline dropped in a deep V almost to my navel, exposing the beautiful chemise there, and at the sleeves. The lacing down the back emphasized my narrow waist in relation to my hips and bust.

I stood looking in the mirror struggling to believe that the woman before me was actually me.

"Jess, you are a miracle worker." The younger maid blushed at the compliment.

From behind me there was a sharp sound of breath being sucked in quickly. "Lillian, you look amazing..." Tallyn's words trailed off as he stared at me awestruck. "If this is a small glimpse of what you will look like tomorrow I may have trouble waiting another day."

His words warmed me to my core. I had a million feelings but at that moment the only words I could find were, "Thank you." He nodded at me and disappeared into his closet.

When Tallyn finally emerged he wore pair of dark chocolate leather leggings with a matching undertunic and overtunic in the same ivory and gold fabrics. As he tugged on his boots Beni stood patiently holding a thin gold circlet for him as well. His long dark hair was pulled back with a thin piece of leather, allowing a few braids to hang free at his left temple. I tried to hide my smile but couldn't.

"You approve?" he asked, doing a little twirl so I could take it all in.

"Yes, very much so." I allowed him to take me in his arms and kiss me lightly at the words.

"Are you hungry?" He tipped his head to look into my eyes.

"Yes, but not for food. I have a sneaky feeling they won't let us go back to bed to sooth the hunger I'm experiencing." I looked around him to stare at the maids.

"No, you're probably correct, they most likely won't allow us to go back to bed. What about going downstairs and breaking our fast before the day becomes a never ending hell of smiles and ass-kissing?"

Jess jumped, obviously startled by his choice of words.

Walking arm in arm we made our way down to the great hall. Both Maerryn and the King were already at the head table eating. We went to sit with them, allowing kitchen workers to fill plates for us. When I finally saw James and Fairwynn step into the hall, I asked for them to be seated at the head table with us as well.

Fairwynn smiled widely at me. "Good morning! I love your gown, it's stunning." I blushed and thanked her.

"So, have you decided on what you are wearing tonight?" she asked. The other four men quickly fell into their own conversation, ignoring us.

I looked at them and rolled my eyes before answering her. "Yes, I'm wearing the purple gown with the gold sleeves. It's one of my favorites and surprisingly comfortable."

We exchanged knowing looks and laughed. "So, if it would please you, I would like to offer to be your Lady-in-Waiting for the next few days. I know there is a lot to do and while maids are wonderful, sometimes you just need a Lady to light a fire under people or save you from awkward social moments."

I grimaced. "You heard Gabriella will arrive today, didn't you?"

"Yes, but not to worry, I will be at your side to help defuse her." I actually felt myself relax a little at her words.

"Thank you! You have no idea how much better that makes me feel." She and I giggled knowingly and dug into the food before us.

"Oh, I can guess how you feel. I've had to mingle in the same social circle as Gabriella for over a hundred years." The tone in her voice conveyed just exactly what those years had been like.

I finished the last of my food and even had a chance to request a cup of tea to help settle my nerves before the hustle and bustle of my day could begin. Tallyn, Maerryn, King Naelym, James, Fairwynn and I were set up comfortably beside the fire to greet guests.

The first to arrive was an entourage of willowy thin Fae. Their wings glittered in the morning sunlight that poured into the hall from windows above. Tallyn and I greeted them with smiles. They seemed to hover just slightly above the ground, but their wings never moved.

A woman who looked barely in her teens stepped forward. "We are excited to hear that a Soul Mate has been found for your royal family once more. We have brought many gifts from the Fae to celebrate this grand occasion. Also, we bring word that the Fairy Queen Mab will be along tomorrow before the ceremony begins. She wants you to know she wouldn't miss it, but apologizes she will be late arriving."

I stepped forward and allowed the young-looking Fae to kiss my cheek. I wanted to reassure her. "Please rest assured we are honored to welcome the Queen whenever she is available to arrive. We understand that responsibility frequently must come before pleasure."

The Fae shifted nervously back and forth looking at me and then the King. "Oh, she has this diplomacy thing down. You are blessed to have such a new addition to your family."

The King laughed and took over the welcoming of the many Fae nobles that had arrived with the group. We made it a point to meet and greet each member of the party, including their servants.

When they had been escorted to their accommodations Fairwynn leaned over to squeeze my arm. "You handled that brilliantly." Tallyn beamed with pride.

In a moment of reprieve I sank into one of the high-backed chairs beside the fire and reached for my cup of tea. Its sweet strong flavor revitalized me and woke me up. "Mmmmm, I love this tea," I mumbled to myself.

Three more parties of various creatures arrived that morning. By the time the last ones were taken to an inn to settle, I was already exhausted. At some point during the morning Jess had arrived with a tray of cheese, meats, breads and dried fruit. I was quickly nibbling some sort of dried fruit when the announcement of the next set of guests came. I turned abruptly causing me to choke on my bite.

In a fluorescent pink dress Gabriella stood holding onto the arm of a person I assumed was her father.

The Lord approached us, offering a bow. Gabriella had a large smile on her face that turned my stomach. She looked far too happy for anything good to come of it.

I almost screamed when she threw her arms out to the side and yelled, "Lillian, you look beautiful.

Congratulations!" then hugged me. I stood stiff in her grip, staring terrified at Fairwynn, who looked just as scared and shocked as I felt.

When she finally let go of me I thanked her for the compliments and gladly passed and her father off to the King to speak to. Tallyn looked at me and shrugged. James, sensing the situation, quickly took the attention of Gabriella and personally saw her and her father to their chamber within the castle.

"I feel like I dodged a bullet," I said turning back to Fairwynn. She nodded but gave a knowing smile that encouraged me to not say any more. Knowing she was right I focused on snagging another bite or two before our next guest arrived.

Just before dinner another large party appeared in the great hall. When both James and Fairwynn raced forward, throwing their arms around the VIP's at the group's center, I knew their family had arrived.

When Fairwynn returned she held the hand of a woman whose smile was soft and inviting. Just looking at her dimples and large eyes I could tell she would be one of those women you hear described as a "cute little old lady" someday. "Lady Lillian, this is our Aunt Ethba." She looked over her shoulder at a man who looked just like an older version of James, only with a thick beard and deeper smile lines. "That's our mother's brother, our uncle Kenthur, King of the Dwarves." My jaw dropped.

"Two Kings in the same castle, one to be my family and the other family of my dearest friends in this realm. Truly, our ceremony will be blessed." I smiled warmly and didn't resist when Ethba pulled me into a tight embrace.

"Thank you for welcoming us and our family so warmly. I've heard only the most wonderful things about you." She leaned closely and whispered in my ear. "We also brought some of the best brew and entertainment for tonight." When she leaned back she gave me a sharp wink that warned of shenanigans.

Naelym and Kenthur embraced tightly in a bond that spoke of a long friendship of brotherhood. The queen soon joined them and all the "youngins" were left to see to the rest of the party. The Dwarves were so friendly, they reminded me of cousins and family you are always excited to see at the holidays. For a moment it made me long for my own family.

Once everyone was settled in and the tables in the hall could be set, dinner was announced. Every spare inch of the hall was crowded with people eating, talking, embracing and laughing. Never in my wildest dreams could I have imagined something like this. Fairwynn and I sat at the far end of the head table speaking with her aunt Ethba about the evening's plan.

"So an hour after dinner a bunch of the women are going to join you in the Prince's chamber for drinking, desserts, music and games, correct?" Fairwynn and I exchanged looks then nodded at her.

"We have some games from up north I think would be better for your last night as a single woman. Does Tallyn plan to have you under lock and key to keep you from other lads tonight?"

"I don't think so. Although, I promised him I planned a relaxing evening in. You know, with chocolate and girl talk." I nervously wrung my hands.

"And so you did lass, but as a queen I am overruling those plans and giving you a night to remember." The mischievous gleam in her eye told me I may not only miss sleep tonight, I would be lucky to be sober for the ceremony.

"Are you sure that a wild night is necessary? I mean, I want to be at my best tomorrow." I nodded as if to reinforce my decision.

"You do know what happens to you at a binding ceremony, right?" I shifted uncomfortably under her gaze but nodded.

"Good, they didn't keep you in the dark like they did me." I swallowed hard knowing that about her own experience. "We'll make sure that we keep you as relaxed as possible for the event." She smiled again. I looked from her to Fairwynn, then sighed heavily, resigning myself to my fate.

There was a sound of tapping on glass. When I turned to look at the King a hush fell over the great hall. He stood behind the table holding his goblet high.

"Friends and family, thank you for traveling great distances to come celebrate this momentous occasion with us. I will not keep you long from your festivities, as I have no doubt there will be no shortage of toasts tomorrow, but for now let's all drink to the happiness of my son Tallyn and his Soul Mate, my new daughter Lillian." There was a hearty cheer followed by the familiar clink of glasses, tankards and goblets around the hall.

Dinner was filled with stories and laughter, but before I knew it Jess was tapping me on the shoulder to leave the meal and go get ready for the party. I leaned over to kiss Tallyn on the cheek before I departed.

He captured my hand before I could go. "I love you. Have fun tonight and I will see you tomorrow." He gave my hand one last squeeze that sent warm tingles all through my body.

I hurried quickly away from the table with Jess, then up the stairs. When I reached Tallyn's large chambers I was surprised that it had already been decorated and was covered in food, sweets and every type of drink imaginable. Before I could sample a chocolate cupcake Jess and Beni were stripping me naked and redressing me quickly.

Once I was laced into my purple gown I was shoved down on a stool where Jess rearranged my hair up into a neat bun of braids. She smiled. "I figured you would want it up off your neck and out of your way."

I laughed. "You know me so well," I teased.

"Well, as your maids, we aim to please. May Beni and I be excused to go change clothes now?" she asked. I gave them a nod and fluttered my hand towards the door.

The door had just clicked shut when there was a knock. "Come in!" I called over my shoulder.

Fairwynn giggled behind me. "Are you ready for tonight?" I turned to face her, confused by a box she held.

"Ready as I'll ever be." I continued to stare at her mystery box.

"All of the women in attendance tonight have prepared gifts for you. This is mine, but you must wait to open it." I laughed but agreed. Her eyes glowed brightly as she took in the decorations and sweets surrounding us in the rooms. "Promise me, that should I ever have a binding ceremony, you will plan a lovely party like this for me too?"

"Absolutely. You have my word." I motioned for her to have a seat with me on the small sofa that had been pushed back against the outside wall to make more room available for guests.

We had about twenty minute before the guests started arriving. Many of the Ladies I had only met in the last day or two as they had arrived. Fairwynn was an excellent Lady-in-Waiting, helping me to keep each guest straight in my mind.

Before long I had a tower of gifts in the corner and most of the women had drinks in one hand and cupcakes in the other. Gabriella kept looking over at me and smiling in a way that made me very uncomfortable. When Fairwynn told me to have a seat on the sofa so we could open gifts, I watched with horror as Gabriella's eyes flared with jealousy as she looked over the pile. She sneered something and moved to the back of the group.

I leaned close to Fairwynn. "Can you take notes of what I got from whom? I want to make sure each person is thanked properly." She nodded, understanding my wish to not make a grand gesture of writing it down.

One by one I opened the gifts to find silk, jewelry, pottery, artwork, embroidery and dozens of gifts that a woman of this realm may need. At the end Fairwynn handed me the present she had brought with her. The box alone was amazing. Intricate metalwork fitted with a large sapphire on the front was held in place by a silver dragon.

When I lifted the lid to peek inside my heart skipped a beat. My cell phone was there, but its case was covered in scrolling glyphs. As I touched it, it glowed to life. "Fairwynn, you were able to fix it?" My eyes filled with tears as I threw my arms around her.

"Aye. It should work for you from here on out. If it seems to be getting weaker, set it in the window seat where it can get some sun." Her smile spoke volumes. I mouthed the words thank you again.

Standing up I looked around the room at all the smiling faces. "Thank you everyone, I am touched by your gifts and the outpouring of enthusiasm you have all shown me." I motioned to Ethba who sat just to my left in a chair. "Queen Ethba has planned some games and activities for us tonight. She will now fill us in on all that."

Ethba stood up, draining the last of what was in her tankard before addressing the crowd. "Just outside the gate to the inner bailey I have set up a series of games with prizes to entertain us and make us laugh. If you will all put on your coats and cloaks I will lead the way to the music and the rest of the festivities." With Jess's help I shrugged on my heavy wool cloak, smiling at the weight of it on my shoulders.

Quickly we all filed out of the chamber and down the large stone corridor to a back exit of the keep. Following a dirt path we arrived at a back gate which stood wide open and was illuminated by the light of many torches. When we arrived, the sounds of playful, energetic music stirred and hot mulled wine was passed out to us all. I laughed as the women scattered to a variety of games, all of them run by handsome young scantily clad men. I felt bad for them, considering how cold it was, but doubted the girls would let them freeze completely.

Beni smiled cheerfully while sipping her drink, watching as Jess, Fairwynn, Ethba and I went from game to game. On an archery game featuring small child-sized bows I won a few small sacks of that wonderful spice tea I had grown to love. At another game where you had to catch swimming fish in a pool with your bare hands I won a small pendant.

We were all having such a wonderful time that everybody missed when we were suddenly surrounded by Goblins in hooded cloaks. I wasn't sure how they got in, or when, but our night of fun erupted into a night of terror. There were screams and cries as we were set upon. As soon as I realized what was going on, I yelled for the women to head for the gate where there were guards stationed, then turned to look for the Queen and Fairwynn.

They were making a run for the gate, but sure enough there were two Goblins behind them. I ran as fast as I could and just as the Goblins reached them, I reached the Goblins. Throwing all my weight into it I tackled the nearest one screaming loudly as I yanked at its hair and clawed for its eyes. Fairwynn and Ethba turned to help, both joining in the brawl. I heard the alarm sound and knew some of the women had gotten to the guards, but that was the last thought I had as a sharp pain rang through the back of my head and the world went black. I heard Fairwynn scream my name as the darkness closed around me.

Lillian, Lillian answer me! Tallyn's voice rang in my head as I slowly returned to consciousness. I could feel his panic and anger. I tried to open my eyes but it hurt too much.

Tallyn?

Yes, love, where are you?

I processed his question slowly. If he didn't know where I was, it meant he hadn't found me yet. I became more aware of myself in the seconds that followed. I was sitting with my hands tied behind my back and my ankles bound together. Cautiously I opened my eyes to look around, opening one eye and then the other. I was in some sort of cell, the only illumination coming from a single torch overhead. Slouched against the other wall was another still form. I focused on it for a moment, then realized it was Fairwynn. I watched her closely and noticed her shoulders rising and falling.

"Good, she's alive," I whispered.

It was then the entire world rolled beneath me and the cell shifted with it. "We're on a ship," I said out loud. *Tallyn, Fairwynn is here but she's out cold. We're on some sort of ship, I can feel it moving...*

My thoughts were cut off as a familiar voice cut in. "Very good. You're smart enough to realize you're on a boat."

I looked in the direction of the voice but couldn't see anything. "Gabriella? Are you safe, did they knock you out too?" I waited for a reply but when the cackling sound of laughter came my stomach turned over inside of me.

"Here I give you credit for being smart and you go and ruin the thought before I hardly take another breath." The door to the cell swung open and Gabriella stepped in.

"Good of you to finally wake up. You've been out for hours." She looked at where Fairwynn still sat and sneered. "It figures."

"What's going on?" I demanded.

"Ah, now that sounds more like the tone befitting a princess." She gave me a sinister grin. "It's simple really. I've brought you here to kill you," she nodded at Fairwynn, "and brought her along to take the fall."

I blinked at her. "Is this about Tallyn? Why are you doing this?"

"You don't get it, do you? They were supposed to be mine. One of them, should be mine. I'm an Elf from one of the richest families in the realm. We control more than sixty percent of all the farming land in this Kingdom. I would be an excellent fit for either one of the Princes, but no, you just had to screw it all up." She threw her hands up before resting them on her hips. "And you, just keep refusing to die. Granted, I was surprised it was you and not Fairwynn, but still, why won't you just die?"

I didn't want to be the one to tell her she sounded like she had lost her mind, but I also knew the longer I kept her talking the longer I had for Tallyn to get here. *Please come soon my love, Gabriella has captured us and she plans to kill us.*

Why would she do that? he asked.

I don't know? Because bitches be crazy. Please hurry up, I am ready to be rescued.

"What? Nothing more to say to me?" she taunted. "I knew Tallyn felt some call from another woman. I could never get him to commit to me. I mean look at me, I'm perfect!" I resisted the urge to roll my eyes. Gabriella turned and glared down at Fairwynn. "I thought for sure it was her. She was always following Tallyn around ever since they were children. Maerryn dotes on her, and her Uncle is not only the King of the Dwarves but Tallyn's father's closest friend."

At this point, Fairwynn began to stir. "Oh, my head is killing me," she said as her eyes fluttered open.

"So good of you to join us, Fairwynn. I was just explaining to Lillian why I thought you were Tallyn's Soul Mate." The Dwarven woman looked up at Gabriella unimpressed.

"Are you daft?" she asked without any tact. "He's like a brother. That would be disgusting."

Gabriella threw back her head and a thick round of laughter rang out again. She spun on her heel to face me, pinning me with her crazed glare. "I called an Itheaga to kill his Soul Mate. When you returned from your little adventure dragging the creature's body I thought you had saved Fariwynn, not that it had been after you. It wasn't until that night with the dancing that I realized what was really going on. My father urged me to stay, but I wanted to leave so I could plan your death. You even managed to sweet-talk the Dragon Lord I sent after you."

Fairwynn turned to shoot me a look of shock. "You didn't tell me that happened!" she asked accusingly.

"Honestly, I didn't think it was that important. Sorry," I shrugged.

Gabriella, unable to stand not being the center of attention even for a moment, stamped her foot. I looked up at her. "We were in the middle of a conversation, do you mind?" In retrospect, tormenting the person who planned to kill you may not be all that wise.

"I do mind, but soon you will be quiet forever," she hissed.

Fairwynn looked back at me. "What is she talking about?"

"Oh, she's going to kill me and blame you. I could be wrong, but she will probably kill you too just so you can't tell the truth." Gabriella leaned in and kicked me hard in the ribs. I sucked in a deep, painful breath.

"Are you alright?" Fairwynn called. I tried to smile to reassure her. Her gaze turned angry as she looked up at Gabriella. "And just what do you hope to achieve by killing us?"

Gabriella's sinister smile was back again. "That's easy. I'll take the throne."

I laughed as I straightened, leaning back against the wall. "You'll never succeed."

"What do you know? I've known Tallyn longer than you've been alive. First he will be heartbroken over the loss of you, but I will be there to comfort him and he will grow to love me without the Soul Mate bond there to get in the way. Then once we are married, I will arrange for Rowena to bond with Maerryn. She's easy enough to control, she'll let me call the shots from behind the crown until she and Maerryn can be disposed of. The grief-stricken Kingdom will need my and Tallyn's strong rule to get them through the tragedy." She threw her head back and laughed again. It was like a bad episode of Scooby-doo.

Fairwynn snorted, suppressing laughter. "It will never work," she stated flatly.

"What do you know?" Gabriella stopped laughing.

"Many things actually. I know that Maerryn can't stand Rowena and would never agree to marry her. I also know Rowena has someone she loves who is already in talks with her father." Fairwynn shifted again, a determined and angry gleam in her eye.

"I also know that Tallyn will never marry or bond with you. If you kill his Soul Mate, you'll be lucky if he doesn't run himself through. Don't forget, my parents were Soul Mates. When my mother died, my father couldn't go on and even though he loved us he killed himself to be with her." I stared in shock at Fairwynn. That was such a horrible thing to have gone through.

"You're wrong!" Gabriella looked like she was seconds away from foaming at the mouth. I bit my lip to keep from chanting mad cow disease at her. "You'll see, I can save him."

If we were going to play the Torment-Gabriella game I was going to get in on it. "Ha! That's what all women think. A man will change for me, because I'm special. News flash sweetheart, men don't change unless they want to. He won't change just because you want him to."

"What would you know about men?" Her eyes were filling with rage as quickly as a shopping basket on Black Friday.

"Obviously more than you. I've been in love before. He wasn't a horrible person, but like you, I thought I could change him if I just loved him enough. Love doesn't work like that though. All that happens is you end up bitter." I laughed this time as the angry emotions came flooding back. "If it's not right, no amount of love or effort you put in will be enough. He will find someone else, and leave you broken."

My words seemed to do the trick because she screamed angrily and stormed from the cell, slamming the door behind her. I breathed a sigh of relief as I had half expected her to fling herself on me to hurry along my death. The wood of the cell around me shivered under the force of the slam.

"Thank heavens, I thought she would never leave," Fairwynn mumbled as she pulled her freed hands and the rope that had bound them from behind her back. She dropped the rope and began to untie her ankles.

"Funny thing about Goblins, they are fierce warriors but they can't tie knots worth crap." As soon as she was done she crawled over to me and made fast work of my own knots.

I breathed a sigh of relief. I lowered my voice to a soft whisper. "Now, shall we figure out how to get out of here?"

"Well if she plans to kill you, then we must either still be docked or close to shore, because she will want to catch me red-handed." She rolled her eyes.

"So, jump her or a guard, get out of the cell and get over the side of the ship so we can swim to safety?" I looked at her, she shrugged and nodded.

"It's as good as any plan I would come up with. Do you know how to swim?" she asked.

"Yes ma'am, been doing it all my life," I smiled.

"Excellent, it saves us having to hijack a boat to get to shore."

Just then there was a sound from outside the cell. Fairwynn and I quickly resumed our earlier positions to keep from giving away that we were free of our ropes, but nobody came. We sat there still and quiet for what must have been ten minutes.

"Where are they?" I asked her in a whisper.

"I don't know." she said quietly with a shrug.

"She seemed so determined to get rid of me, I thought she would be well on her way to doing just exactly that." There was nothing quite as rude as a homicidal villain delaying your death scene. We slumped against the walls, minutes passing like hours. "How long do you think this is going to take?"

Fairwynn grinned. "Maybe she broke a nail or stained her dress?"

"Dear lord, we'll starve to death forgotten if that's the case." Exchanging looks we both giggled. I closed my eyes and reached out for Tallyn again. *Are you there?*

Yes. You don't happen to know where you are, do you? His tone felt annoyed.

Nope, Gabriella isn't telling us too much. She left about fifteen to twenty minutes ago. I wasn't sure if that would help any.

She's here now, so at least we know you are within the Kingdom. Now to fan out and see where-all she could have come from between now and then. I smiled knowing Tallyn was coming for us. I looked at Fairwynn. "Tallyn is organizing a search party to find us right now. He said Gabriella just arrived, so we can't be too far from the castle."

She stared at me like I had horns growing from my head. "How do you know all that?" Her voice was confused and louder than a whisper.

In hushed tones I quickly moved to sit beside her. "Tallyn and I can feel and share our thoughts and emotions. We can also talk, telepathically." Now that

I was saying it out loud I understood why she thought I was crazy. "I know it sounds crazy, but really, we can."

She considered me for a moment. "Tell him to check Gray Cove. It's a ten minute ride to the castle but not connected to any of the local docks. When my Grandfather went to war with the Elves he hid at least a dozen ships there."

"When did the Elves and Dwarves go to war?" I couldn't help but ask.

"It happened around the time the gates to your realm were sealed. So maybe a thousand or so years ago. Certainly before either of us were born." She turned her head to look at the door.

Tallyn, Fairwynn says try Gray Cove. There was another sound from outside the cell, and before I could convey any more, three large Goblins burst into the small room. Along with them came a thick scent of something rotting and unwashed. My stomach lurched so much I almost tossed my cupcakes.

"Ah, there you are, pretty girls. We were told not to eat you yet, but the Lady Gabriella didn't say we couldn't have our way with you before we kill you." The largest of the trolls looked at us and licked his lips while rubbing his hands together.

The middle one looked at the tall one. "You go stand guard. When we're done you can have your turn." The tall one looked like he wanted to argue but he obeyed.

I glanced at Fairwynn who showed no signs of fear. I had to hand it to her. She was looking rape and death in the eye and she didn't look worried at all. She just stared at me intensely telling me what had to be done. When the talkative Goblin reached out, pulling me away from the wall I grabbed the ropes behind my back that had bound my hands. While he shoved my skirts up my thighs he didn't seem to notice my feet were no longer bound. He ripped open the front of my dress and I stared at him with anger. I wanted him to know he was going to die.

"What's wrong little girls, not going to scream for us? Maybe you like Goblins." He leaned down to bury his face in my cleavage. I turned my head and took action.

I pulled my arms out from behind me and flipped the rope around the Goblin's neck. Then, bringing my left knee up quickly under his arm, I used the momentum and rolled him onto his back, using both of my hands pulling in opposite directions to choke him. He clawed at the rope, making gurgling noises until he turned purple and his eyes rolled back in his head. As quietly as possible I stood up and pulled the rope free.

I snuck up behind the Goblin who had Fairwynn pinned. He had her arms pinned on either side of her and was leaning down to smell her hair. I snapped the rope around his neck and quickly yanked it closed, pulling back on him with all my strength. Fairwynn climbed to her feet and gave him a swift kick to the crotch. She pulled his long knife free from his belt and plunged it deep into his chest. The creature struggled to gather enough breath to scream, but couldn't before he died.

I let go of the rope and straightened. Fairwynn pointed to the door and I nodded in understanding. She pulled the knife free of its bloody resting place. I turned to look at my earlier victim to see if he had anything useful. My search proved useless. I looked around the room and found the ropes that had bound Fairwynn. "Better than nothing," I whispered.

I led her to behind the door then pounded loudly on it. As predicted the other Goblin raced in, already untying his pants. His eyes flared wide when he realized his friends were dead. Before he could turn around we both rushed him, knocking him to the ground. I took a sharp blow to the stomach but never loosened my grip on him. Fairwynn made quick work with the knife.

As we got back to our feet we looked at the open door. "Let me go out first," I said. "I'm a little taller, maybe they won't see you if they rush me first."

Fairwynn pulled a small axe free of the most recent Goblin victim and handed me the knife. "An axe is better for me anyway. You or me... it doesn't matter. Let's just get out of here."

I nodded and stepped through the door into a narrow corridor. For good measure, I pulled the door shut behind us. At the end of the corridor there was a set of steps that sounded like they led above deck. Sounds of drunken singing, fighting, and male fish stories surrounded us like bilge water on a sinking vessel. "Ugh, do we have to go out there?" Fairwynn asked.

"I'm not sure there is another way above deck. I'm not familiar with ships in this realm, but in my own it's not uncommon for there to only be one way out and one way in." A particularly off key note made me shudder. Taking my courage by the hand I was reaching for the door at the top of the stairs when we heard a half-gurgling scream. I jumped down the stairs and pulled Fairwynn with me behind them just as the door above us burst open.

We stayed still, huddled together behind the stairs while sounds of a battle raged on above us. A Goblin came staggering down the stairs, screaming, two crossbow bolts protruding from his back. He turned, panic in his eyes. When he saw us hiding there he took a step in our direction and another crossbow bolt plunged deep into his heart.

"Now is our chance. They sound distracted. It may be our best hope," I said cautiously. With a nod we darted around and up the stairs pushing through the door carefully.

The deck was teeming with Goblins, Dwarves, Trolls and all other manner of bipeds doing battle with one another. I looked around trying to figure out just what had caused this outburst and if Tallyn was at the heart of it, but a tug on my arm reminded me I needed to keep moving. Fairwynn and I had made it to the side of the ship unnoticed when a loud noise behind us served as the needed motivation to make the dive.

The water shocked my system as we collided. Its icy cold grasp forced me to fight with all my might against inhaling lungs full of the salty freezing liquid. When I popped above the surface I looked around for Fairwynn, frantically searching. With a sudden splash she breached the surface sputtering for breath. "Gods it's cold."

"Are you alright?" I asked her.

"I'll be better when we make it to shore and can find a way to dry off." She pointed to the shore and then I followed her lead as we made the swim.

With sand beneath me again I collapsed on the beach gasping for air. Before I could really rejoice in our freedom Fairwynn was over me holding out a hand.

"It's too cold for us to be standing about out here sopping wet. We need to either get somewhere safe and build a fire or find shelter where we can dry off."

"You're right!" I clasped her hand, glad for the help to my feet. I followed her past sand dunes and to a small rocky path. "Do you know where we are?" I asked her.

"I won't until we get up higher, but I think I was right about the cove." We climbed the steep, narrow path up the side of a cliff. When we reached the end she tugged me into the woods and put a hand over my mouth. We could hear someone speaking as they grew closer.

"What do you mean the Prince seemed to know where we were holding them?" Gabriella's angry question cut through the silence of the night.

"Gabriella, be sensible. If the Prince knows she is here, he knows you're behind it all. If we leave now, we can flee this realm and keep you safe." Gabriella's father pleaded with her for some sense of sanity.

"No!" She stomped her foot. "If I can't have Tallyn and the Kingdom, Lillian must still die. We need to go to the ship and see that it's done." Gabriella and her father moved to the path and made their way down towards the beach. We watched in silence from the cover of the trees.

I looked at Fairwynn, tugging on her hand this time. "If they're here, it means they must have horses tethered up somewhere." The light bulb clicked on and we made our way in the direction Gabriella and her father had come from. Sure enough, a short distance down the path we found two horses tied to a tree.

Making quick work of the knots we climbed on horseback and headed for the castle at a feverish pace.

Lillian, Lillian, I found the ship, where are you? Tallyn's concern rolled over me, causing me to all but glow with love. His warmth flooded my icy body.

We escaped. We're on horses headed back to the castle. I smiled as the flood of his relief filled me.

Woman, can't you ever let me rescue you? Get home, bar the door and stay safe. I resisted the urge to argue.

Fairwynn proved her ability to navigate and knowledge of the land because fifteen minutes later we were at the front gates of the mighty palace. "Hark, who goes there?" came a cry from atop the wall. I smiled, thinking it was funny to hear it used seriously and not in a bad historical movie.

"Lady Lillian and Lady Fairwynn, we have escaped our captors. Please open the gate." Moments later several large and well-armored men from the royal guard stepped through the door of the gate. Relief covered their faces as two of them helped us lead our horses into the gates and up to the stables.

One of the men held up his arms to help us down while sending another man with word of our return. "Will the Captain be along soon?" he asked.

"I don't know, I didn't really see him," I explained to the young man.

"So you and Lady Fairwynn escaped on your own?" He shook away the shock that threatened to spread across his features.

"I guess that shouldn't surprise me considering all I've seen and heard of you doing." I smiled, and thanked him for his assistance.

I turned right before we made our way to the great hall and called to him again. "Make sure all members of the guard are aware that if they see Lady Gabriella, her father or any other member of their party they are to be brought to me under escort. Do you understand?"

The man nodded. "Yes My Lady, but the treatment sounds a little discourteous for a Lady of the court."

"Not when her plan was to kill both Lady Fairwynn and myself in a play for the throne." I noticed that the guard paled a bit but made haste to leave with my orders.

Fairwynn waited for me by the doors to the Great Hall. "Are you ready for this?" she asked.

"Yeah, why wouldn't I be?" She laughed with a knowing smile I didn't quite understand. Together we pushed open the heavy doors and entered the Hall. Gasps came from all around and before I could take another breath we were surrounded by people asking us a million questions and hugging us.

I glanced at Fairwynn, who leaned close. "I'm not sure who I feel worse for, us or your Prince."

"Why do you say that?"

"Because to date you have saved yourself twice and taken down an Itheaga. A lesser man would feel more than a little threatened." I laughed at her statement as I turned it over in my head.

Tallyn had been this realm's Hero before I arrived. Now, I'm sure there were more than a few jokes about how he couldn't keep his woman safe and she had to save him. When I considered it, I thought myself lucky because he had never had a sexist thing to say about it, other than having been concerned for my safety.

Chapter Seventeen

Beni and Jess managed to beat their way through the throng of people and wrapped blankets around both of us. Ethba parted the crowd and led us to sit by the fire so we could warm up and get dry. "You girls look half frozen. The last day has been a nightmare."

"Day? How long were we unconscious?" I looked at Fairwynn who seemed as startled as I was. I looked around the room at the many concerned faces. Pulling the blanket tighter around me I stood to address them all.

"I'm sorry to have put you all through so much worry. I also apologize that the ceremony everyone came for must be postponed for a few days."

The King's rough voice cut in behind me. "We hope you will all enjoy our hospitality until my new daughter-in-law and son have recovered enough to complete the ceremony." He came to stand by me wrapping a warm fatherly arm around me.

I looked up at him. "This was the work of Lady Gabriella and her father," I whispered to him.

"Are you sure of this?" he asked.

"Yes. She's not really one for competition. Gabriella feels like she is entitled to a kingdom because of her family's role. Her plan was to get rid of me because I was distracting the prince." I squared my shoulders back. I couldn't imagine treason was taken lightly here.

Fairwynn reached over and touched my arm before addressing the King. "She speaks the truth, Your Majesty. Gabriella admitted it to both of us while she held us on a Goblin ship." The King stiffened noticeably but nodded.

"My ladies, I think you should both return to your chambers where you can clean up and get warm. I will see to it that food is sent to you both." King Naelym then turned and left the great hall. I didn't struggle as Beni and Jess led me out and up to Tallyn's chambers.

With the door closed firmly behind us the two maids made fast work of stripping away the tatters of my beautiful purple gown. I looked sadly at it. "Goodbye pretty dress, I will miss you." I waved in its direction as Beni threw the foul-smelling, bloodstained gown in the fire with a curse.

"Stop being so dramatic. I'll make you another like it next week. I still have the silk sitting in my fabric pile up in the sewing room."

"Sorry," I said looking down at my hands.

"Don't be sorry. Just don't be overly dramatic about a dress that can easily be replaced when your safety is far more important." I understood her tone and didn't disagree. She was right. "Come now, let's get you clean and warmed up."

I took a shower first to remove all the grime before settling into a warm, steaming bathtub. I think my favorite part of this realm besides a loving Soul Mate, amazing friends, a huge library of books I've never read, and all the new foods, had to be the amazing bathtub. Oh, how I loved this bathtub. I sat there stroking the walls of the bathtub.

Jess rushed in. "I'm sorry to disturb you - Lord Tallyn is home." I sat up quickly, reaching for the towel.

"Quick, help me dress." Jess gave me a hand out of the bath and helped me towel off. She held up a heavy velvet dressing gown, then stood back when I ran through the door barefoot with wet hair.

My feet beat against the cold stones underfoot as I almost flew down the stairs and pushed through the crowds. My breath caught as I saw Tallyn walk through the door dressed in his armor. He had a nasty looking injury on his right thigh and a cut above his eye that was still bleeding. Our gazes locked, he tossed his sword and helmet to the floor, and despite the grossness of his post-battle look we wrapped our arms around each other in a tight embrace.

"I was so worried," he whispered, stroking my hair.

"I know. I'm sorry I worried you." He shushed me and just held me close.

"Excuse me love birds, but have you seen Fairwynn?" I looked up to find Maerryn just as armored- and blood-covered as his brother.

"Yes, she's fine. She is probably in her chamber getting cleaned up." Maerryn and James, who stood behind us, both gave me a nod and quickly headed in the direction of the Dwarf lady's chamber.

The cheers of the crowd around us were forgotten now that Tallyn and I were together. It was as if the world stood still and nobody else was around. "I love you," I whispered.

"I love you too," he said, lowering his lips to mine. It was a kiss so soft and so loving that it caused tears to prick at my eyes. He kissed the tears from my cheeks.

"Go run a new hot bath. I need to speak with my father, then I will shower and join you there." His smile spoke volumes.

I left the hall without delay to set about my new chores. I tossed the dressing gown over the back of the sofa and ducked back into the bathroom. With the hot water refilling the bathtub and steaming up the room, I added in savory herb oils that made the water smell wonderful and left the body feeling relaxed.

I heard the door behind me click open then close. "Wow, that was really fast," I called over my shoulder. "Hurry up and take a shower then come slip into the tub. A nice hot bath will make everything better."

"I don't think so." The hair on the back of my neck stood up.

I didn't even have to turn around to know who was at my back. "How did you get in here, Gabriella?"

She laughed coldly. "It wasn't hard. This has been my home for several years now." Something cold and sharp pressed at my back. "Why couldn't you just die quietly?" she hissed.

"Rumor has it, it's just not my time." I winced as the blade pressed into my skin.

"It didn't have to be like this," she insisted. "If you had just died like you were supposed to, I wouldn't have to get dirty doing it myself."

"Gabriella, if you turn and walk out that door now, and swear never to come back, I promise not to come looking. However, if you make me choose between me and you, *I will* choose to save myself."

"Listen you little half-breed whore..." She never finished the sentence because I hopped over the side of the tub into the hot water and away from the blade. I whirled around to face her, stepping deeper and deeper into the water. If she wanted me, she was going to have to come in and get me.

She stared at me for a moment, then decided she wanted me dead more than she wanted to stay dry. So with one hand, she tried to hold her skirts up out of the water and with the other she charged in swinging a sword at me. Now, to her credit, she did have her Elven speed and strength behind the sword. On the other hand, we are talking about a woman who struggled with cutting her own meat at dinner.

I was able to sidestep her charge, thankfully. When she turned, I took advantage of the wet footing and shoved her. As expected, she stumbled, and dropped the sword. My hope was that she would look for it, but instead she turned and jumped on me, angrily pushing me face-first under the water. She pinned me to the bottom of the tub, both her hands on the back of my head. My lungs were burning from holding my breath.

I abandoned the idea of removing her hands from my head. Instead I pulled my knees under my body and with a burst of strength pushed up out of the water. As soon as my face broke the surface I sucked in a deep breath of air then began the battle against her. On my knees now, I brought my elbow back swiftly into her gut, the pivoted, grabbing her hair and dragging her down face-first into the water. She struggled against me, throwing all of her strength at me. I captured her closest arm and used it as leverage. When I felt her choke a little I pulled her head back allowing her air. "Knock it off. I don't want to kill an unarmed, untrained assailant."

"Rot in hell!" she screamed, flailing at me. I dunked her head back under the water. It was then I realized I wasn't alone in the room.

"That's enough!" a woman's voice bellowed. I grabbed Gabriella's head and pulled it out of the water.

I let go of the obnoxious Elf, suddenly very aware of my nakedness. I stepped out of the tub and quickly grabbed a dry sheet and wrapped it around myself. "Guards, take that woman into custody." I looked at the older woman whose face rang with a note of familiarity.

"You're the shop owner. The one that sold me that beautiful gown. How did you get here?" I stood confused as she smiled at me. A paunchy cat rubbed against my legs before jumping up into the older woman's arms. I recognized the cat.

"Your cat!" I pointed at it. "You had it at the store. It protected me from an Itheaga attack in the closet."

"Did he?" Her smile broadened as if she knew a secret I didn't.

"Yes, he did, but how did he get there?" I was so confused. If the realms were sealed, then how did he get back and forth?

"Oh, Sheldon here gets around, dear. Most of the time he stays with his own pet back in your realm, but every so often he does favors for me, or just comes to visit."

"How does he get back and forth between the realms?" I tried to keep the shock from my voice.

"Magic, dear, how else?" Her matter-of-fact tone told me it was old news.

Tallyn pushed through the throng of people. "What's going on here?" he demanded.

"Oh nothing we couldn't handle, lad. Calm down, your Lady is safe and sound." The woman's voice was motherly.

When Tallyn saw her, he dropped to one knee. "Your Majesty, thank you for your assistance."

She beamed down at him. I looked back and forth between the two. "Your Majesty?" I asked out loud without meaning to. The shop woman took one look at my face and burst into laughter. "I'm sorry I don't think I get the joke."

Tallyn stood up beside me. "Lady Lillian, may I present to you Queen Mab. The oldest and wisest of the Fae."

I laughed again. "Oh, honey, I think you're mistaken. This is a very sweet shop lady from my realm, although I'm thinking now she may be some sort of a witch. She's got a magical cat," I said, pointing at Sheldon in her arms.

Tallyn turned pale. "I'm sorry, she's new here and sometimes doesn't realize..." The queen held up her hand to calm him.

"She speaks the truth, lad. In her realm I have a very special shop. I enjoy playing Fairy Godmother from time to time." She smiled softly as she turned to me. "And here, I am the Fairy Queen."

"I didn't just get a Fairy Godmother, I got Queen Mab for my Fairy Godmother. Score!" I threw my hands up at the last part of the statement. She chuckled as Tallyn just seemed to pale more.

"I was passing by when I heard the struggles in here, so I opened the door to investigate."

She took a deep breath, casting a glance in Gabriella's direction. "And you, you tried to kill two highborn ladies today. You'll spend a night in the dungeon and then I will conference with the Dwarves and Elves and we will decide your punishment. Take her away." The guards left, dragging Gabriella from the room. The hatred in her eyes burned brighter than ever as she glared at me.

"Thank you!" I said, stepping forward and hugging the older woman. I could feel everyone's eyes bugging out as I did it, but the Queen just hugged me tightly and laughed merrily.

"You two should get cleaned up and go to sleep. You have a big day tomorrow," she added as she turned to exit.

"I think the plan was to postpone it a day or two until everything has been resolved," I mentioned.

"As you wish my dear. I will see you in the morning. I have a very special set of gifts for you. Come find me after you eat," she called over her shoulder.

Tallyn and I opted for a shower then dressed for bed. Before I could rest though, he insisted I get checked out by Grelyem. "She looks healthy to me," the old Dark Elf commented. He eyed Tallyn's still bleeding wound. "You, on the other hand, need stitches."

"I'll be fine. Did you check the bump on the back of her head?" Tallyn pointed the elder back in my direction.

"Turn around my dear. I fear if I don't check you over with a fine-tooth comb, your Prince may not let me stitch him up so he doesn't bleed to death."

I gasped, then turned to glare at Tallyn. "You hear that, you could bleed to death! I'm fine, you should get some stitches." Grelyem's hands parted my hair and I could hear him clicking his tongue. "What?" I asked.

"You have black and blue marks all over you and a knot the size of my fist on the back of your head. They really clobbered you good. You feel fine now, but tomorrow isn't going to feel very nice. I recommend getting plenty of rest tonight and tomorrow. Make sure to drink plenty of water. I will prepare a tea to help prevent blood clots."

He shifted back to Tallyn. "Now for you, Sire."

Tallyn, exasperated, flung himself back on the bed. "Really, I swear I'm fine."

"Relax, Sire, you want to be at your best for the Binding Ceremony, don't you?" Tallyn stiffened and stopped fighting. Soon he was stitched and bandaged.

"Now off to bed with both of you. Take your morning meal in here and join us after you are properly rested." We both nodded and bid him good night.

Snuggled beneath the sheets and blankets Tallyn ran his hands over me. "What are you doing?" I asked playfully. "You're supposed to be resting."

"I can't sleep until I check every inch of you to make sure you are truly alright." He rolled me over and looked deep into my eyes. Tears streaked his perfect cheeks. "Don't ever scare me like that again. When you didn't respond that first day I was afraid you were dying somewhere, or that you were frightened and used the chance to run away." He sobbed into my shoulder. "I was so worried I had lost you."

"Hey, I'm alright. I'm here and fine." I reached out and cupped his face in my hands. "I'm not going to leave you. You're stuck with me." I smiled and wiped away the few tears that ran down his cheeks. I was reminded of the story Fairwynn had told about her parents. As Soul Mates they just couldn't go on without each other. I really understood now. Tallyn would have given up if I were dead. I pulled him close and held him tightly.

The night passed and it was late morning before either of us woke up. The sun was already high when I opened my eyes. Tallyn rested peacefully beside me. I sat up and grabbed for the bed when the whole world shifted. Grelyem was right, today was going to suck. I tried again, glancing slowly around the room. Jess or Beni had brought us food and left it on the small table. I climbed out of bed, careful to avoid Tallyn's injuries.

I sipped on the tea that was now cold, then enjoyed some buttered bread. It was sweet and fresh, making my mouth water more. Before I knew it, I had eaten four slices of bread with butter, an apple, a large hunk of soft cheese, two pickles, and consumed an entire pot of tea.

"I guess I was really hungry," I mumbled to myself.

I pulled a chemise on over my shift then pulled on a heavy jumper over that. I combed my fingers through my hair and quickly braided it. I slipped my feet into a soft pair of leather slippers and quietly stepped out into the corridor.

"Tallyn, keep sleeping," I whispered into the door. Ignoring the throb in my head I went to look for Queen Mab.

The great hall was quieter than I had expected. Very few people were around. I caught sight of one of the guards from the night before and made my way over to him. "Good morning," I chirped.

Then man bounded to his feet. "Good morning, My Lady. I trust you are on the mend?"

"I am, thank you. I seemed to have consumed all the tea, cheese and so forth that was sent up for me. If you happen across a kitchen maid before I do, can you have more food sent up for your Captain?" The man nodded. "Oh, and do you know where everyone is?"

He stared at me for a moment, processing my words. "Each Kingdom is hosting refreshments in their Royal's chambers. The King is in his Solar. The Dwarves are in the West chambers and the Fae are in the East, near my Captain's chambers."

"Just further down the corridor?" I asked.

"Yes, you'll know it when you see it. There will be a dozen or more Fae and lots of flowers. Queen Mab always has her chambers decorated with lots and lots of flowers." I almost laughed at the glum way he said that.

"Thank you." I smiled and went off in search of the queen.

Sure enough, the guard had been right. It was very easy to find. The closer I got, the more the corridor smelled like roses. When I arrived at an open door I peeked at the many people inside. Knocking on the door frame I stepped into view.

"Come in, Lady Lillian," Mab called from behind several people.

I wove my way through the Fairies and the flowers, taking the seat beside her. "Thank you," I said.

"How are you feeling, dear?" she asked, pouring me a cup of tea.

"I have the worst headache I've had in years, my whole body is covered in bruises and aches but other than that I feel wonderful. Gabriella has been captured, Tallyn came home safe and Fairwynn did as well. I can't ask for much more." I took a sip of the tea. "All is well in the world."

"I see. Is there nothing else that would make this all better?" she asked. Her mouth turned up in a mischievous smile.

"Not that anyone can change, no." I answered.

"Oh my sweet child, don't underestimate what I or even you can do." She turned and motioned for someone to come over. A Fairy appeared carrying my blue ball gown and accessories.

"Please wear it for your party after the binding ceremony. I know you have a dress for the ceremony and claiming, but please do give life to this beautiful dress. I made it as a gift for my great-great-great granddaughter-in-law when she married into the family. Only, because of politics she never wore it, and left England for the United States."

"That must have happened a lot. My mom's parents did that." I looked at the dress and smiled widely. "I do love this dress." I said as I ran my fingers over the bead work. "I would be honored to wear it."

She smiled. "Of course your grandparents did, your grandfather was my great-great-great grandson. Your grandmother was the one I made the dress for."

I almost spit out my tea. "Wait a minute. I'm your granddaughter?"

"Yes, dear," she said reaching out to pat the back of my hand.

"I'm related to THE QUEEN MAB!" I took a deep breath, still in shock.

"Yes, dear. I also have another surprise for you." She motioned again for someone to come forward. I wasn't sure how many more surprises I could take in one day.

"Hello sweetheart! I've missed you so much." I looked up, frozen in the moment. There, with her auburn hair and blue eyes, stood my mother. Pain and dizziness be damned I threw myself off the chair and into her arms.

"Mom! I've missed you too. Where's Dad? What does he think of all of this?" I leaned back then hugged her again.

"Your father is here but he's a bit... glamoured. There are parts of what's going on we aren't mentioning. He thinks we're in Europe and everyone is Human." She shrugged, wearing the same mischievous smile I had seen the Queen wear moments ago.

"I'm not sure I condone you lying to Dad, but I don't really care right now because you're both here." I turned and smiled at the Queen. "Thank you. I've missed them so much."

"It's nothing, child, and once the ceremony is over I can take you and Tallyn out to unseal the portals. Then you can freely visit each other as you see fit." Once again I found myself hugging the Queen. Everyone held their breath but she wrapped her arms around me and squeezed affectionately.

"It's been a long time since one of my grandchildren showed me any affection. I'm afraid I'm a little out of practice." She took my hand and motioned for my mother and me to sit down.

"Your brothers are off flirting with girls. I'm sure they will wander back at some point." Mom picked up a cup of tea and took a sip.

"Do they know what we are?" I asked, afraid of the answer.

"Heavens, yes dear. They are half of this realm too. After you made me realize I had made a mistake I sat them down and explained everything. When they found out where we were going they insisted on coming too." It didn't surprise me in the least that my brothers had come along. We have always been close and they have adventurous spirits.

There was a knock on the door. I turned to see my brothers come in with a tall man in a kilt. He had long dark hair that fell nearly to his waist and wore heavy motorcycle boots with thick wool socks peeking out over the top that drew attention to his legs. His face was handsome but looked sad. Tattoos covered his shoulder, and down the side of his body I recognized the binding brand of a mate.

My brothers rushed forward to hug me. They were sweaty, and smelly and big, just like my favorite puppies growing up. Matt, my baby brother who was the size of an Ogre, leaned back and motioned to the man who entered with them.

"This is Ian MacGregor. He's the son of Cariss, who happens to be a Chieftain of Werewolves up in Scotland. He doesn't really have an accent though. It's really sad." Matt actually looked pouty.

I extended my hand to Ian and he just looked at it. I withdrew it slowly. His voice was thick with an edge of sadness. "Congratulations on finding your Soul Mate. It's a special bond that few will ever share. I am here on behalf of my clan. We have worked a long time with your Uncle and I was sent as a representative." He looked at my brothers and his face brightened a bit. "Your brothers remind me very much of my own family. They are a welcome change from the pageantry and boredom that are frequently part of these celebrations."

"Thank you for coming. Will your mate be joining us?" I asked, eyeing the branding down his side.

He stiffened considerably. "No, I lost her and my sons a few years ago." My heart broke seeing the pain that flickered across his face.

"I'm sorry. It must be hard coming to these types of functions." I reached out and took his hand, giving it a squeeze. My older brother, who was just as tall as Ian, patted his shoulder and gave it a reassuring squeeze.

"Have your brothers always been this big?" Ian asked, eyeing them both. "Normally neither Humans nor Fae get this big." I laughed along with them.

"Mom fed them Miracle Grow with their formula." We all laughed again. "If there is anything I can do to help make your stay more comfortable, please let me know. I know what it's like to be far from family."

He thanked me politely then disappeared off with my brothers. I was just settling into my seat again when there was another knock at the door. I turned to look that way and my heart immediately started to race. There stood Tallyn, handsome as ever. I waved to him and he stepped in.

I rose to wrap my arms around him when he approached. "I woke up and you were gone," he said, hugging me closely.

"You were sound asleep. I figured it was better to let you rest. Besides, I had to go find someone to take you more food - I ate almost everything. I was very hungry this morning." I beamed up at him. "Oh, there is someone I want you to meet. Actually, there are a couple someones, but only one of them is here right now." I turned to face my Mom. "Tallyn, this is my Mom. Mom, this is Tallyn."

"How is this possible?" To his credit he didn't struggle when my Mom reached out and hugged him, then welcomed him to the family.

"Grandma brought her. She brought my Dad and brothers too. I'll introduce you all later." The queen chuckled softly behind me at the use of Grandma.

"Grandma? Your Grandmother came as well?" he asked with an astounded tone.

"Of course I came. I would have come if it had been just you, but because it's Lillian too, it meant I had to bring several cartloads worth of presents for your celebration." She never looked up from her needlework but the smile was still there, and hard to miss.

"You're the granddaughter of Queen Mab?" He stumbled back a step.

"Technically, I'm the great-great-great-great-great granddaughter of Queen Mab, but I'm going to go with

Grandma. It's a lot easier to say." I smiled and pulled him down to sit beside me.

"Does my father know?" he asked Mab.

"No, I thought it would make for entertaining dinner conversation tonight. I wonder if his eyes will pop out of his head. Your family has been trying to plan a binding between our houses for centuries." She snorted a cheerful laugh at the idea.

"He's going to be stunned," he whispered.

"I sure hope so. He's been rather boring the last day or so with all his worrying." She shrugged. "Now, you must promise me, young Prince, that when you two have children, you will raise them with me as a grandmother. I have missed out on the lives of so many of my offspring. I rather like this girl, so you had better keep her happy." She leaned over and patted him on the knee. There was no missing the warning there. All I could do was laugh.

After a few hours I bid everyone a good day and asked to be excused. "I'm really worn out and want to get some rest before dinner and the judgment for Gabriella. I want to be as fair as possible and the more tired I am, the crankier I get." I waved good bye and departed.

Tallyn escorted me back to our chambers. "Are you really going to rest?" he asked.

"Yes, what else did you think I was going to do?" I playfully pushed him in the shoulder.

"I don't know. Get kidnapped, slay a dragon, or rescue a fair maiden.... Something dangerous that will send me to an early grave with worry." His tone said he was teasing but his eyes denoted real worry.

"I was going to lay down and take a nap. Maybe you should nap with me so I don't do any of those other things." I leaned up on my tiptoes and pressed my lips against his.

"Mmmmm, yes, I think I should stay and keep you out of trouble." He followed me into the chambers and helped me peel down to my shift. I quickly climbed into bed and he soon joined me.

I awoke with Tallyn lightly caressing my neck. "Wake up sleeping beauty. It's dinner time. We wouldn't want to miss the show, would we?" he asked playfully. With his help I redressed and re-braided my hair.

With all the visiting royals, Tallyn, Maerryn, James, Fairwynn, my brothers, Ian, Rowena and I were all put at what I lovingly called the "kiddie table". Ian and my brothers laughed at the joke but nobody else got it. I shrugged it off. Dinner was pretty quiet overall. Lots of friendly conversation, excellent food and of course all the toasts from people there to celebrate. Nothing, however, will top dessert.

We were quietly sitting there eating cupcakes (which the chef was now obsessed with making) when there was a loud curse from the high table. We all turned to watch.

"What are you talking about, Mab?" Tallyn's father demanded.

"Just that you had best be good to my Granddaughter and let me have equal time with my future grandchildren." Queen Mab remained seated. Her face gave away no sign that she was anything but calm.

"What granddaughter?" he demanded.

"Lillian, of course." She pointed me out.

The King's eyes flew to me. His brows lifted high. "Lady Lillian, did you know about this?" he demanded.

I stood, popping the last bite of cupcake in my mouth as I did. He stared at me expectantly but I held up my hand so I could finish chewing. "Sorry about that. I only found out this morning, Sire." I cleared my throat. "Grandma asked me to allow her to tell you."

The King sank back down into his chair silently. I did the same. Tallyn leaned close while Maerryn shook with silent laughter. "Nobody shocks our father like that. Priceless!" Tallyn pressed his lips against mine.

After dinner was finished, everyone at the high table, along with Tallyn, Maerryn, James, Fairwynn and I all went to the King's Solar. The room was warm with a large fire glowing in the low light. Maerryn made a motion with his hand and the room brightened considerably. I sat with my mother and Tallyn along the large table at the back of the room.

When Gabriella and her father were brought forward the room was hushed. Her father stepped forward and dropped to his knees before the king. "As a father to another father, please punish me, but spare my daughter."

Queen Mab rose and stepped forward. Turning, she addressed Gabriella. "Young Lady, do you realize that you committed acts of treason against three Royal Houses? When you thought to kill Lady Lillian, you wanted to snuff out MY grandchild, his mate and their niece." She motioned to all of us who had been affected by Gabriella's plan. "The punishment for treason is public execution, are you aware of this?"

Gabriella's father burst into heavy sobs. Gabriella on the other hand, showed no remorse. "For years the royal families have picked exactly who they wanted on the throne. My family has supplied this Kingdom for centuries with the fruits from our fields and people. I deserve to sit on the throne and be called Princess more than any half-blooded whore!" she shouted.

I looked at Fairwynn, who gave me a nod telling me to go ahead. Slowly I rose from my seat and walked around the table. I approached the royals where they stood before the accused. "May I say something?" They all appeared surprised by my request but motioned for me to speak.

"I believe death is too kind. She endangered people I care about in her constant pursuit to destroy me. I would ask if possible some sort of magical imprisonment and permanent banishment from her home and family. I know firsthand how painful that can be." I turned and looked at Gabriella. "It's my wish that you live for a long time, alone, knowing that I live happily. Knowing that Fairwynn lives happily. I want you to go to sleep at night thinking about how you failed in your quest for greed, and if I ever see you again, I will slay you where I showed restraint and mercy before." She paled at my words.

I knelt beside her father. "Children make mistakes, but parents are there to guide them. I know you tried to get her to flee when things started falling apart, but you should have kept her from doing it in the first place. Your life would be wasted if we ended it. I would request to the royals here that this man be stripped of his title, given a home on the outskirts of one of the kingdoms and allowed to live out the rest of his days without the privileges a title brings."

The man's face softened when he looked into my eyes. "Thank you for trying to spare my daughter," he whispered.

I turned to face my soon-to-be father-in-law, my grandmother, Kenthur and Ethba. The four exchanged looks and shrugged. Kenthur leaned forward and looked at Fairwynn. "What say you to these terms? Would you feel justice was done?"

Fairwynn stood and looked at Gabriella. "Lock her in an old Magic Mirror. That way she can watch life happening without her."

Kenthur looked at the others. "We will accept these terms and allow her to keep her head."

Queen Mab stepped forward. "Gabriella, you have been found guilty of treason across three kingdoms of this realm. Your punishment will be to live out the rest of your days in a Magic Mirror." With a crack of lightning the room flashed and Gabriella screamed, a blood curdling sound. There was a puff of smoke where she stood and in her place was a small, round, golden mirror. "So it is done."

Gabriella's father was removed from the solar and the mirror sent to the vault for safe keeping.

"Now what?" I asked.

"Now, you two go get some sleep. You have a big day ahead of you tomorrow. Morning will come far too early," my mother explained.

I started to argue but thought better of it considering our present company. I turned and offered a bow to the monarchs. "I guess I will be taking my Mate and heading off to bed. I will see you all tomorrow. Thank you for your mercy."

"Like you said, death would have been too easy." James corrected from across the room. "Plotting to kill my sister and my friend, then to think she would use and discard Row like that. She deserves what she got and more." He stormed out still muttering.

I turned and looked at Fairwynn. "Who's Row?" I asked.

She smiled. "My brother has loved Rowena since we were children and she has always cared for him as well." It all clicked into place - the things she had said on the ship.

I looked at Maerryn as I left the Solar. "Can I talk to you? Sister to brother?" Tallyn nodded and went along ahead of me. I took Maerryn's arm when he offered it. As soon as we were out of earshot and headed up the stair in the great hall I stopped him. "How do you feel about Fairwynn?" I asked bluntly.

He paused. "I'm very fond of her and have been for a long time. I backed off because I knew she liked Tallyn and would rather see her happy with him. Now that he's out of the picture maybe she will give me a chance." He smiled that secret smile, the one that warms your cheeks when you are thinking of someone you care for.

"What if I told you it has always been you?" He looked at me funny, not understanding. "She knew you were always busy because you were the first born son, so she would follow Tallyn around all the time drilling him for information and stories about you. She thinks of Tallyn as a brother." I began walking up the stairs again but Maerryn didn't move.

"I think you are wrong, Lillian," he said, his face flickering with pained emotions.

"I'm not. She and Tallyn have both told me as much." I stroked the back of his hand. "If I get through this ceremony tomorrow I will personally approach

Fairwynn and her family about a binding of your own. If you're interested?" I grinned the best devilish grin I could.

That's all I had to say. Maerryn picked me up in a crushing hug and spun me around there on the stairs. "You, Lady Lillian, may be the best little sister in the history of sisters." With that he walked me back to Tallyn's chambers and bid us both good night.

As I shut the door Tallyn came over to help me out of the gown I wore. "He was in a good mood."

"He should be," I told him as I slid out of the wool gown. "I told him after the ceremony was settled I would approach Fairwynn and her family about their own binding ceremony. I'm pretty sure he likes me more than you now." Tallyn laughed as he tugged the outer chemise off over my head.

"Go get into bed, I'll be there soon. I just want to clean my cut and change the bandages. Then I will be right in." I slapped him on the backside as he turned to walk away.

He joined me in bed shortly thereafter, pulling me into a spoon against his body. "This is pretty darn close to heaven," I said as the call of sleep wove its spell over me.

"That it is, my love. That it is."

Chapter Eighteen

When I woke up the next morning Tallyn was already gone, but on his pillow sat a small wooden box. My name was carved into the top of it. I ran my fingers lightly over the indentation. Looking around to make sure I was totally alone I opened the box. Inside there was a small golden bracelet. The strands of gold were delicate and twisted back and forth around each other. I slid the cuff on my wrist. It glittered in the sunlight. At the bottom of the small box there was an inscription carved.

"Two hearts made forever one"

I slid the cuff off my wrist and back into the box before heading to the shower. I wasted no time in scrubbing my hair and body. When I stepped out Beni and Jess were there waiting for me, both dressed to the nines in green silks. I smiled at them before they descended on me like birds of prey.

First I was laced into the underdress that looked and felt like I was wearing nothing. My skin just seemed to shimmer with a purple and blue sheen. Then the vivid aqua blue velvet dress was laced on. As promised, the V at the front was deep, showing the shimmer of the Fairy Silk below. The sides were fully open with a thin silver thread laced between them, causing it to hug me tightly. The last components of the gown were the heavy thick sleeves that were tightly laced onto my upper arms. The sleeves trailed down almost to the floor. The blue velvet on the outside and Fairy Silk on the inside were covered in fine silver and gold embroidery and beading. I was fixated on running my fingertips over the patterns.

"Lady Lillian, please have a seat so we can prepare your hair and makeup." Beni guided me to a wooden stool where she pushed me down to sit. I watched in the mirror as the two women pulled and braided my hair in a variety of directions. When it was done my hair was secured in a high bun made up of probably one hundred little braids. Beads and gems were then stitched into the bun and surrounding hair.

My face and shoulders were powdered with a fine dust the looked like it had been made from pearls. Then without warning Jess painted silver markings down the back of my neck and along the tops of my brow bones. "What do these markings mean, or are they just decoration?" They looked like Elven Script but I couldn't quite make it out.

"They are prayers for a happy life." She smiled.

"Ah, thank you." I glowed warmly back at her. "All I need now is my jewelry and I'm good to go."

On cue Beni stepped forward and secured my necklace. She pulled out a small crystal headband that looked like something from my own world. Beni must have sensed my fascination with the item because her next words answered my unasked question. "Your mother brought it with her. I thought you may enjoy wearing it today."

"It's beautiful." I smiled.

"My Lady, you are the definition of beauty today. Our Kingdom is blessed," the older woman said with a tear in her eye.

"I'm not the definition of beauty every day?" I asked. "Why is your Kingdom only lucky today? What about the days I saved Tallyn or defeated the Itheaga?" I had to bite my lower lip to keep from giggling.

The older woman became pale and started apologizing. I bust out in a fit of laughter then stood to hug them both. "I was teasing, Beni. Thank you, you have done an excellent job of making this sow's ear into a silk purse. I'm sure Tallyn and everyone else will be thankful for your hard work."

"We should get going so we can escort you to the temple," Jess spoke up.

"Temple?" I asked, then shook my head knowing I would figure it out soon enough. "One moment, then we can go." I rushed into the sleeping area and pulled on the cuff Tallyn had left for me. I then pulled out a small bag I had worked on during needlepoint chatter. It had Tallyn's crest on it, which I had spent hours on and lost much blood trying to recreate. Inside I had tucked my ring from home on a cord. I had wanted to have something more grand made for him but life just sort of happened. It was one of the few things I had brought with me of any meaning or importance. I tucked it into my dress and stepped back out. "Ok, I'm ready to go."

When I stepped into the corridor three men-at-arms stepped forward with a large gray cloth. Beni and Jess also took sides of it. "It is to veil you from view until we arrive at the Temple of our Ancestors. Don't worry, I'll help direct you on where to go until we get there," Jess chirped happily.

Ok, I learned some valuable lessons today as we walked through the castle and out to the Temple. One, trying to walk while surrounded by a curtain sucks. Two, Jess sucks at directions. I was incredibly happy when we finally arrived.

"Are you ready?" Jess asked.

"As I'll ever be." I stopped. "You don't have any fruit or anything do you?" I heard her eep.

There was a mutter back and forth whispers. Finally Beni leaned in. "I'm sorry, we totally forgot to feed you. I will make sure there is something for you between the ceremony and branding."

I shivered at the thought of the branding and thanked her. It was then some sort of music sounded and the veil was dropped. I looked around at the inside of a building that was as white as shell and stood almost to the sky. Light flooded the Temple from every angle with candles and sun uniting to make the place feel like we were standing within the clouds.

When I looked to the right, there stood Tallyn, dressed to kill. His own clothes had been made to match my own. When he extended his hand to take mine he noticed the cuff and smiled at it. "Do you like it?" he asked.

"It's beautiful." I squeezed his hand warmly. Quietly he lead me down the center of the grand temple to a raised platform at the front where his father stood along with several men and women all dressed in white, whom I guessed led the Temple.

The King's voice was deep, mellow and welcoming. "What is your intention here today?" he asked Tallyn.

"To bind myself forever to my Soul Mate," he responded. It was then I realized I had no clue what I was supposed to say.

"Do you both come here of your own free will?" we were asked by one of the men in white robes.

"I do," I responded.

Tallyn answered with a simple "yes."

King Naelym looked at us both closely. "Then speak from your hearts and go on with my blessing." At these words the King stepped off of the platform and went to sit down. A man and a woman stepped forward. One was holding a dagger and the other was holding a chalice of wine.

Tallyn took the dagger in his right hand, pierced his fingertip, and made a small cut on the palm of his left hand. He did these actions slowly and deliberately so I could follow along. Turning, he dripped the drop of blood from his finger into the chalice. "I, Sir Tallyn of Vesaria, bind myself to you, Lady Lillian." He handed me the dagger, forcing me to take it in my left hand.

I pierced a finger on my right hand and made a small cut on the palm. The man who had held the dagger stepped forward to take it back. I leaned forward and squeezed a drop of my own blood into the chalice. "I Lady Lillian of.... not here, bind myself to you, Sir Tallyn." I heard a swarm of amused chuckles run through the crowd that was watching.

Tallyn beamed at me, his own amusement lighting his eyes. He reached out and took the chalice, offering it to my lips. "From this day forward we will drink of the same cup, shelter below the same roof and bind our lives together forever." I took a sip of the wine. It was sweet and as I swallowed it I felt as if a fiery warmth ran through my veins and made me glow from the inside out.

I took the chalice, holding it to his lips, smiling. "From this day forward we will drink from the same cup, shelter below the same roof and bind our lives together forever." I handed the chalice back to its bearer when he had taken his sip. He held out his left hand to me, blood covering his palm. I placed my right hand in his. The last of the priests stepped forward and tied a long embroidered cloth around our hands.

"Who will bear witness to this joining?" asked the priest.

"I will," said Maerryn as he stepped forward, placing a hand on his brother's shoulder.

"And I will," came Fairwynn's voice from behind me as her hand rested on my shoulder.

"Then as it has been written and as it has been done, may the world know that these two are forever sworn to each other by body, mind and soul." The crowd behind us erupted in a loud cheer. Tallyn leaned forward and captured my mouth with his. I melted against him.

Fairwynn, chuckling, untied the cloth from our hands and folded it neatly. The four of us were seen to an annex while the excited crowd left the temple to go await news of the claiming and branding.

Grelyem was waiting in the annex when we arrived. I looked around, expecting more people. "Where is everyone?" I asked.

Tallyn leaned back against the table. "You seemed hesitant to have a large audience, so I made the arrangements to have as small a group as possible. You have two royal heirs to stand witness and a royal physician to administer - that's as small as it can get."

Maerryn smiled. "I swear we are going to sit quietly out of sight and entertain ourselves. When the time comes Grelyem will apply the brand and then Fairwynn and I will look at the brands and announce that it is done and the brands match."

Fairwynn smiled. "I promise we won't peek more than the one time to make sure it's really you who is naked. I will make sure they don't peek either." I laughed as she eyed Maerryn and Grelyem. The old Dark Elf just rolled his eyes.

There was a knock on the annex door. "Come in," I called, already knowing it was food. Sure enough two young maids entered with trays of fruits, nuts, cakes and tea. "Thank you," I said with a smile. Both girls giggled but quickly disappeared.

"What's this?" asked Grelyem. "I've never seen refreshments offered at this stage of the ceremony."

"This is me breaking my fast," I said as I popped a slice of apple into my mouth. "I sort of forgot to eat this morning." I motioned to the trays. "Please, everyone feel free to grab something. I'm not sure how long this next part is going to take and I don't want anyone starving on my account." My words must have made sense because everyone sank into a chair and made quick work of the snacks on the trays.

"For the record Lady Lillian, I think the snack was brilliant." Grelyem licked his fingers after the last bite of a honey cake.

"To be honest this was Beni's idea. I just asked if she had some fruit because I was hungry." I took another sip of tea. "She's the one that sent the food."

"So how does this work? Is this done in here or do we go to a different room?" I was trying to picture a room in the temple with a large bed and chairs like a movie theatre so witnesses could watch with popcorn. Or maybe if it took place in this room Tallyn would lay me down on this very table. I hoped we moved the food first.

"We'll go back to your chambers where maids will have prepared the bed. You two will make with the claiming and we will sit awkwardly on the couch until we brand you and get this all over with." Maerryn's voice actually conveyed his emotions on the subject well. He felt much like I did.

"Not an exhibitionist?" I asked him.

He shrugged. "I talk a good game, but I don't like sharing what is mine."

"Ok, so shall we get this over with?" Tallyn asked.

We walked back as a group to the palace. We discussed in detail our feelings on chocolate cupcakes vs. traditional Elven honey cakes. People were already celebrating in the great hall while the maids and pages bustled quickly trying to finish setting up and preparing the meal.

From somewhere in the crowd I heard my brother's teasing shouts. "Woooo, go get him tiger! Ride him cowgirl!" My face blushed a bright red.

"What is a cowgirl?" Fairwynn asked as we navigated down the corridor near the chambers. "Did your brothers just call you fat and ugly like a cow?"

I burst out laughing. "No, no. Nothing like that. Years ago the country I'm from had an area that was sort of wild and untamed. There were men called cowboys that would ride horseback to herd cattle and keep them in formation. Well, in later years we picked up the term 'cowgirls' because we believe anything a man can do a woman can too."

They all eyed me still not understanding. "They were saying I should ride Tallyn hard like a horse."

There was the moment of the universal "Oh!" and the group became awkwardly silent. Luckily we had arrived at the door. Pushing the door open I was overwhelmed by the smell of flowers.

Every available surface where there could be flowers displayed now held flowers. Everyone's eyes rolled.

"This must be my Grandmother's doing." I offered. It didn't seem to help anyone. I gave an apologetic smile to the group.

"You two, strip so we can get this over with. I've heard they are serving more of the mac and cheese stuff from Lillian's home world and I want an entire plate of it this time." I laughed as Maerryn made a face reminiscent of Cookie Monster when he wanted a cookie. Big googly eyes and a ravenous smile.

Tallyn took me by the hand and led me into the room with the bed. He helped me unlace my sleeves and overdress, letting them fall to the floor beside me. He looked at the small pouch tucked beneath the edge of my nearly transparent chemise. "What's this?" he asked, tugging the pouch from its resting place.

"Oh, that's a wedding present for you. I embroidered it myself. That's why it sort of sucks. I'm sorry, I guess I need to work on that skill." I bit my lip, watching carefully as he ran his fingers over the small bag. His smile broadened with each passing second.

He carefully opened the bag and pulled out the ring on the cord. He looked at it closely. "It's my family crest. My Mom gave it to me when I finished grad school. I was going to have something made but life and stuff sort of happened faster than I had expected. If you don't ...." He cut me off with another kiss.

"I love them and they are perfect," he whispered resting his forehead against mine. He handed me the cord. "Will you help me put it on?" I nodded, and with shaky hands I reached up and tied the cord behind his neck. "Thank you."

"Why are you wearing so many clothes?" I asked him. "I'm practically naked and you're still standing there fully covered, that's so not fair."

"I require your assistance, wife." The last word sent a chill down my spine. I wasted no time in pushing the jerkin off his shoulders and unlacing his pants. Soon he was bare for me to see and explore. I ran my hands over his bare chest and grinned as he sucked in a deep breath when I trailed my hands down his stomach.

In a fluid motion and a slight ripping of seams the transparent chemise joined the rest of my clothes on the floor. Sliding his hands over my skin he cupped my backside in his hands and lifted me against him. In two long strides we fell on the bed together. The soft silk against my back combined with his calloused hands running over my skin made me quake and ache for him. When his hands came up to cup my breasts I arched my back to press them tighter against his palms. His thumbs brushed over them each causing my nipples to harden and tingle under his touch, when he lowered his mouth to lay claim to one I moaned gasping for breath.

"I didn't know you were going to make this so easy. You must really be looking forward to those cupcakes," he teased.

When I slapped a hand playfully against his chest he caught it and held it to his heart. "Do you feel that?" he asked as the pounding rush of it pumped beneath my hand. "It beats for you." He was so corny and sweet, how could I not love him?

With a wicked grin he pushed my legs wide open. Laying down on his stomach he grasped me by the hips and slid my apex towards his mouth. His tongue scorched me like fire as it shot out to taste my core. With slow deliberate actions he circled and nipped at the bead of my bloom. When he suckled it I threw my head back and moaned. I reached down to run my hands through his hair but all I could do was hold on.

He took my moan as a signal for an onslaught of pleasure, and fast and hard his mouth moved over my sex. His tongue was taking special interest at the bead between the folds. When he nibbled on it next I felt like I was on fire and climbing towards the sun - the higher I climbed the hotter it became. Then finally when I was on the brink he plunged his tongue deep within me to taste me at my very center. I exploded, screaming as my hips left the bed. I pleaded with him to slow down but he pushed on, opening his mind to me, sharing in my own pleasure but also allowing me to feel his. I came again harder than the first time.

"Please," I begged him. "Take me, join with me, and complete me." So great was my need that I was trembling in his arms as he encouraged me to turn over. Moving behind me, he lifted my hips. I was unsure if my knees would support me. Then he drove deep into me and I cried out. He filled me so completely I felt ready to burst. He slowly withdrew and then plunged deeply into me again. The slow pace was maddening. As he withdrew a third time I tried to follow him but he held me in place, and when he reentered me again it was with such hunger and need I felt we were one body.

Tallyn's speed quickened as I could feel his pleasure growing along with my own. Soon we were panting, teetering on the edge of one final release that would surely burn us both alive. Without losing his rhythm he pulled me back against his lap, reached around cupping a breast in his palm, and with his other hand stroking me again so I couldn't take it anymore. I screamed release and he did too. The muscles of my body tightened around him, holding on and refusing to let go. Behind my closed eyes there was an explosion of fireworks, a moment of slight discomfort that washed over me and darkness took over us both as we collapsed on the bed.

When I woke up we were still joined, and Tallyn was trailing little kisses over my shoulder. I tried to sit up but a burning sensation in my side stopped me.

"Shhhhh, lay still just for a few more minutes. Grelyem has already applied an ointment which will take the sting out, but it needs just a little more time."

"It's over?" I asked.

"No." He kissed my ear. "It's all just beginning. This was just the start to a long, happy life together."

I laid there in his arms for what felt like hours but it never would have been long enough.

Grelyem poked his head back in. "Yup, I thought I heard you up. Let's take a look at those brandings so these two can go make the announcement."

Fairwynn and Maerryn entered the room with large grins. Maerryn stroked his chin while Fairwynn leaned close looking at the brand.

"I don't know, what do you think? Do they match?" Fairwynn asked Maerryn.

"Oh, they match, but is it just me or do they look really girly?" he replied.

"Men can wear flowers too, you know," she argued back.

Tallyn and I both stiffened. "Flowers?" he said.

"Yeah, it looks like a whole bouquet little brother." Maerryn laughed.

Grabbing a sheet to wrap around his waist Tallyn rolled of the bed rushing to a long mirror. I eyed the mark from where I lay on the bed. It looked like a cross between a vine and a daisy chain. One of the leaves at the bottom seemed to bear the marking of Queen Mab. Tallyn swore under his breath. "Trickster fairies..."

I laughed and walked to the mirror ignoring the other people's stares in the room. Standing side by side the marks ran from the bottom of our rib cages and stopped just above our knees.

"I think they're pretty." I turned and softly ran my hand over his.

He looked down into my eyes and started to say something that I had no doubt was romantic. Instead I leaned up and kissed him.

"I love you. Now let's get dressed and go party."

"We've got some good news to go share. You two should hurry up and get redressed, nobody can eat until you get down there." Maerryn said before slapping my butt and leaving the room. Grelyem and Fairwynn were tight on his heels.

"I'll kill him for that later." Tallyn insisted.

"Nope, no bloodshed on my binding day. You will let it go. Besides, you've seen my brothers. They're as big as werewolves, let them handle it." We both laughed.

Tallyn redressed in no time. I, on the other hand looked at the corseted ball gown and grimaced. Trying to explain to an Elven warrior how to tie a corset and a corseted gown is a whole new level of challenging.

"I know how to take these things off, not put them on. I was never trained on this." He fumbled with the laces. When we both became ensnared in laces with knots binding us in a whole new way I saw Tallyn do something I had never before seen. He poked his head out into the corridor.

"Maids! Lily's Mom! Grandmother Mab.... Some woman.... Any woman.... HELP ME!!!" The pleading tone was so sincere it was sweet.

As luck would have it my mother came to the rescue. She wrestled the laces away from him and was able to untie all the knots. Making quick work of it she tied me off, then helped me into the dress.

"Seriously, how do you ever put on armor if you can't handle simple lacing?" She teased my new mate.

"It was dangerous, that thing is a death trap. Why would you women willingly put that on?" His eyes were wide and horrified.

"Because it looks pretty." I held the dress in place while my mother laced me into that too.

"Ok, turn around let me look at you." I did as I was bid. Her eyes washed over me. "That is an amazing dress. I can't believe Mom didn't want to wear it." She shrugged talking about her mother. "I'll see you kids downstairs," she said.

With one last once-over in the mirror we stepped out into the corridor. As we approached the top of the stairs leading down into the Great Hall a hush fell over the crowd.

"Whooooo, you go get him girl. Ride that man!" I looked straight at my little brother who was standing tall and the only one making noise.

I looked over at Tallyn. "And you thought your brother was embarrassing." I took another step down and before he could say anything else I saw Ian clamp a hand over my brother's mouth.

"Are we still sticking with the whole not killing our siblings' thing? I mean, I could polish him off after Maerryn." I shot Tallyn a dirty look. "I was just offering."

"No, if anyone is going to kill him, it's going to be me," I said forcing a big grin on my face.

Tallyn chuckled and tightened his grip on my arm. I wasn't sure, but it might have been for Matt's protection. At the bottom of the stairs the room erupted around us with cheers and well wishes. A wall of happy Otherworlders rushed us to offer their congratulations. There were hugs, handshakes, kisses, tears, laughs and even some random butt slaps between the men.

Dinner was amazing and would have been a culinary taboo at home. However, here it was a night filled with exotic foods like crunch rolls, fried mac and cheese, lasagna, chocolate cupcakes, lemon tarts, and chicken noodle soup. I laughed as people filled plate after plate of my favorite foods gulping them down greedily. Sure enough, Maerryn ate an entire plate of nothing but fried mac and cheese squares.

The party continued well into the night with games I had never heard of or seen played. My grandmother performed magical tricks for the children, my parents danced and looked happy, and I didn't say a word when Maerryn and Fairwynn snuck away from the festivities hand in hand. This was my home now, and these were my people. I almost laughed to myself.

I wandered out onto a balcony away from the noise. I was really surprised to find Ian MacGregor out there reading. "Whatcha reading?" I asked.

The Scot marked his page and closed the book. "A Tale of Two Cities." He crossed his arms over his chest. "Why aren't you inside celebrating?"

"It's a lot to take in. I just needed a moment that wasn't loud and overwhelming." I considered him for a moment. "So what's your next big move? Go home, go to another party, or get into a fight with a Vampire?" I said the last part as a joke but noticed he didn't crack a smile.

"I've accepted a teaching position in Seoul. I need a change of pace and luckily, there aren't really many Vampires there for me to slay." His jaw hardened.

"You slay Vampires?" I asked a bit amazed.

"Among other things. My job has been to protect my clan for the last couple hundred years. It cost me my family." His eyes looked sad. He looked through the doors at Tallyn. "Just remember duty is great but it doesn't love you back. Protect each other." He started to go back inside.

"Hey Ian, be careful in Asia. Also, don't close yourself off. You'll never heal or find anyone else again if you do." My heart went out to him.

"I doubt that, but it's sweet of you to think that, My Lady." He turned and before I could say more he was gone.

Tallyn came out to join me on the balcony. "I'm not sure what I think about the Werewolf. They are native to this realm, but have a rough reputation. He seems pretty honorable. What were you two talking about out here?"

"He said to love and protect each other." I smiled and was glad when he wrapped his arms around me to protect me from the cold.

"I will always protect you because I won't go on without you." He pressed a kiss to my forehead before taking my hands and leading me back inside. "Now come on, you still owe me a dance from the last time. I even decked my brother for his kiss. I think you owe me, don't you?"

I laughed. "Yes my Prince. Whatever you say, my Prince."

"Now that's more like it," he teased as he pulled me into his arms for a waltz.

ABOUT THE AUTHOR

Isabelle Saint-Michael is a cupcake enthusiast, shoe addict, and world traveler. She is known for her sense of adventure and geekier hobbies. She is frequently seen haunting coffee shops and pubs in the wee hours of the morning. No matter where she goes, shenanigans and laughter are never far behind.

www.ingramcontent.com/pod-product-compliance
Lightning Source LLC
Chambersburg PA
CBHW051321250626
47155CB00007B/2396